I0749205

THE UNIVERSE CRACKED

Written by

ESSEL MACBETH

Edited by M.K.V.P Macbeth

Grosvenor House
Publishing Limited

This book is published by
Grosvenor House Publishing Ltd
Link House
140 The Broadway, Tolworth, Surrey, KT6 7HT.
www.grosvenorhousepublishing.co.uk

A CIP record for this book
is available from the British Library

Hardback ISBN 978-1-83615-352-8

THE UNIVERSE CRACKED

SEQUEL TO

THE UNIVERSE BLINKED

CHAPTER ONE

The fleet of twenty Clariziane spaceships left spaceport as normal, on a routine patrol mission of the galaxy. Spirits were high, the pilots happily chatting over their radios, relating what they did with their downtime. It was a relaxed atmosphere among the fourteen men and six women pilots; all well acquainted with each other and good friends for the most part. The mission as always to take three weeks, patrolling space, then returning home with nothing to report; same as last time and the time before that, and so on. Always nothing to report, their galaxy was empty of life, no intruders, everything was normal.

Into the second week, patrolling near the edge of the galaxy, something did happen. The sudden disappearance of the lead ship with Commander Sol Nussar aboard was anything but normal, it took everyone by surprise; terrifying to say the least. His fellow crewmen were stunned.

Nussar's one-man ship vanished without a trace, one second he was there ahead of the fleet, in formation still; then in the blink of an eye – gone. Initially unable to speak for several seconds, each pilot thought their onboard monitors had suddenly stopped working. They were frantically pressing every button, flicking every switch, checking the helm controls for a malfunction. Nothing.

An immediate search began for Commander Nussar, his ship couldn't just vanish; no sign of debris floating about, no wreckage, nothing untoward except the fact the commander was not there anymore. His radio crackled before falling silent. Panic set in among the pilots; the single crew ships were not designed for extended periods in space. They had to find Nussar fast; with only limited supplies for the three-week mission, including the oxygen supply, finding the ship was a priority.

The search went on for days with no success, the pilots were unable to locate Nussar's ship or reach him on the radio. They had no choice but to return to spaceport before their own air supply ran out; agreeing to refuel and return to that sector of space and resume the search. No-one was giving up on their friend. The mood was very subdued heading home; the concern was not making it back in time to save Nussar before his oxygen ran out, yet they had to try; he would have done the same for any of them.

Not one pilot had an explanation for the strange unnatural occurrence they all witnessed; they all saw it, not one believed it and were certain it had nothing to do with Nussar's disappearance.

A baffling phenomenon manifested itself just ahead of Nussar's ship. For a moment, the pilots stared in utter disbelief at their monitors, stunned into silence.

Did that just happen, or didn't it?

Some even questioned their eyesight – or their onboard computer system malfunctioning. It came as a complete shock simply because nothing ever happened on these monthly patrols.

Why this time?

A section of space inexplicably became distorted; twisted out of shape with a misalignment of the stars and for a second, a black void appeared. Onboard computers failed to register any anomaly, it shouldn't have happened, but it did. Now Commander Sol Nussar was missing.

The fleet, as per instructions from spaceport officials were clear and simple; patrol Clariziane space, maintain law and order, and peace. Ludicrous orders really, a pointless task as always, the pilots thought. Doing the same mission every month without fail, patrol an empty galaxy; Clarizia being the only planet in the system with sustainable life. But they were paid well, so naturally no-one questioned it.

Why would they?

Unaware of the real purpose for the missions was much more sinister than the pilots could ever imagine. They were told to patrol round the perimeters of the galaxy to ensure no-one entered Clariziane space; intruders were not welcome. The pilots on their part were naive to think anything untoward about their missions. They simply did as instructed; the money was good, loyalty blinded by the insanely high wages.

*

The supreme hierarchy of Clarizia deemed it necessary to protect their privacy from off-worlders; but also, to keep prying eyes away from the real reason of their secret activities. It did occur to them there was other life in the universe beyond their own galaxy. It was necessary to keep all away from the Clariziane space. While the fleet of ships did their duty without question, it meant illustrious leaders could continue their clandestine experiments. The rest of the universe was irrelevant to the plan.

*

The universe was watching, furious with the Clarizianes. It didn't like what they were doing. Repercussions were inevitable. Their preposterous plan was going to encroach into another universe with disastrous results. Why couldn't they stay in their own universe and stop meddling with the laws of nature. Their actions threatened the very existence of life in two universes if they persisted with their foolhardy quest for life in another time. There were consequences to consider, the universe had already experienced one rift in space; it would not and could not allow these disruptions to go unpunished.

The Clarizianes were not welcome in this universe, they needed to stay in the parallel universe – where they belonged and stop meddling in science they didn't understand.

*

The fleet headed home to Clarizia, now led by Don Kant, Sol Nussar's closest friend. He was more subdued than the others. How could he lose his friend so suddenly in mysterious circumstances? He worried aliens from outside their galaxy had somehow secretly entered their space. It seemed unlikely, he thought; but it was the only conclusion he could think of. The fact remained, Clarizia was so remote, so isolated on the very edge of the universe, off-worlders wouldn't know of their existence.

The universe knew.

The pilots never spoke on the return journey, preferring to switch off their radios and silently contemplate losing their commander, mentor, and friend; then feeling guilty for going home and leaving him in outer space, alone in the darkness; no communication with the fleet.

What must he think of them?

The pilots had no idea how they would explain Nussar's disappearance to spaceport officials. Would the ground staff even believe what happened? It wasn't an easy homecoming.

Kant finally summoned up the courage to radio ahead to inform the spaceport commander the fleet was returning without Commander Nussar, saying he was missing; lost somewhere on the outer limits of the galaxy. He requested permission to refuel and immediately return to space to continue the search. Kant didn't see a problem with that, a reasonable request under the circumstances. The intercom stayed silent, no reply, no acknowledgement. He assumed his radio might be on the blink, so he transmitted the message again, with more urgency in his voice; again, he waited for a reply. Nothing. Checking the onboard instruments, everything was functioning normally, yet still no response from spaceport. Now he was worried, ground staff always answered. *Why was this time any different? Did they not understand the urgency in his request? Why were they ignoring him?* Kant's anguish was slowly turning to anger. Fearing the crew might be in trouble over this – although he couldn't think why. Losing Commander Nussar was hard to stomach, but it wasn't a capital offence.

Touching down at spaceport was smooth, nothing like the mood the pilots were in as they exited their ships in silence; at the same time trying to think what just happened out in space, and how to explain what they saw. The onboard computers wouldn't back up their story, there was an anomaly that needed an explanation they didn't have.

Straightaway Kant realised something was wrong, they weren't greeted in the usual manner by ground staff; they were conspicuous by their absence. At that point Kant wasn't sure if Commander Rab Diamont, chief spaceport officer, received his message or not, he also hoped the refuelling crew would be on hand, no sign of them either. The pilots assembled in the docking area; the usual debrief procedure. Again, the place was deserted.

"What is going on Kant?" asked Rol Cheda, one of the male pilots.

"I wish I knew Cheda, something is very wrong, and I don't like it" replied Kant, frowning at the prospect of being snubbed. None of the pilots were happy about the situation, voicing their concerns to each other. Looking around, waiting for someone to appear, it was several minutes before Commander Diamont headed their way and he wasn't too happy to see the pilots. Then again, Kant couldn't recall a time when the miserable bugger actually smiled, a grumpy sod even on a good day.

Diamont approached the pilots, stony faced as always; flanked by several faceless armed guards. That wasn't normal procedure; the pilots started to feel nervous. Quantum energy blasters pointed directly at them was not a good sign.

'This is not going to plan' Kant thought. *What had they done wrong?* It wasn't the plan for any of them, staring at each other with confused expressions; wondering what they did wrong to warrant weapons being shoved in their faces. Just what had they walked into? The pilots returned from a routine patrol, everything normal – except for the bit when they lost Nussar; armed guards at spaceport was not normal. The energy blasters were deemed too destructive and shelved a long time ago.

Kant signalled to his fellow pilots not to make any sudden moves, especially the women pilots; they could be volatile in a situation, their short fiery tempers could land them all in hot water. He would do the talking; they had to find out what was going on first. Then he wondered if Nussar made it back safely ahead of them. *NO*; he quickly dismissed that idea; this was way more important to bring out the energy blasters. Kant couldn't understand why, they were no threat to anyone.

Answers were needed now, the pilots had to get airborne immediately, Nussar was out there somewhere waiting for them to rescue him. Kant had no chance to speak.

"You will all come with me, now!" said Diamont in a harsh gravelly voice.

That didn't sit too well with the pilots for a start, it sounded more like an order than a request. The pilots didn't move, not until the guards prodded them with their weapons. They had no choice, as they hesitantly followed Kant who tried to make eye contact with Diamont. It was impossible, he was flanked by his guards, front back and sides. Kant counted at least fifteen of them. He opted to call out to him. "Do you mind telling us what's going on Diamont? What is the meaning of this?" Kant got no reply. Diamont didn't even bother to look round. *'What was his problem?'* Kant couldn't fathom the man's attitude. *Did he not care about Commander Nussar not returning? What hadn't he asked about him?*

For his part Diamont wasn't interested in anything Kant had to say, they were irrelevant to the situation now. Kant refused to let it go. "Why are we being treated like criminals Diamont? You can't do this, we are dedicated elite officers of the fleet" he shouted furiously, only to get a stiff jab in the stomach when he tried to push past the guards to reach Diamont. He was certain they wouldn't actually use those weapons, but he didn't want to risk it and held back; his stomach hurt, and he was getting nowhere anyway. He scanned round at the guards, faceless public servants hiding their identities with helmets and a visor shielding their faces. He wondered how much they were getting paid.

'Idiots!' he thought.

It was soon evident they were being taken to the conference hall, not the right place for a debrief, Kant risked another jab in the stomach – or worse, but he wanted answers for the pilots, they were close to the edge, he could feel tempers rising to boiling point.

"Diamont, what's the bloody matter with you man? Can you not stop and talk to us. We have to refuel and return to space. Commander Nussar is still out there and he's running out of air. We have to go!" Kant couldn't make it any clearer, he was angry at the continued silence. Why wouldn't Diamont answer him? Did he not understand the gravity of the situation, or was he just plain stupid? Kant opted for the latter. "I want answers, damn you." No response came from Diamont. *Yes*, Kant thought, *the man was a complete prat at times, but this behaviour was out of order. Who the hell authorised it?* Diamont couldn't do it alone, he hadn't got the bottle, someone else was pulling his strings for sure. The pilots deserved better than this; forcibly taken by gunpoint for simply doing their jobs was a farce from start to finish.

As the pilots were ushered into the building leading directly to the conference hall, the women pilots were abruptly pushed further along the corridor, manhandled by the guards and shoved into the next room and locked in. their tempers could explode all they liked, the women were not getting out of there anytime soon. Diamont didn't want to deal with their volatile tempers' which soon became apparent with the loud screaming and banging on the door. So much for staying quiet and allowing Kant to speak for everyone. That really worked. Now the men stood around wondering what Diamont was going to do with them. Clariziane super hearing meant anyone in the building could hear the women screaming to be let out, that extra hearing not always an advantage.

"What was that all about Diamont? Why are the women locked up?" Kant didn't hide his anger, it was totally unnecessary, he clenched his fists, so wanting to wipe that smirk off his face – if only he could get near enough. Six of the guards stayed close to Diamont as he waited for the last guard to enter the hall who then slammed it shut and stood guard at the exit.

"Diamont! I demand you release the women" shouted Kant, it did no good.

Diamont stood behind the large conference table, well away from Kant and his motley crew. He still refused to speak. Kant understood the guards staying silent, they never spoke, but Diamont, he sure was playing them all for fools. His blood was boiling; he still motioned his pilots to stay quiet, he would sort this. They weren't happy, glaring at Diamont with evil intent. Kant was asking all the right questions, just not getting the answers.

Finally, Diamont decided to speak, the pilots gathered round the table waiting for his explanation but really wanting to punch his lights out. The guards moved in closer, any wrong move by the men and they were gone. Diamont had yet to mention they were actually all under arrest, charges to come later. He thought it best to delay that part. He was instructed not to reveal too much, so decided to stay quiet. The pilots didn't need to know details – or the truth; they wouldn't handle it anyway. Diamont was at that point fed up with Kants incessant questions, it was getting on his nerves.

"I was ordered to bring you here by senior Commander Neal Polton. He will arrive shortly; he has some very important questions to ask you." Diamont leant over the table, glaring at Kant. "I for one can't wait to hear your answers." He was taunting Kant into doing something stupid but knew he couldn't with the guards breathing down his neck. Kant was too busy thinking, he didn't like that nasty smirk on Diamonts face, and seriously wondered how he could get away with murder. It didn't answer the question why the women were taken away; they were pilots too.

What had Neal Polton to do with spaceport business he wondered. The man had no jurisdiction here, although he had close connections to the government. That bit did worry Kant.

"So, are we under arrest or not? Because it sure as hell feels like it."

"All in good time" came a short brusque reply from Diamont, he didn't want to give too much away. The strong bulging ridges on his forehead suggested he was lying his arse off. *What was he hiding?* Kant suddenly had a horrible feeling they were being made scapegoats for something sinister, a dodgy plot no doubt. Something happened in their absence, and he'd had enough of this fiasco. "Look Diamont, stop playing games with us, we really do need to leave, get back into space. Did you not get my message?"

Diamont still refused to answer. He did get the message, the look on his face said so; he was behaving rather shifty, shuffling his feet, not standing still for a second; a sure sign he was up to no good. "Oh, come on man, give us something, and why lock the women up? They should be here with us?" Kant was fuming and he wasn't the only one; all the pilots were seething at this idiot official. There was no reason for it.

Diamont was visibly rattled with the persistent questioning; it made no difference; the pilots were going nowhere. He did however decide to give them something. "You don't seem to understand the severity of the trouble you're in Kant. You and your little band of pilots are finished." He almost broke into a snigger at their plight.

“Finished? What are you talking about?” yelled Kant, followed by several expletives from Cheda, Fisah Selan and Hanzo Gato. Kant held his hand up to cool them down; it didn’t help him; he was furious with the little weasel.

Diamont refused to elaborate; he was getting bored waiting for Polton to arrive. That man was late, and he’d always blame government business for his own tardiness. Diamont for his part was afraid of letting something slip out; the pilots were all collateral damage in the grand scheme of things. Nothing could stop the exodus now, least of all a bunch of pilots with too much curiosity.

“Just tell us what we’ve done wrong” Kant demanded.

“Yes, we have a right to know, and why you deem it necessary to have banned weapons pointed at us” said Selan, unable to stay quiet any longer.

“We are just doing our jobs, like you ordered” added Cheda. The lack of communication was ridiculous, none of it made any sense. Worse still they could hear the women going ballistic in the other room. No chance of them calming down any time soon.

The pilots were tired, hungry, but more worried about Nussar all alone in space. They were quite willing to forgo shore leave to go back for him. Diamont however was having none of it. The pilots couldn’t understand why the man didn’t ask about Nussar. *Did he not care?* What was really annoying was the simple fact he was behaving weirder than usual, like he was someone in authority; instead, he was a jumped-up jerk, full of himself and actually a nobody. His title was just that, a title.

Eventually Neal Polton arrived, breezing into the hall, knocking one of the guards with the door swinging open. He made no apology, he never did. Approaching a lot of angry faces at the table, it was no more than he expected. Kant thought *‘here we go, another jerk in uniform. How could a couple of idiots be put in charge of important jobs involving spaceport or the government?’* It baffled him, but he kept his thoughts to himself, it would do no good to air them right now. He still had questions. "Well, Polton, now can we have some answers? What is the meaning of this?" he asked, slamming his hands on the table, thinking it would get a response.

Polton took a seat, Diamont decided to stand back, Polton could take the flak now. He would enjoy watching their faces.

Kant was still waiting, the pilots weren't leaving without answers, not intending to stay any longer than they had to, not sure how that were going to leave the room without being vapourised. Kant had yet to work that one out.

Polton casually opened a file he brought with him, scanned over the contents once more, before looking up to angry faces bearing down on him, he just smirked back at them; if they were hoping to intimidate him, they were wrong. He wasn't afraid of them in the least, not while the guards were present.

"I come directly from our illustrious leader, Chane Auston" he made the announcement without any emotion, he wasn't giving anything away at that point.

'Another jerk in authority' thought Kant. He did admit the highly insane wages they were paid made the pilots blind to the incompetence of the ruling government.

Polton continued. "Firstly, several serious violations have been committed by you pilots."

The pilots were shocked into silence again. *What was he talking about? What Violations?*

Gathering his thoughts Kant was first to speak. "What rubbish are you spouting Polton? We have always done our duty by the book" he wanted to make it absolutely clear, there was never a question of the pilots breaking the rules. "Where are you getting this information from?"

Polton ignored him and carried on. "You have been charged with stealing a fleet of spaceships, taking unauthorised trips into space without the relevant documentation. You have further been charged with violating a direct order from a senior officer and shown a total disregard of government protocol."

After reading out the charges, Polton looked up, he was holding something back. The pilots could tell by his manner. Yet it was hard to get their heads round the absurd charges against them. Some of the pilots not entirely taking in what they heard, they could see Polton was serious – if smirking could be taken as serious. It was too ridiculous to be true, these charges had no base in reality. Kant tried to plead their case. "This is all nonsense, and you know it, we have broken no rules. How can we steal spaceships when we were on a normal routine reconnaissance mission, authorised by spaceport?"

Polton was about to reply with something sarcastic, but Kant hadn't finished. "We were on patrol when we lost Commander Nussar. Why aren't you concerned about him?" A valid question he thought. *It did seem strange neither Polton nor Diamont weren't interested in what happened to Nussar. Why were they behaving so hostile? What was the problem?* More importantly, Kant thought, *where did these outrageous accusations come from?* Polton had no time for the poor deluded fools, they had been missing for five years; then suddenly turn up out of the blue. He did realise they could cause trouble; he could not allow them to leave spaceport, their appearance now would raise too many questions.

Looking at the file again, Polton delivered more bad news. "You may wish to know Commander Nussar disappeared in space five years ago while out on such a mission. So, you see Kant, your story doesn't add up. Nussar was never on the mission with you in the first place. As for you and your team here, I have been reliably informed, no authorised space flights have taken place in the last five years. All space travel was halted after Nussar went missing. Whatever your game is Kant, you are finished with spaceport." Polton was actually laughing at the pilots, it seemed one big joke to him, and not a very good one. He enjoyed making them squirm.

"Furthermore, all ranks will be stripped, and you will be detained here overnight, then taken to prison to await your sentence." Polton closed the file, sat back, and folded his arms; that last statement was brutal, he relished dishing it out.

The pilots didn't.

"That's crazy man and you know it, none of the charges are true." Kant went from angry to scared, this was turning into a nightmare. He turned to Diamont, still standing behind Polton, trying to hide.

"Come on Diamont, tell him it isn't true, you saw us off at the beginning of the month, you were there talking to Nussar."

Diamont stayed tight-lipped, he wasn't backing up his story, shuffling his feet again. He had his orders from above; besides, he had no explanation as to why the pilots were back from space five years after they left, and without Nussar. Something was going on and it seemed he wasn't privy to all the answers. The pilots were on their own.

The pilots were horrified, they were being treated as common criminals; knowing full well if they went to prison they would never see the light of day again. It was a death sentence. How could a jerk like Polton strip them of their ranks? That certainly wasn't protocol. Each and every pilot trained hard to become elite space pilots, the government couldn't take that away without the proper procedure in place.

Several pilots pulled out a chair and sat down rather heavily, rocked by the shock announcement. Polton was wrong, he was lying through his teeth. They did leave spaceport three weeks earlier as usual, that was fact. The rest was pure fiction. Polton and Diamont were holding something back, but Kant couldn't fathom what their game was.

Diamont still refused to back up the pilots story, he couldn't, they had been missing for five years, presumed lost in space. He told Polton he hadn't seen them at all in those five years, so they had no reason to be on spaceport property. He was mystified at their reappearance, but still reacted in a shifty manner that made the pilots disbelieve every word he said. Besides the alleged theft of the spaceships Diamont even suggested to Polton he add the charge of trespass, which Polton was happy to do.

"As I said, you will stay here under armed guard until morning. This meeting is concluded" said Polton, he couldn't explain they reappearance; didn't want to know, but they would still be a threat. He mentioned prison in the morning – that was never going to happen; the pilots would not be allowed to leave spaceport. He left that bit out.

"You can't do this!" snapped Kant, "we are elite pilots of the fleet with impeccable records. The charges are bogus, we have done nothing wrong; you know that Polton, why are you treating us like this?" Kant reached out over the table to point a finger in his face, only to get dragged back by a guard.

"You are no longer pilots; your elite status had been revoked by order of Chane Auston himself." Polton was aggressive, he had no love for these worthless pilots appearing out of nowhere. It did disturb him where they'd been, but he had his orders; in the end he didn't care.

Even Kant had to take a seat, shocked to the core; it was a complete stitch up. They couldn't spend the rest of their lives in prison, he had no idea how they were getting out of this one. Polton refused to listen any further, he had other matters to attend. He stood up, file under his arm and waved the guards to do their jobs. The pilots were forcibly taken from the conference hall by way of a couple of digs in the ribs with their blasters. Kant stared back at Diamont, thinking he had to be in on this conspiracy. *Why didn't he back up the pilots?* Diamont in return gave Kant one of his stupid sideways grin; but it was a look that really said, *'where have you been all this time?'*

Kant had his suspicions about Polton, he was a sycophantic idiot obeying orders, he still knew what was going on, there had to be more in that file. As for Diamont, he was lying through his teeth – which Kant so wanted to knock out there and then, that would wipe the smirk off his face.

Suddenly alarm bells went off in Kants brain. *What did Polton mean when he said Nussar disappeared five years ago?*

That didn't add up, Diamont spoke to Nussar at length the day they left – it was definitely three weeks ago. What were they covering up? He couldn't get his head round it; they were being played for sure.

The pilots were moved down the corridor, flanked by the guards; they were a bit subdued by now, Kant warned the men not to say a word. It was pointless to provoke the guards, who still gave them the odd poke in the back – just because they could. The pilots knew not to mess with quantum energy blasters, get hit with one of those, there would be no evidence left behind – no bodies.

Once the conference hall was empty, Diamont decided it was time to take his leave, he'd done enough lying for one day. He wasn't entirely sure what was going on with Polton, he knew not to question anyone from the government, but he also wanted to know where Kant and his fellow crew appeared from, five years was a long time to go missing. Nussar's disappearance was an even bigger mystery. No wonder he was told to say nothing, which was just as well because he knew very little; and Polton wasn't giving much away.

Polton called out to Diamont as he was leaving the room, "Make sure they are guarded well Diamont, no visitors or interaction with anyone. We can't have them talking out of turn. Chane Auston assures me their disappearance and reappearance is in hand. We don't want the awkwardness of disposing of anyone else."

"I know my job Polton, just make sure you do yours. Secrets have a nasty habit of slipping out" replied Diamont, "and I don't suppose I get to see what's in that file?"

"No Diamont, you don't get to see." Polton wasn't too pleased with Diamont's attitude, but silently he agreed with the man, they had to be careful, the pilots asked too many questions, and they weren't buying the story even if it was true. He couldn't have them working it out, the truth wouldn't go down very well. *'Never mind'* he thought, they would be disposed of first thing in the morning: Problem solved.

Polton left spaceport in a hurry, he didn't like the idea of the pilots turning up out of the blue, it would cause complications if it came out. Secrecy was all important until the time was right; not every Clariziane would approve what the government was doing. The exodus had to stay on schedule, survival of the citizens was the ultimate goal, at least most of them. It would all happen when the new messiah arrived.

The file Polton had with him needed to be shredded when he returned to his office, the information inside was far too sensitive to fall into the wrong hands. There was not as much in the file as he wanted, he wanted to know more; even he was kept in the dark by the government officials, who deemed him a liability – he would not feature in the end plan. Details were kept to a minimum; problem was the government didn't know everything either. Details were kept from them also. The scientists thought they were in charge. They got a bit too cocky; something went wrong with their experiments, a miscalculation in the initial trials went undetected until it was too late.

The research was flawed.

A time discrepancy happened in space so serious, it echoed back to the planet with a time shift no-one could have foreseen. Time travel was Clarizia's only option to maintain their survival. It was uncertain at the time, the scientists caused the anomaly in space, or even how it happened; they just hoped to get away with it by saying nothing. The scientists hadn't realised a warp near the edge of their galaxy twisted the universe out of shape, causing a tear in the space time continuum. It affected another universe – and that universe was far from happy.

*

The universe suddenly got a bad bout of hiccups, reverberating across the cosmos, then it blinked. That only made it worse. It watched the Clarizianes. They failed to make amends and simply carried on; they would pay dearly for their stupidity.

If they thought it was okay to meddle with the natural order of existence – the lifeforce of the universe, they were wrong. Disappearing into their own past just so they could do it all over again, was not an acceptable solution.

Not this time.

CHAPTER TWO

Locked up in a windowless room for the night, with only one flickering light, all nineteen pilots crammed in, they felt utterly despondent, abandoned, betrayed by their own people. *How did it come to this?* They desperately wanted to prove their innocence, whatever it was they were guilty of, that was still a mystery and impossible to do while stuck in that room. None of them completely sure what was going on. Everything said by Diamont and Polton was all lies; it was difficult to know what the truth was.

The pilots weren't even offered food and drink. It was bad enough losing their friend, but not being able to head back out to look for him surely sealed his fate. Those idiots in charge had condemned Nussar to death and maybe he already was. It was a haunting thought, hard to get out of their heads.

Kant felt particularly responsible for not doing more; he felt he should have tried harder. Quantum energy blasters have a nasty habit of keeping one quiet. He'd let his crew down, it was especially hard for the women, all six of them had suddenly gone very quiet, huddled together in the corner. Something was wrong with them, they made no attempt to vent their anger like true Clariziane women; renowned for being bold and brassy, fearless and tempestuous, their manner often volatile. This wasn't their usual behaviour. Kant worried for them deeply. He couldn't help them, or the men. Suddenly he felt strange, not his usual self; a bit off but nothing he could put his finger on. None of the pilots had eaten, but it was much worse than that.

Something dreadful was happening to them, something very disturbing and sinister; some beginning to experience a change in their mental ability to function rationally. No wonder the women were acting out of character, so timid, frightened of their own shadow; the flickering light didn't help their mood.

They seemed lost.

A plan was urgently needed, the pilots had to break out, get away from spaceport; their lives depended on it. Trouble with that idea, Kant thought, *if they did manage to get the door open, they would be vapourised in seconds and if they managed to escape spaceport, where would they go?* The whole scenario was killing Kant, he struggled to think straight, his mind was fogged up, his whole body was out of sync with his brain. He guessed the others were feeling much the same; then he had a sudden feeling they had to leave Clarizia altogether. He wondered if something did happen on the return journey. The strange anomaly they all saw, and the subsequent disappearance of Nussar had to be connected. *Was it having an adverse effect on everyone?* He hoped not but couldn't rule it out. Divine intervention was needed, something to aid them in this hellhole.

Nothing was forthcoming.

None of them had a clue what to do but stay put and await their sentence.

Every pilot started to feel wretched, they had no idea why and at that point didn't really care; they were all screwed. If only they knew, they did actually enter a time warp on the return to Clarizia and arrived home five years in the future.

That same time distortion was now playing havoc on their body clocks, as well as their mental capacity to deal with the situation. It was only going to get worse the longer they stayed on the surface. They were in serious trouble because of the spatial distortion putting the timeline completely out of phase. The pilots physical beings didn't match up with the planets magnetic field; they were out of alignment with their own world. Worse, they didn't know it was happening.

Kant stood by the cell door – to him it was a cell, not just a locked room; his mind drifted away for a while, it was difficult to concentrate and keep his sanity in check. His thoughts were getting jumbled into one, *how could he sort his head out feeling like he did?*

Glancing round the cell, some of the men sprawled out on the floor, the mood wasn't great; the women still in the corner, having no interaction with the men. There wasn't even a chair to sit on, it appeared protocol didn't extend to trumped up charges. They were allowed no privileges, no food, no drink, and no furniture to sit on. *What a way to end the day on*, Kant thought.

His mind returned to his friend once more, and how he might be feeling, he must be scared out there in the darkness all alone. That was the moment Kant felt a sudden sensation, a real sense Nussar was still alive. He didn't know how or why, just a strange awareness. Kant muttered to himself.

"Hang in there Sol, hang in there my friend."

*

The night dragged on painfully slow, no one slept. They couldn't, minds went into overdrive, racing out of control – except the women whose minds went into meltdown. They couldn't think for themselves at all. The men were different, thoughts of murder crept into their heads. *Who could they kill? Each other maybe?*

No, suicide was a better option. No, they couldn't do that either. Decisions were increasingly unavailable to them. They were still elite pilots whatever Polton said, they had to hang on to that one thought: their one piece of sanity.

One or two of the men tried to engage in conversation, if only to stay alert through the night; nothing meaningful. The women unfortunately were feeling the effects of the distortion far worse than the men, they stayed huddled together for comfort, too frightened to talk, petrified of everything.

Kant looked across in their direction, in between the flickers of light he smiled, wanting to make them feel a little easier.

It made them feel worse Kant truly felt for them. *How did they get roped into this fiasco?* It wasn't fair. He and Nussar fought hard to get women to train in the elite space programme. The women proved themselves beyond all expectations and passed with flying colours. It was horrible to see them so distressed in this manner. He could do nothing to help them.

Again, Kant called out to his friend across the vast emptiness of space. *Would Nussar be able to hear his plea?* Even if he did, Kant wasn't sure he could help them out of this mess.

It was a stupid thought.

His mind was stuck in limbo, as his thoughts slipped away again, back to the events in space. He couldn't get that image out of his head. *What did it mean? Was there really a connection with Nussar going missing and their strange behaviour?* Kant wasn't sure, his fogged-up brain refused to clear. He wasn't even sure how much longer he'd be able to think for himself.

*

The hours ticked by, still Kant couldn't rest, on his feet continuing to pace up and down the cell; stopping at the door each time, then back again trying to burn off the excess mental energy built up in his brain. It didn't do any good, and certainly didn't make him feel any better.

"Kant, why don't you sit down, rest man" said Selan. The pacing up and down was doing his head in, making him nervous. It didn't serve any purpose.

"I can't Selan, sorry" said Kant as he stopped by the door for the umpteenth time. He could just about hear the guards doing their rounds, but not what they were saying. The voices muffled, his acute super hearing failing in this instance. He really wanted to know what they were saying. It somehow seemed important to him.

"Does anyone else have a problem with their hearing?" he asked. Several of them nodded, suddenly realising their impairment.

"I'm so glad it isn't just me then" he said, then carried on walking around, going from wall to wall. Any thoughts of escaping going out of his mind. They had no chance with the guards patrolling all night.

A tiny shaft of morning light shone under the gap of the cell door. Dawn was breaking over spaceport. The guards would come soon, the pilots were getting anxious and dreaded the moment the cell door swung open. Once inside the prison walls, that was it. They would never see the light of day again, or their families. Options were down to zero, Kant was so despondent he failed to come up with any kind of plan to save their skins.

The time and space distortion was taking full effect, rational thinking was almost non-existent for most of them. Kant was hanging on to his last shred of sanity, apologised to his crew for not coming up with an escape plan. He tried to think what Nussar would do in such a crisis. That didn't help in the slightest.

In sheer desperation he called out to Nussar in his mind, asking for help. If ever he needed his friend it was now.

CHAPTER THREE

Outside the main spaceport building, dawn was fully over the horizon. It was suspiciously quiet; the usual change of personnel had not happened – they were late. No security at the main gate either, or anyone to question the absence of guards. They were all missing. The only guards left were inside the conference hall building, waiting for the changeover. Every single guard had fallen asleep, not one expected trouble, so deemed it safe to sleep on the job.

They would be paid regardless.

As the eerie silence descended over spaceport, not a single person reported for duty. The place was deserted. Inside, Kant was still pacing the floor, unable to rest his tired body. Nothing would make him feel better, knowing the guards would come soon, it made him feel worse thinking about it. Some of the pilots had managed to fall asleep, probably through sheer exhaustion; some partly to forget the horror of where they were. No-one wanted to wake up to face the day, the nightmare would still go on.

Having walked around all night, Kant stopped and propped himself up against the wall for a moment. He soon realised he was shattered. Maybe he should have rested, his head was fit to burst, his body completely at odds with his brain and now his hearing was greatly reduced; still he could hear someone snoring – it was probably Gato he thought, typical of him. Kant nearly nodded off stood up, but something alerted him to a faint noise from outside the cell. He couldn't make out what he heard, it was a strange noise. It was the guards coming for them, it had to be.

Cheda and Selan got to their feet having heard a faint sound, followed by Nadal Lanke and Shan Tayon; they had enough of the hard floor anyway. Nice of Diamont not to give them anything to sleep on. Then again spaceport wasn't designed for overnight prisoners. Selan made it clear he wasn't happy about the floor; his back was aching. Cheda told him to get over it, at least they were still alive – for now at least.

"What is that Kant?" asked Lanke, "is it the guards?"

Kant didn't answer, he had his ear to the cell door but still struggled to hear anything definite. His hearing was down two thirds now, it felt isolating to feel such deafness.

"Well? –" said Cheda, he was desperate to know if their time was up or not.

"I don't know" said Kant, "it seems to have gone quiet now. It was a weird noise though, not voices."

Selan and Cheda put their ears to the door, maybe they would have better luck.

"Something is going on out there" said Cheda, he was sure of hearing a scuffle. Then it went silent again.

"Nothing, damn it" said Kant. He was disappointed not to hear; at the same time not wishing the guards to turn up.

They continued to listen at the door. Footsteps could be heard and getting nearer; it sounded like heavy boots, similar to what the guards wore. This was it – they were coming. Time had run out for the pilots.

Seconds later a key went in the lock, turning slowly, the pilots stepped back from the door, panic was setting in; they didn't know how the guards would react, they certainly wouldn't be worried about the pilots well-being.

The cell door opened gradually, a single guard entered holding a quantum energy blaster, pointed at the pilots. No-one dared to make any sudden moves, getting vapourised after such a shit night wasn't to be recommended.

"Hello" said the guard unexpectedly.

"What? –" said Kant in total shock, guards don't speak.

"Who the hell are you?" Selan wanted to know, risking his life even speaking to a guard, but it sounded like a woman's voice. That couldn't be right. The other pilots began to stir, only to see the menacing looking guard standing there, that blaster was a bit intimidating. They stayed on the floor, afraid to move. Still holding the blaster at the ready, the guard suddenly removed their helmet.

"I said hello."

"Stella!?" Kant blurted out, shocked for a second; what the hell was she doing there in a guards uniform, and a badly fitting one at that. She shouldn't be there; she was just a kid. As far as he could recall in his hazy state, Stella wouldn't know which end of a weapon was the dangerous end.

"Well, are you pleased to see me, or not Don?" she asked, it wasn't exactly the warm reception she was expecting.

Kant had to pick his bottom lip of the floor before coming to his senses. It was Stella, but different, he threw his arms round her and hugged and kissed her. It was such a shock to his system to see her there, but in a good way.

"What are you – I mean, how did you –?." Kant struggled to get his words out, he was speechless for a second. His brain went into overdrive. Stella couldn't have done this alone, someone had to be with her. She in turned hugged Kant, pleased he was okay, pleased they all survived the night.

"Excuse me Kant –" said Cheda, "you know this girl?" even he barely managed to keep his composure, she was drop dead gorgeous and she was hanging on to Kant rather affectionately.

"Of course I do, this is Stella Nussar, Sol's cousin" replied Kant finally, still holding her tight round her slender waist. He wanted to make sure she wasn't a dream. Then he made a mental note to find out how she got into spaceport property and then get past the guards.

Jaws dropped all round the cell, the pilots didn't know Nussar had a cousin – he kept that one quiet. She was beautiful, and the ridges on her forehead very prominent – very appealing to the men.

"Okay guys, close your mouths" said Kant, managing to raise a smile. He couldn't blame them though; Stella was a lovely girl, but she was still a teenager – not quite worldly-wise yet; or so he thought. He let her go to ask the obvious question.

"Am I allowed to ask what you're doing here Stella? And how did you get into spaceport and then what happened to the guards?"

Cheda was already out the door to check the corridor. No guards. *Strange he thought, what kind of female was she? Should he even ask?*

"Tell me what you did?" Cheda asked, coming back into the cell waving his arms at Kant. "Nobody out there, it's deserted." Kant looked at Stella.

"Best you don't ask Don, but the guards won't be bothering us anymore" said Stella, pleased with herself and giving the blaster a gentle tap. The pilots were left in no doubt what happened.

Little did the pilots know, Sol had taught his cousin well, he hoped one day she could enlist in the space programme and become an elite pilot like him. Stella was his only family now; he would take good care of her.

"Stella, do you realise what you've done?" Kant was worried for her safety. "You shouldn't have got involved; this is no place for a young girl; you could have been shot on sight. I'm still trying to work out how you didn't."

"I'm okay Don. Really."

"Now what Kant? I'm afraid to ask how this little lady got into spaceport, and I can't see how it's going to help us" said Cheda, an extra person, a kid almost, was only going to complicate matters, they were in enough trouble as it was.

Stella didn't like his patronising manner, and certainly didn't like the way he was looking at her. She was stronger than they all gave her credit for.

"Listen Don, I'm here to help you, because of what I heard from my friend Ariel, I don't care what happens to this place, but I do care about you guys, and I care about Sol."

Don admired her grit and determination but felt it wasn't enough to get them out of there.

"I don't know Stella, you shouldn't –" suddenly Don stopped mid-sentence, his head was spinning, he couldn't think straight and the pain – it was getting worse.

"You okay Don?" asked Stella putting a hand on his arm, he obviously wasn't. Cheda leant a hand to steady him also. He looked wobbly on his feet. Then Cheda too was light-headed, something serious was wrong, the pain in his head unbearable. It wasn't just the hearing loss now. Suddenly the other pilots were holding their heads in pain, their brains felt like bursting out. It was fleeting, in seconds the pain was gone, but none of them felt quite right. Kant nodded to Stella he was fine, but didn't know how long for.

"We have to leave Don; I felt a calling from Sol. He's alive and needs our help, and judging by you lot, you need help too." Stella gave him a comforting squeeze on his arm. She was adamant they had to go.

"Sol needs us. What about someone helping us first?" chipped in Gato. None of what was going on he understood. They were all doomed to die in this pitiful makeshift cell. *How was this slip of a girl going to help?*

"Just how do you expect us to escape from spaceport undetected?" he added, thinking it was safer to stay put; he was certain they had no chance of making to the exit without being shot – or even vapourised. He didn't fancy his options one bit.

Many of the pilots were now on their feet, the conversation didn't appear to be going too well, and they couldn't quite hear clearly enough from where they sat. None of them knew why their hearing was so limited to the point of partial deafness by Clariziane standard. It was a strange feeling to have. The women remained seated in the corner still huddled together and not wishing to participate in any discussion; and they weren't too sure about Stella standing there waving the blaster about. All their courage and spirited nature evaporated during the night; they were disorientated with the surroundings – nothing was real to them. The women were affected by the time and space distortion in a different way, they were pretty much helpless.

Cheda for once was with Gato. "Even if we do get away from here, where could we go? We don't have a spaceship big enough to take us past this system. It's pointless. We were all screwed the moment we landed."

"He's right, we can't do this" said Kant, still trying to regain his senses; his fears running riot in his head. It was a crazy plan that Stella hadn't thought through properly.

"Bloody hell you lot, where's your backbone?" snapped Stella, furious with their cowardice, not the reaction she wanted. She didn't break into spaceport, steal a guards uniform, then dispose of a few bodies just for the men to take a wobbly.

"We are going after Sol and I have just the spaceship to take us" she said with confidence, looking round at the men hoping for a more favourable response.

"You do? I mean you do!" said Kant with utter surprise, this wasn't the Stella he knew. She was a kid, and he was still afraid to ask what she did to get her hands on that blaster. She didn't even know how to shoot. *Then again*, he thought, *there was the question of the missing guards. Surely she didn't do all that alone. Could she?*

"Well, are you wimps coming or not?" Stella asked, urging them to make a decision; because if she had to go it alone, she would, but experienced pilots would be better, besides, they hadn't much time left before the authorities realise something was wrong at spaceport.

They needed to be gone, now!

"Okay, okay, I take it you have a plan Stella" said Kant, who was still struggling to believe Sol's teenage cousin could get them out of this mess, let alone get them out in space. He couldn't remember her growing up; but if she had a plan it was better than the pilots had, which was basically nothing. They'd be lucky to find their brains the state they were in.

"I thought we could work it out on the way. Firstly, we get out of here before Polton or Diamont turn up."

Kant knew Stella was right, she sounded so grown up, it was like she was in charge. He wondered if they really did have half a chance; but then he spotted a big problem, the women pilots would be reluctant to go anywhere, they didn't want any involvement in an escape plan.

"What about the women, I'm not sure about them Stella, they're not coping for some reason" said Kant, pointing to the women sitting in the corner. Suddenly Kant couldn't continue, the pain in his head was back. He screamed in agony, a pain like he never felt before, nauseating for a second. Then it was gone. He couldn't explain it. Stella knew more than he realised, she guessed they were all suffering similar symptoms. She knew why, it was the reason she had to act swiftly and get everyone back into space; it was their only chance of survival. It did feel strange to her, rescuing the pilots – after all they were supposed to be lost in space five years ago; but in her heart she always felt Sol never died.

"I'm fine Stella," said Kant, "I can't understand why we're experiencing these strange feelings, or why we're in so much pain. It's ever since we came back." He shook his head, wishing his fogged-up brain would clear. It was only going to get worse, and he couldn't stop it.

"That's probably because you returned to Clarizia five years in the future, but your mind is still in the past. Don, you're supposed to be dead."

Kant was confused, and it showed.

"Yes Don, I know everything from Ariel, my friend. You think you left three weeks ago because your brain is telling you that, unfortunately you came back through a time distortion and landed in the future. The so-called expert scientists are fully aware what they did and are trying to hush it up."

Kant was even more confused; Stella wasn't making sense.

"Don, your bodies are operating in a different time zone to your minds, you're not coping with the imbalance."

The men definitely heard that bit, still they struggled to believe it. Or even understand it. *How could it happen? Could they time travel and not know it?* It didn't sound good news whichever way they looked at it.

"Just a second Stella, so what are you saying? Are you thirteen years old, or not, because you sure as hell don't look it." Kant had to ask, he needed to put it all in perspective; not sure how it was going to work in their favour – because at present, it wasn't.

"No Don. I'm eighteen, my timeline is fine, it's yours that's screwed up – the whole bloody lot of you."

"Thanks Stella" said Kant, that didn't make him feel any better to hear that, probably made him feel worse.

Suddenly Gato collasped on the floor, appearing to be in pain. "Oh, my head hurts, I'm totally confused with this shit. Somebody wake me up when this nightmare is over" he couldn't take much more, his understanding of the situation just hit zero.

"Is he always like this?" asked Stella.

"Usually" said Kant, he couldn't blame Gato, nothing made sense to him either.

Stella sort of felt sorry for the wimp, but this wasn't the time for dramatics. "Come on big guy, get your arse in gear" said Stella sternly, at the same time grabbing his arm to help him up. "We leave now, okay." She gave him a look to reassure him it would all work out.

Cheda was stood close to Selan, watching Gato make a fool of himself as usual. He admired the way Stella handled herself with Gato, firm but sensitivity, he leaned into Selan. "That is my future wife, she is so masterful, so beautiful."

"I heard that –." said Stella, there was nothing wrong with her hearing. "You make one wrong move buddy; you will find this blaster pointed at a strategic part of your anatomy. You got that!"

"Yes ma'am." He said, but too late. He was in love.

Stella did think he was cute, good looking in a boyish way, but they had no time for that sort of thing. She thought it best to keep him in his place – for now at least.

"Right, come on then, you men help the women up, we're not leaving anyone behind." Stella said in a commanding manner. She led the way out of the cell and along the corridor to the exit, it was deadly quiet. Kant couldn't believe what he was seeing, Stella was behaving like a mercenary, way, way beyond her years – whether she was thirteen or eighteen, that was going to take a bit of getting used to.

Having left the cell behind Stella led the pilots to the main exit doors, there was no opposition, except perhaps from the women protesting about being dragged away. They didn't take kindly to being manhandled while feeling very vulnerable; it unnerved them even more. But with Stella in charge shouting at them to move, they didn't have a choice.

Spaceport was completely deserted, it shouldn't be. Even with a fuzzy head, Kant knew it was wrong, the main exit doors should be locked and the guards patrolling inside and out.

There was no-one.

Just what had Stella done?

Stella pointed to a neat stack of quantum blasters propped up against the wall. "Pick those weapons up guys, the guards won't be needing them anymore – we might" she said, realising for now she had to take charge. Half the men were unable to focus properly, the others struggling with the women. The time lapse was affecting them worse than before. It was going to be hard work to get them to function. She prayed at least one of them could find his brain well enough to pilot out of spaceport. Hopefully then they would recover, the opposite she didn't want to think about.

*

Stepping out into the early morning sunshine, the air was crystal clear, the silence over spaceport was strangely eerie.

It certainly didn't feel natural. The men started to panic, worried guards would show up any second, it would prove a bit awkward to explain their presence.

"Where are we going Stella?" Kant asked, as he watched her ushering everyone away from the building, towards open land behind the complex.

"We are heading for the very edge of spaceport Don, there is a huge alien spaceship waiting for us."

"Alien?" Kant stopped in his tracks; things just got a whole lot worse. *What was she talking about?*

Stella carried on, but shouted back to Don, "Yes, an alien spaceship Don. When the time and space distortion occurred, this weird alien ship arrived close to our upper atmosphere. There was no-one aboard, the authorities were in a panic at the time, they brought it down and left it at spaceport for the last five years where it wouldn't be seen. The fact is Don, the scientists didn't know what to do with it. At first it was assumed to have something to do with your disappearance."

Kant caught up with Stella, he heard most of it but wanted to know more. "Then how did you find out about it?" he asked, this he had to hear. Stella was certainly full of surprises.

"I'll tell you later Don. The ship is unguarded, no-one knows of its identity, but it's fully operational and equipped to take us beyond our galaxy."

"Wow!" said Kant, astounded by Stella.

"I thought you would appreciate a big ship to make our escape."

Stella was pleased; everything was going to plan. They would soon be airborne, then the search for her cousin could start.

"No, I mean wow! How did you come to know all this Stella? Spaceport is supposed to be off limits, and top secret I might add, and heavily guarded. Where are you getting your information?"

Kant realised there was a serious breach of security, it would not go unnoticed for long. Things must have been bad if this slip of a girl could simply walk onto spaceport property so easily. He was frightened to ask about the guards, she couldn't have done it alone. Then again –.

"Let's just say I have a friend in the government office records department."

"Ariel?" asked Don.

"Yes" was the reply.

Kant was still shocked by Stella, the last time he saw her, she was rather shy and awkward, and most certainly not this confident – outgoing and brave enough to risk her own life to help them. Then he thought, *when was the last time they met?* The time discrepancy was distorting his memory.

Had he and the crew really been missing for five years?

He didn't want more headaches on top of everything else.

CHAPTER FOUR

Finally arriving at the perimeter of spaceport, having trudged over the dry dusty barren land for over two miles and grudgingly dragging the women most of the way; everyone was fatigued, hungry and very thirsty. The trek was harsh on an empty stomach, and a lot longer than the pilots first realised. They were however relieved when Stella stopped. It was alright for her; she wasn't halfway to being dehydrated. Stella saw the state they were in and hoped to remedy it very soon. In the meantime, the pilots looked around, there was nothing to see but space and more space, as far as the eye could see. The vast emptiness stretched for many more miles. Nothing ever grew on this landscape. Hearts sank, the pilots couldn't go on, they'd had enough; the dust was getting in their eyes, in their mouths, it was unbearable.

"Where's the bloody spaceship then?" called out Selan, he was sure he didn't sign up to stare at the wasteland and eat dust. He dropped to his knees in despair. Kant looked about, suddenly realising Stella had disappeared. Nobody saw where she went, through the choking dust swirling in the breeze. It got very disturbing to think they were left alone. Was this the beginning of yet another nightmare? She had abandoned them.

In an instant a huge black alien spaceship materialised in front of the pilots towering over them. The smooth outer hull reflecting back the sunlight. An imposing vessel with no distinguishing marks, the pilots were unable to gauge it's true size as they couldn't see either the stern or the bow. It was a monster of a vessel. They stared open mouthed, trying to fathom how it appeared out of nowhere. Some of the pilots thought it was just a mirage, it couldn't be real, how did it stay hidden, that size would be difficult to keep under wraps for long.

Stella was back, she was definitely real, walking back to Kant with a smile on her face.

"Double wow!" said Kant, "how did you do that?" he was impressed.

"Simple refraction of light" replied Stella, "it was here all the time, I just reversed the light source, how else could the authorities hide a ship this size."

Now Kant had a dilemma, concerned how they could get this monster of a ship off the ground, then somehow pilot it in space with some degree of accuracy; especially when their brains were partially fried at present.

"And you say it was abandoned in space?" he asked.

Stella nodded. Kant was still sceptical; how would they understand the alien technology. He had serious doubts about piloting it. The pilots had only ever handled single crewed ships. This was the mother of all vessels ever created, and way out of their league.

"So, will this do Don?" asked Stella.

Kant was speechless, thinking how they were going to survive this suicide mission. It wasn't how he envisaged his life going. A month ago he had everything he needed, a well-paid job he loved, a comfortable lifestyle and good friends. Now he was an escaped prisoner on the run, about to steel the biggest spaceship in history and the fact he'd missed the last five years of his life. Then he thought, *it was only an alien ship, so he wasn't sure if stealing was the right word.* If it were really abandoned, technically they could claim it as salvage. None of it would help them to pilot it. Suddenly he got a heavy tap on the shoulder.

"Don, snap out of it, this is our ticket off this piece of rock. What do you say?" asked Stella. It would do no good staring at it. They had to move. Kant was about to make a point when an unfamiliar voice called out. Stepping out the airlock, a young woman appeared.

"About time you got here, I was getting worried."

"Is everything aboard Ariel?" Stella asked as she went to greet her best friend, and now fellow conspirator.

"Yes, everything we need is loaded and ready to go" replied Ariel.

Kant looked on with astonishment, thinking, *'this can't be right, not another bloody teenager.'* A sense of inadequacy came over him; to be rescued and ordered about by a couple of kids didn't feel comfortable. It wasn't right.

"Come on guys, get inside" waved Stella, "food and drink is waiting for you." She turned back to Kant, "It's time to go, Don." He just shook his head, not knowing what to say.

"I hope one of these men can fly this metal box Stella. I couldn't make head or tails of the controls" said Ariel, concerned with the condition of the men. The thought of food and drink got the pilots moving, still dragging the women with them.

"Stella, care to introduce us" said Kant, beginning to wonder how many more were enlisted in this breakout.

Ariel started to usher everyone through the airlock, some needing a little encouragement, a colossal spaceship like this was overpowering, never mind it was sitting there in plain sight all the time.

"Come on, keep going" urged Ariel, as vulnerable as they were, there was an urgency in her voice; the sooner they were away from spaceport the better.

Not for the first time Kant got a nasty twinge of pain in his ears, he couldn't shake it; his hearing fading badly. He tried hard to hold it together for the sake of his crew, but he was struggling just as much as they were.

"Come on Don, let's get you inside and I'll explain everything, and by the way, this is my best friend Ariel Zanet. She works for the government."

"Hi," called out Ariel as the last few were coming aboard. "Well, I used to work for the government – I resigned. They just don't know yet." She took Don's other arm and assisted Stella to get him aboard.

Stella soon realised that Don was in bad shape, worse than the others, his mind not fully functioning. In fact most of the crew were not the full shilling, she would have to take charge and organise everyone as best she could and pray one of them could operate the ships controls, if not his brain. The women would need nursemaiding for now, Stella soon realised the size of the job she and Ariel had taken on. They couldn't do it alone, they knew that. The men somehow had to snap out of it, time for a big announcement.

"Right, listen up guys, anyone who can function – in fact, anyone who can't even, we have to get airborne as soon as possible. Get to the control section and get this ship moving." Stella had to be brutal, this was no picnic. Because they took so long getting there, she was concerned someone might arrive at spaceport main complex and discover the empty buildings, no guards, no-one patrolling the main gate, and no prisoners. It was a well-known fact Commander Diamont was a lazy sod and wouldn't arrive too early; anyone else she couldn't be sure of. After what she did, she didn't want to hang around.

Kant allowed Stella and Ariel to take charge, he had to sit down before he fell down. He was in no fit state to control himself, let alone the others. For the women, it wasn't so good either, they took their seats quietly albeit with reluctance. It wasn't where they wanted to be but then hadn't the courage to argue. Their inner emotions were shot to pieces, making it difficult to function properly. An irrational fear of anyone close by was disturbing to them, they didn't seem to mind Ariel, so she stayed with them to aid their comfort. Stella assured Ariel it would get better once they got back into space.

That was the plan anyway.

*

Selan, Cheda and Gato found the control section and settled in to study the instrument panels. They hoped between them to work out the alien technology. The helm looked rather complicated to begin with, even for elite space pilots; with their mental ability under par, it was going to take time.

"Don't suppose it comes with a manual?" asked Gato.

"If you can't say anything constructive Gato, sod off" said Cheda, infuriated with his silly comment, normally he'd let it go, but with scrambled brains he could do without idiotic remarks.

"I was only thinking if we could locate the start button" Gato suggested, he was trying to help in his own way.

Selan looked at him as if to say, *'if you don't leave right now, I'm going to throttle you.'*

Gato raised his hands. "Just saying guys" he got the message he wasn't wanted. They weren't happy with his presence, so he left to find food, he was hungry, they could fathom out the controls on their own.

Everyone else found a seat, all feeling worse for wear, their entire bodies out of sync with the timeline; and all at different levels of confusion. Selan, Cheda and Gato seemed less affected; still they struggled, but someone had to pilot this monster out of Clariziane space. It was a calculated risk by Stella, one they had to take. Staying on the planet surface was not an option, the pilots would have gone completely nuts.

With Gato taken his leave in a huff, another pilot entered the control section to help, Shan Tayon, barely functioning but he thought he could help, it was better than sitting and doing nothing. Everyone was out of their comfort zone, they just had to keep at it.

"Hi guys, how's it going?" asked Tayon, glancing over their shoulders at the helm controls. It was certainly a lot more complex than their own one-man ships.

"Slow going, Tayon, but I think we can do this" said Cheda. He'd been trying a sequence of switches and coloured buttons to see what would light up, something had to kick-start this thing. Tayon noticed a large red button neither

Cheda nor Selan were touching; *pressing that one might start the engine* he thought, so reached over to try.

"Don't touch the red button!" screamed Cheda loudly.

Tayon jumped back, startled by his outburst.

"We're not sure what it does" said Selan.

"Sorry, I was only trying to help guys" apologised Tayon.

"Yeh well, Gato tried to help, and he was useless" said Cheda, he really didn't want any more interference, the job was hard enough as it was.

"It's ok Tayon" said Selan "we think we have it down to two options, it's either weapons or a self-destruct button."

"We think –" said Cheda.

"Oh shit man, that's heavy" said Tayon, he was glad he didn't get the chance to touch it.

"Look Tayon, Selan and I have got this, go away, and leave us to it. Go and annoy Gato or something."

"Okay, okay, no need to bite my head off Cheda" said Tayon annoyed at being spoken to like that. If they wanted to do it alone then so be it. The effects of the time lapse wasn't doing much to help their mood swings. Everyone was a bit tetchy, Cheda the worst. He was taking this mission seriously, if they didn't get it right, they were all screwed – that much he was certain of.

Going back to the controls Cheda did one more check, he was sure he got it this time. "Right Selan, I believe we may have ignition." The control panel suddenly burst into life, clicks were heard, then a faint humming sound filtered through the helm, it seemed to be coming from beneath their feet.

"Well done Cheda, let's see if we can get this baby off the ground."

Selan got excited, their perseverance had finally paid off. The ship started to move, everyone felt the vibrations, it was a good feeling to finally be on the move.

Stella was particularly pleased, the sooner they were away, the better, time was limited. Perhaps then the pilots would start to get their minds back in sync with their bodies, whatever time zone they end up in. there was no guarantee of a quick fix, they might have to live with the consequences, then live with the uncertainly of outer space and the unknown.

A delay in lift off sent Stella along the corridor to get an update. The ship was moving but it was still on the ground. It seemed mastering the alien ship was proving trickier than first thought. Stella started to get impatient, they needed to go.

"Hi guys, what's the problem, why aren't we airborne yet?" she asked Cheda and Selan. As far as she was aware from Ariel, the ship was operational, they didn't need hiccups now. Ariel's information was rock solid.

Cheda felt his heart miss a beat with Stella so close, she was leaning over between the pilots seats for a better look at the helm. He could feel her warm breath on his neck, his body clock was already a mess, now Stella made it go into overdrive with passion leading the way. It was left to Selan to answer.

"Yeh, sorry about the delay, a few minor glitches to sort out, like we don't really know what we're doing. Some of the technology is a complete mystery. But rest assured Stella, we'll get there, give us a couple more minutes and the ship will be airborne" said Selan with some degree of confidence, although he had a sneaky suspicion he might be piloting alone for a while.

"Brillant, as quick as you can then" said Stella, then patted both men on the shoulder and left. Cheda was in a complete daze, now she touched him.

"You are so sad mate" said Selan, "can I be your best man?" he asked with a smile. His friend got the love bug really bad; this was the real thing.

*

Stella returned to sit with Kant, he was still waiting for answers and getting impatient. There was so much he didn't understand about the situation the pilots found themselves in, it was surreal, very confusing for an already muddled head. No way could he work it out on his own.

Ariel continued tending to everyone's needs, making sure they all got rehydrated and plenty to eat. She spent most of the night before loading provisions on board. She was tired herself, but the pilots welfare was a priority. All the while she was feeling sad inside, sad at the fact they could never return to Clarizia. This was a one-way ticket to destination unknown. She and Stella had no choice but to go with the pilots, they knew too much anyway to stay. They also knew there would be nothing to come back to. Ariel was grieving for her family, unable to tell her parents what was going on. That was hard for her, Stella had no-one, only Sol. Soon they would all be homeless refugees in space. Not a nice thought Ariel wanted floating about in her head, but it was their new reality. There had to be more out there in the black emptiness, she was sure the pilots would find it, at least she hoped they would.

Kant sat looking around his new environment, his crew now in the hands of a couple of teenagers, who appeared to be managing very well. He wasn't sure how they could cope all together in one big ship, there didn't appear to be much in the way of sleeping accommodation for a huge vessel this size, it seemed odd. He wondered what kind of aliens occupied the ship before, maybe they didn't sleep. His head was full of questions.

"How are you doing Don?" asked Stella, putting an arm round him, it was obvious he needed comfort. She always regarded Don as a surrogate uncle, she liked him, and he was supportive whenever she needed it. Now Don needed that support, he put on a brave face for her, but couldn't disguise how wretched he felt, useless came to mind. His hearing almost gone and distorted, he thought for a moment Stella was whispering even though she was sat right next to him. His fogged-up brain needed sorting badly.

"Tell me what you know Stella, how did you and your friend get mixed up in all of this?"

"Well for a start I do know Sol is alive, but he isn't in this universe."

Kant gasped; his bottom lip nearly hit the floor. *What was she talking about? There was only one universe, and they were in it.*

"I don't understand Stella, you're being cryptic. Explain again what you just said."Gato walked past at that moment with food in his hand, munching away as he spoke, "Don't worry Kant, she lost me when she said five years have passed. We'll never get that time back. Believe me man, another universe – we're screwed." Then he carried on walking, always the sceptical one, totally unconvinced about what they were doing. Being on the run wasn't quite what he had in mind for his life.

"Ignore him Stella, carry on. I need to know everything" said Kant. He was still trying to come to terms with her last statement, and was certain he wouldn't get it. Another universe was not something he could believe or even visualise, it wasn't real. Their galaxy was the only one, and no-one else existed but the Clarizianes. *Why was he so stupid to go out on those monthly patrols at all*

Clarizianes were made to believe the universe was empty. Had the authorities been holding out on the people for centuries? He did wonder. Then how far back did the lie go. The whole experience was making him even more wretched if that were possible. Apart from the women Don was suffering the effects of the distortion the most.

"Don, Don –" Stella shook him, trying to get him to focus; she couldn't have his mind wandering off.

"Sorry, what did you say?" he was back.

"As I was saying, Sol is alive. I know he is, I never believed any of you died. Ariel came across some confidential files while working in the government offices, she has a photographic memory by the way and remembered every detail before being told to shred the evidence. They didn't suspect her Don, those idiots regarded her as a dumb teenager. Then she was transferred to Neal Polton's office –"

"That idiot –" interrupted Kant, he was sick of that man.

"Don, what she found out will blow your mind."

"You mean, more than it already is" said Don, Stella wasn't helping his nerves.Stella did have sympathy for him, it was hard to take in. "I'm sorry Don, I know it's not what you wanted to hear, but it seems our scientists have been experimenting with time travel, and they are already building a huge portal in the city. The government are telling people it's a new municipal building; one with no windows would you believe."

Kant listened, he didn't fully understand everything Stella was saying, she seemed so sure of her facts. The whole universe thing sounded ludicrous; it could actually be true – even if he didn't want it to be.

"Go on Stella, what else?"

"Don, they messed up big time, the experiments were flawed, the galaxy is now in total disarray. Distortions of space and time have been reported but hushed up. It might even have gone past our galaxy. The problem was you pilots returning in the wrong time."

"We went forward five years?" questioned Don.

"Yes, exactly, but anyone questioning it are never seen again."

Kant didn't like the sound of that last bit. *How could the authorities do that?* Making people disappear was alarming.

"Is that why we were locked up on our return? We did witness some weird anomaly in space, didn't know what to make of it at the time. That was when Sol vanished."

"Yes, but it gets worse, I'm afraid you and the other pilots were not going to prison, just disappear." Stella ran her fingers across her neck, Kant got the message.

"Bloody hell!" he was shocked, *how could the government just murder people and hope to get away with it?* Now he understood the shifty behaviour of Polton and Diamont, it all made sense; they were merely following orders, but Kant deemed them just as guilty.

"There is more Don, much more" said Stella sounding more serious than before. Kant didn't think it could get any worse. It just did.

"Ariel had been suspicious of goings on in the government offices for a while, everything was getting secretive, she began to investigate –"

"That was highly dangerous under the circumstances" interrupted Kant, Ariel should not have got involved, she was too young. It wasn't her problem.

"Yes well, she did Don and I'm glad she did. She read reports, historical documents, stuff that hadn't yet happened but will. The timeline was messed up. I think Clarizia got caught up in a time warp, that's why you slipped five years into the future – and that's why I have to get you all back into space, to hopefully put your minds back in sync with your bodies. Then we find Sol."

Stella thought it best she tell Don the raw truth as she saw it.

"After that?" he asked.

"Sorry Don, this is going to be hard for you. Clarizia is doomed, the portal is almost complete, and they are waiting for the new messiah to lead the chosen ones into history."

Kant hung his head down; his whole body was racked with pain, and it wasn't just the distortion causing the problem. Stella hit him with the biggest bombshell in Clariziane history.

How were they supposed to deal with something like that?

Now he also had two teenagers on board to worry about.

"Won't leaving Clarizia affect you and Ariel?" asked Kant, they risked so much to help the pilots. He thought they should really stay behind. Stella did point out they couldn't under the circumstances. "As for whether Ariel and I being affected, I don't know Don. Whatever you're thinking we're coming with you, we have to, besides, I need to find my cousin, Sol is the only family I have. Ariel can't stay behind; she knows too much. She read Polton's file he left on his desk. It's why we had to act quickly, before anyone found out what we've done, and they will know for sure it was Ariel who found the location of this alien ship."

"What did those damn scientists think they were doing, messing with time travel in the first place?"

"Exactly Don –" said Stella, "Clarizia will become extinct soon. The portal is a means of escape, not everyone was invited for the journey, that's why it had to stay secret to the very last."

Stella was bitter at the fact her name wasn't even on the list Ariel showed her, but Ariel's was. It didn't seem right.

"Oh Stella, this is bigger than I first thought" Kant felt very down, his feelings for his fellow beings diminished greatly, in a way he was glad to have no part of it.

"You do believe me, don't you Don?" asked Stella, "that Sol is alive."

"At the moment I'm not sure what to believe."

"Don, he's alive. I feel it, trust me" Stella was steadfast in her belief. She felt a deep connection to her cousin, something she didn't understand at first. Now she was certain Sol was out there, alive but alone – but not for long.

In a strange way Kant did understand Stella, he had a sense much the same about Sol. He thought at first it was his distorted brain cells playing havoc, but not now, Stella was right, they had to go in search for him; the problem was where to look.

"How the hell do we find Sol if he's in another universe Stella? Don't get me wrong, I do believe what you're saying, even it's hard to swallow. I'm hoping you have the answers." Kant realised it was all real and there was no going back now, it was the forward bit he had difficulty with.

"Well, I don't have all the answers Don, I thought we could get airborne and wing it – maybe." Stella shrugged her shoulders, being a little vague, she hadn't thought that far ahead. She then took a deep breath to deliver another bombshell because she hadn't told Don everything. She was about to when a loud voice boomed out from the control section.

"We have it!" shouted Cheda, he wanted to make sure they all heard the good news. Finding the switch to start things up was easy, it had taken ages to find the buttons to actually lift off. They still don't know what the red button was for, deciding it was best not to touch it for the time being.

"Well done guys" called out Stella, she was pleased for them, maybe now the pressure would ease a little.

Another quick check of the instruments and Selan was happy with his section. "Better fire it up then and get this tin can off the ground. Are you ready buddy?"

"Ready as I'll ever be" replied Cheda.

"I'm so glad we're moving at last Don" said Stella.

Kant nodded, also relieved but nervous; the great unknown awaited them. He was scared what they might find, the idea of another universe didn't give him any confidence for the journey. Then he remembered Stella was about to say something.

"Oh, it's nothing really, I wanted us airborne before someone finds out what I did at spaceport." She had a look of guilt that suggested to Don trouble with a capital T. He looked her in the eye, *what had she done that he should know about?* He still hadn't asked about the guards, that was obvious now.

How did this slip of a girl do any of it?

And just when did she grow up?

That bit obviously by-passed him.

"Stella – what have you done?" Kant asked hesitantly, he wasn't entirely sure he wanted to know, but felt he had to ask.

"Okay Don, nothing much, well sort of nothing much –"

"Spit it out Stella, now!"

"Alright – I sort of rigged spaceport to blow, happy now."

"What? How?" Kant thought his hearing let him down again.

Did she really say, rig spaceport to blow? It had to be wrong.

"I'm almost afraid to ask –"

"Don, if the authorities intend coming after us, they can't do it without spaceport or spaceships."

"Where did you get the explosives from, and how the hell do you know about bombs and detonators?"

"You don't know me as well as you think Don" she declined to elaborate further, except to say the detonator was timed to go off in less than an hour. They had to reach past the upper atmosphere at least, there was enough explosives to flatten spaceport.

Kant was shocked, she was right, he didn't know her at all.

Stella got to her feet, needing to check on Ariel, then the control section to make sure Cheda and Selan knew the urgency. As she left Kant's side, she turned back to say she had one request to ask. "Do you suppose we can dispense with surnames; it sounds so formal, stuffy, don't you think?"

Kant looked at her as she raised an eyebrow that made the ridges on her forehead wrinkle up, in a cute way. He then wondered where she got her brains from, she was going to be a handful. And it hadn't gone unnoticed how Cheda behaved around her. He had his work cut out for sure.

Poor man.

CHAPTER FIVE

Leaving Clarizia behind was a dreadful wrench for the men and women, the hardest decision they had ever made but the right one. Seeing their home disappear from the rear-view monitors was heartbreaking. They watched as a huge fireball was detected in the upper atmosphere, that was obviously spaceport gone. It must have been one hell of a bomb; Don declined to ask Stella just how much she used to blow the place; it was best he didn't know. Tears were shed, mostly from the men, some had families, their lives torn apart through no fault of their own. They never had the chance to say goodbye.

On the upside they were slowly beginning to feel more like their old selves the further away they got from the planet, without realising the pilots slipped back through the time warp, back five years to reconnect their minds with their bodies. It was time now to relax a bit, the immediate danger was over; now the unknown future lay ahead, that thought terrified them. Routine missions were one thing, travelling beyond their own galaxy was daunting, and as Cheda pointed out, they didn't know which direction to take.

Space was still a dangerous place, a spatial discrepancy that had not corrected itself, as well as a time distortion occurring would not help the situation. Aboard the alien ship they were blissfully unaware of what lie ahead. They were happy at least for now to have full mental capacity back, bodies finally back in sync with their brains, it felt so good to feel normal. The pilots were confident they had the ability to deal with any situation, even if they didn't understand the complexity of existence in the order of life.

They had to keep going, no choice.

Don was glad his hearing was back to near normal, the deafness he found frightening, he suffered more than others, especially the headaches. For a while he thought he would go mad with the pain, his brain got so muddled. Each crew member suffered different degrees of impairment, all luckily seemed to have recovered, even the women. It was good to see them back to their energetic confident selves. Even their volatile tempers was good news, not so for Tran Fiba who connected with a right hook from Cora Lisles. He made a bad comment, and it didn't take much to set off a Clariziane woman. He should have known better than to tease the women over their conduct in the cell. Things could have been a lot worse. However Don was very concerned about Hanzon Gato who seemed to have developed an eating disorder, he always had food in his mouth. Don let it go for now; it was unimportant at present.

Taking Stella and Ariel into space didn't affect them in any way, which was a bonus because none of them were medics. If anyone did get sick they were in trouble. The teenagers were immune to the time distortions happening all the time, how long it would last was anyone's guess.

The alien ship was behaving itself, though with twenty-one people on board, the ship wasn't as big as first imagined, not if the crew wanted solitude now and again. They had to make do because it was all they had. Not knowing how long they would take to find Sol was the hard part; no one dared to ask the obvious question about what to do with their lives afterwards. Finding Sol was their only concern for now.

The crew had finally been briefed on what Stella and Ariel had done to aid the pilots prison break, and what led up to it. The government wanting them all dead was unforgivable, getting angry would do them no good, they were grateful for being alive. Time to settle down to a routine for piloting the ship, there wasn't much else to do, except watch space. Boredom came to mind several times.

*

Two weeks into the journey the edge of the galaxy was approaching, time to make a big decision. It was difficult if not impossible to gauge what velocity the ship was doing, some of the instrument dials were still a mystery. There did seem to be more dials than they actually needed, which didn't really help the pilots. At that point no one was sure if the ship was even capable of taking them beyond their own solar system. It was down to chance and a lot of guesswork. The only dial that looked familiar resembled a clock, it was showing a time and date, but the pilots didn't know whose timeline it related to.

Still no one touched the red button, that stayed strictly out of bounds until someone figured out what it was for.

As far as the pilots could tell, they were approaching the sector where they lost Sol, Don recognised the star formation ahead, at least the one before space got twisted out of shape. The ship reached that point without any obstacles, it was a good sign. Now all Don needed was a sign to show them the way, something to say what direction to take. Slowing the ship down seemed a good idea until they made a decision. Looking out the portholes at the vast black unknown, the pilots were overcome with mixed emotions, mostly fearful and daunted by the fact they had never been any further than this before. Orders were very specific from spaceport to the edge of the galaxy and back again, a three-week journey. Now those decisions belonged to the pilots alone, but that was not forthcoming. Don was hoping something would happen like before; it would at least give them a clue to how Sol vanished.

*

All the while they were being watched, the universe observed the pilots every move. If they made the wrong decision there was going to be serious consequences. A bad case of hiccups from the universe would be the least of their worries. A major catastrophe across the cosmos would unfold, the universe was at the mercy of a right or wrong decision made by aliens in the parallel universe. Their superiors had already made the first mistake.

They should not enter.

*

Rol sat in silence thinking about Don, *what was he waiting for?* It looked like he was expecting someone. Rol stared out his porthole, he saw nothing but distant stars, *what else was there?*

"What are we waiting for Don?" he asked, he felt they should be doing something.

"I really don't know Rol, do we proceed outside our galaxy or not? Will this alien tin can even be able to take us there? Maybe we should wait here for a sign." Don was still reluctant to venture into the unknown, he didn't want to admit he was scared, he didn't realise they were all scared.

"A sign? What do you mean Don?" Rol was puzzled by Don's behaviour; he was being very vague. *What did he think would happen out on the edge of their galaxy? What did any of them know?* Rol started to question himself, surely the whole universe was empty so it seemed unlikely they would bump into other beings, let alone Sol. He was certain it was too late now to save Sol; he had to be dead; he just didn't want to be the one to say it.

For what seemed like hours the ship remained motionless, Don and Rol were about to fall asleep at the controls, mostly through sheer boredom. No one came to relieve them so they sat slumped in their seats, a conversation at that point all but dried up; they hadn't much to talk about and there was only so many times one could count the stars. Don tried to switch off his emotions to fall asleep, at least that way he didn't have to deal with the problem. It wasn't ideal and it didn't work anyway, because suddenly a high-pitched warning siren woke them and everyone else on board, a piercing noise shattering the silence and almost bursting the most sensitive of eardrums. Super hearing wasn't an advantage, they soon came to realise that.

Stella was first rushing to the control section with several pilots behind her, all wanting the damn noise to stop.

"What did you touch?" screamed Stella shouting to get her voice heard.

"Nothing, honest, we did nothing" pleaded Rol.

Don was already checking the dials trying to ascertain which one was causing the awful sound. A red flashing light persisted as it got louder and louder, pressing it made no difference. Rol assisted Don but they failed to work out where it was coming from, nothing stopped the penetrating noise.

"Can't you turn that bloody noise off; my eardrums are going to explode" shouted Hanzon Gato pushing into the front section.

"Don't be so dramatic Hanzon, we're all in the same boat" said Kat Loris right next to him, she was for slapping him right there and then. Fisah Selan looked at her with eyes that said, *'please don't.'* Hitting Hanzon wouldn't solve anything.

Most of the crew were now crowding in and around the control section while holding their hands over their ears, which actually did little to help.

"I don't know what's causing it guys" said Don, he tried every switch, every button in an effort to stop the noise. He avoided the dreaded red button; it wasn't lit up so he assumed it couldn't be that.

"Maybe it has something to do with that" said Rol pointing to the monitor in front of him.

"What is that?" questioned Don, something was happening in the sector of space directly ahead.

Kat pushed in to lean over Rol, for a better look.

"I see it, but don't believe it" she said, shocked at the images. It couldn't be real. Don was busy trying all the switches again, the noise had to stop soon, or they would all go deaf.

A strange distortion in space appeared to be twisting out of shape, the alignment of stars changed, then in a blink of an eye, it was gone. Now there was a new star system showing on the monitor. Everyone stared at it, what they saw was all wrong, definitely not their galaxy, they knew that like the back of their hand. This was a strange star system that didn't match up with what they expected, though at that point it wasn't clear what they were expecting. Don rose to his feet to peer out the porthole, he wanted to see first-hand what was outside, several of the pilots did the same as if they didn't believe what was showing on the monitor. The area of space was new, no doubt about it. Don made a calculated guess this was the other universe Stella mentioned. It must have been how Sol vanished.

The warning siren finally petered out, everyone giving a sigh of relief, now perhaps they could have a proper conversation.

"Well, I think we did it" said Don, "I reckon this is the route Sol took."

"So we're really in another universe" said Fisah, he was struggling like the rest of them to get their heads round what just happened.

"It rather looks that way my friend" Don stood at the porthole realising what they might have achieved, he didn't know whether to congratulate himself or shoot himself. He didn't know what to say next, this was completely out of their comfort zone. He thought to himself *'now what do I do?'* He was stuck for words, he really thought he had a plan when it came to this, however he found his brain not working.

"So what course do we take?" asked Stella, she was eager to go, didn't seem any point in hanging around any longer. Nobody had an answer. They were lost in a universe they knew nothing about, ahead of them lay the unknown, and they had no idea how big this universe was.

How could they hope to search every inch of it if they didn't know where it actually ended? Did it have perimeters? It was whole new adventure for the pilots, and they weren't sure they were ready for it. Eyes went round the control section looking at each other, surely one of them had the answer.

"Well, at least we know it wasn't the red button everyone's been avoiding" said Hanzon attempting to lighten the mood. The warning siren was still a mystery no one could offer any solution for.

"I don't know about the rest of you wimps, but I'm fed up sitting around doing nothing" said Kat, "How about we start the engines and go straight ahead, surely that's what Sol would have done." It seemed the only logical option left. The other women backed Kat up, they were all for action having been so withdrawn in their shells while in prison. They were so pumped up and ready for anything. It was time for bold decisions.

"Whoa, whoa, just a moment –" said Rol, he was having doubts about this whole scenario, he felt the women were rushing it. "I'm going to say what everyone is thinking, are we certain Sol is still alive?"

"Yes!" cried Stella, "Absolutely he is alive, you imply that again you're going to get a fat lip Rol." She was livid at his suggestion, Rol on the other hand thought he'd blown his chances with her, he didn't mean to offend but it had to be said.

"I agree with Stella" said Don, "Besides, where else can we go anyway?"

A moment of silence as the pilots weighed up their options which took all of two seconds because they had no options to debate.

"That's settled then, let's go, beats waiting for the universe to come to us." Stella made the decision, forceful in her manner, adamant Sol was alive out there somewhere.

“Anyone want to argue with that” she said with a fist waving about. At that point, the men really did feel like wimps, though they would never admit to it, truth was no one wanted a fat lip.

They had to carry on.

*

The universe watched, listened to the pilots debate. It was angry with the Clarizianes, they made their first transgression, trespassing. A rift in the space time continuum allowed their passage into another universe. Repercussions were inevitable, the results devastating, there was no other option.

*

Fisah and Cora Lisles, one of the women pilots took to the helm controls giving Rol and Don a well-earned rest. Everyone else settled down, thankful for the silence once more. They prayed the warning siren didn’t go off again, the ear-piercing noise they could do without. Answers was what was needed.

All the pilots were deep in their own thoughts, anxious about what lie ahead in the unknown; what they would do with their future hanging in the balance, and whether Sol was still alive and actually made it this far. Stella resolute he was, backed up by Don. He had a deep-seated feeling his friend was indeed out there, lost in the vast emptiness, and probably worried about them, not himself. In the meantime he told Fisah and Cora to be extra vigilant. This universe, if as expected different to their own, could be hostile, no telling what alien life existed here. They were not soldiers, never trained to be, they had to remember that, merely pilots, elite pilots but that was the extent of their abilities. This was a new experience, a hazardous mission fraught with danger. The pilots would never be ready to fight the unknown enemy, although Stella and the other women had other ideas. Don was sceptical and warned the women of their vulnerability. Stella ignored the remark.

The Clarizianes own galaxy was devoid of other life, so never before had they encountered other beings, this universe could be littered with them. It was a daunting prospect to face; yet they pressed on with no choice but to go forward into the deepest depths of the unknown that stretched out in front of them, all the while wondering what the alien ship was capable of.

Another week passed, and still no clue to the route Sol had taken. It wasn't looking very promising for him; his oxygen supply would be spent by now. That knowledge put more doubt in the pilots minds, but Stella insisted her cousin was alive. She and Ariel pointed out how they risked their own lives to help the pilots, they had to put their trust in Stella, she would never give up until Sol was found.

Kat and Hanzon sat at the controls taking their turn piloting the huge ship while the others rested, or slept, there was nothing else to do but sit around for something to happen and getting very frustrated when it didn't. Feelings were running out of control; tempers got a little frayed now and again with nowhere to hide in a confined space. The doubts reared up again, some started to question it was a mission too far, especially Hanzon who was his usual pessimistic self. He felt abandoned by the others; he was a team guy, but it didn't feel that way. He kept muttering to himself how his life was worthless, all the pilots teased him at one time or another. He also felt ridiculed at the unfair treatment he got, he was after all a first-class pilot, as good as the others. Kat did her best to keep his spirits up seeing how miserable he really was. All the pilots were feeling down, but Hanzon seemed to feel it more deeply.

"Don't give up my friend, we will find Sol, if he came this way we will find him then he will know what to do after that, trust me." Kat said, though in her heart she wasn't so sure.

"Hope so Kat, because I tell you I'm never going on another mission ever again."

“Stop worrying Hanzon, after this mission we’re all done” she said placing her hand on his shoulder to reassure him he wasn’t alone in all this.

Hanzon nodded, but he wasn’t convinced, Kat meant well but something told him they would spend the rest of their lives drifting through space. Suddenly he was hungry again. “What time is it?” he asked, “Must be about time for food.”

“You’re kidding right, you’re always hungry. The supplies won’t last forever you know Hanzon, and besides you better take a look at that dial in front of you.” said Kat pointing to what they had assumed was some kind of clock.

“Whoa! That can’t be good, can it?” if Hanzon was feeling depressed before he just crashed to rock bottom. The dial was going crazy, numbers whizzing round at speed barely registering anything before stopping, then racing forward again before going into reverse. Hanzon’s bottom lip already on the floor in a complete panic.

“What does it mean?” Hanzon asked in a shaky nervous voice, he didn’t want the blame if it all went wrong.

“Hell if I know” said Kat trying not to sound too alarmed for Hanzon’s sake, he was already stressing out, a complete bag of nerves. *Best not to tease him at the moment* she thought, but really he was such a wimp, she had long forgotten how she and the other women felt. That was out of their control, so she reckoned it didn’t count.

Stella popped up front just to check up on the progress and see if they needed refreshments.

“Hi guys” she said light-heartedly in her usual bubbly self.

“Hi Stella” said Kat.

“So what’s happening here? I heard raised voices as I came down the corridor” asked Stella noticing Hanzon looked like he was going into a meltdown. She wondered if Kat had been teasing him again.

“Take a look at that clock thing Stella” Kat pointed to the dial again, it was still moving forward at an alarming rate, then reversing.

Stella leaned over to take a look, then swiftly fisted it hard. It stopped.

"Bloody hell Stella, I hoped you haven't broken it" yelled Hanzon half jumping out of his seat, he didn't expect her to be so brutal.

"It will be fine, calm down Hanzon. I suspect the dial doing that means something is about to happen, you best stay alert." Even though Stella sounded confident she wasn't, blowing up spaceport was one thing, but alien technology, what did she know? She wouldn't let on she was as scared as the men, that would mean she was vulnerable, something she simply refused to be.

"If the star system changes at all let Don know straightaway."

"Sure thing Stella" said Kat and settled back into her seat.

"If I smacked that clock you would have given me a right mouthful" said Hanzon annoyed at the fact that Stella got away with it.

"Be quiet Hanzon and concentrate."

"Well I hope something does happen soon, this is getting boring" snapped Hanzon, he didn't see the point anymore, and he was still hungry, Stella didn't bring him any food or drink, he had to suffer and said so.

"Shut up!" said Kat, now she had had enough of Hanzon, "You sure like tempting fate" she moaned.

CHAPTER SIX

Sitting in a cold dank cell isolated from all other prisoners, two lonely souls awaited their fate: going on trial for kidnapping, false imprisonment, slavery, and mass murder. Two aliens on Earth from another universe who shouldn't be there, they were making the imbalance between the universes a whole lot worse. Now they were locked up in a sparse unfurnished cell, barely any light and a rock-hard floor. They were scared shitless what would become of them.

Qrotei and his friend Oston, Naasooks from the parallel universe, whose planet was knocked out of orbit and inadvertently passed through a rift in the space time continuum. From that moment on the planet Naasook was doomed, heading on a collision course with a nearby sun. the only two Naasooks left alive were brought to Earth to stand trial for crimes by the entire Naasook people. They feared the sentence of death was hanging over them, they had no defence but hoped for leniency as they did try to make amends in the end. Unfortunately it wasn't going to help their plight, the charges were severe. It seemed very likely they would be found guilty even before the trial commenced. Public opinion made it impossible for the verdict to go any other way.

In the adjoining cell sat another lonely figure, who only just made it back to Earth with the Naasook prisoners by the skin of their teeth. Rescue ship Retriever-1 was buffeted almost its entire journey back, navigating past the spatial distortions, and displacement of several meteor showers put in its path. It was done deliberately; something didn't want them to make it.

But they did.

Now former rescue Captain Marc Westler was also on trial for murder as witnessed by his own senior officer Stuart Kranley. His fate already sealed. All retriever rescue ships were grounded for the foreseeable future. It was deemed the selection process for senior commanding officers was flawed. Captain Westlers conduct was not in keeping with strict company guidelines. He acted rashly on numerous occasions, did not always adhere to company procedures as laid out by Earth mission HQ, then he went on to commit cold-blooded murder while in uniform, defaming the company and embarrassing the entire rescue organisation. He was stripped of his rank as soon as he set foot back on Earth.

As for Captain Gram Valmak, he was tried in his absence and found guilty of gross misconduct, disobeying orders, theft of company property, i.e. space rescue ship Retriever-2. On top of those charges he was also found guilty of mass murder of an entire world, Kangis-3. It never occurred to Earth authorities Kangis-3 came from a parallel universe and charges would not apply as they had no jurisdiction.

The news of Captain Valmaks demise never reached Earth; the authorities had no idea they put a dead man on trial. The fact was reports saying Retriever-2 had been destroyed did not reach Earth until after the trial verdict. It wouldn't have made any difference as Valmak had been dead almost a year. To complicate matters the news about Retriever-2 arrived a full two months before some of the crimes actually took place, the time shift having a huge effect, but it was some time before idiot scientists on Earth began to even suspect there was a serious problem out in deep space, and it was heading their way. All life was being disrupted one way or another because the law of nature being controlled by the universe deciding to have one big hissy fit.

Earth authorities were slow to act, even then they didn't know what to do about the timeline and spatial distortions that were rife across the universe. Some didn't seem to think it was even their problem.

That really upset the universe.

Mission HQ disbanded itself in the aftermath, the company decided there was no profit to be had now the entire fleet was grounded. Earth officials were in total confusion, their standing in the known universe was under threat; not controlling their superior officers being a major factor, and a blot on their reputation as guardians of the universe. Fixing it would take more than a few apologies.

The echelons of power crumbled.

Federation police didn't get off scot-free either, destroying an intergalactic hospital ship with a full crew aboard, for whatever reason, did not sit too well with the other planets who relied on their medical assistance. The federation police did have their orders, but with the timeline totally out of sync with the physical side of life, those orders kept being changed with new updates either in the past or in the distant future. Finally the order of shoot to kill was rescinded, unfortunately the commanders of those ships never received such an order, not until after the event. When all federation ships returned to Earth the officers were immediately relieved of duty and summarily charged with the wilful destruction of company property and loss of life, charges just falling short of murder.

Earths reputation was shot.

Planet Earth had no real standing in the universe once the news was out; being isolated from all other civilisations Earth was on the brink of collapse economically. The profitable rescue ships were about the only real income Earth had to rely on. Now that had dried up it meant no work for the masses. It seemed putting aliens on trial for their own crimes was really to save face.

Even that failed.

*

The universe was going to make them pay for their arrogance and stupidity. This behaviour could not go unpunished any longer, the imbalance with the parallel universe made it difficult for the natural order of life to continue in a sustainable way.

The universe was furious, it blinked hard. That had repercussions of its own, nobody was coming out of this unscathed.

CHAPTER SEVEN

Advancing across space, a fleet of heavily armed, menacing looking warships belonging to the Cynturian empire were on a destructive crusade to wipe out all who stood in their way. A trail of death and destroyed worlds lay in their wake as they entered another star system looking for the next victim. All life on many planets were annihilated without a shred of emotion. The Cynturians spared no one. More than fifty spaceships in formation were heading for the ultimate prize in their quest for supremacy.

Planet Earth.

The Cynturians regarded their species to be the most supreme and fiercest fighting warriors of the cosmos, no one had firepower to match theirs. Planet Earth would be a valuable trophy, long sought after. Before reaching their final destination the Cynturians had a little revenge mission to take care of on the way, if only they could find the culprit. They wanted retribution for the death of their supreme commander Emperor Yulan. A hefty price was placed on the head of a certain little alien who was responsible. The alien's identity was only just recently discovered so they knew exactly who to look for, a pint-sized annoying alien in dungarees with wobbly eyes out on stalks.

It was assumed some time ago they had killed everyone aboard the Earth rescue ship Retriever-2 before it disappeared in mysterious circumstances on the edge of the universe. They were certain the ship could not have survived the onslaught on all flanks. Naturally the Cynturians claimed the victory for themselves and departed that sector of space swiftly. The other aliens they would fight another day. But now rumours were rife some may have survived including the dungaree clad alien they so wanted. As no debris was ever found apart from the tailpiece of Retriever-2 the warships re-emerged to search for the survivors and wipe them out once and for all, and if that little squirt of an alien turned up, all the better. They intended to have fun with him before blasting his body to the four corners of the universe. The death of Emperor Yulan would not go unpunished.

While on route several messages were intercepted from various sources, but the Cynturians did not realise that timeline discrepancies were occurring constantly, space also being distorted which they did witness numerous times but chose to ignore it, none of it relevant to their mission. Nothing was going to stop the advance of the Cynturian fleet. The messages they received were out of sequence with real time, something they were unaware of. Nevertheless it gave them the one name they wanted. Xander, the alien Avaan responsible for Yulan's death. If indeed he was still alive, he wouldn't be for much longer.

After disposing of him the fleet would advance towards Earth to wipe it and it's people out, giving them total control of every galaxy. They would reign supreme for all eternity.

Except one minor detail.

The Cynturians hadn't thought far enough ahead, and wiping out life everywhere gave them nothing to reign over. It was in reality a very important factor in their quest for supremacy.

They weren't quite as smart as they thought!

'Stupid aliens.'

*

Continuing the journey deeper into another solar system, it wasn't too long before a new victim appeared on the radar. The

Cynturian warships were quick to pick it up. A single spaceship travelling towards them at a very low velocity, a huge black vessel with no markings on the hull to identify it's origin; it wasn't important who it was. A little target practice was good for morale. Warships at the front of the convoy could have the pleasure. The unknown alien ship was now in perfect range. Time for fun. New Emperor of the fleet Axon instructed his overeager warriors they should not play games with the oncoming ship, as the late Emperor Yulan once did, it cost him his life.

The first seven warships at the front of the huge convoy were ordered to open fire, which they did simultaneously. A barrage of destructive energy blasts rained down on the defenceless alien ship. No mercy was shown, the bright blinding laser blasts lit up space like an emerging new star on steroids, a cloud of space dust and smoke screened the ship, the attack was intense and relentless. Axon wanted his victims obliterated completely. Every single blast found its target and continued for a full five minutes. Axon was happily laughing, whoever it was would be an excellent trophy for him.

Finally the firing stopped, Axon wanted to observe the destruction, a ship that size would have many lives aboard and worthy of a victory for the Cynturian empire. Expecting to see floating debris and not much else, Axon stopped laughing when through the haze of space dust drifting away, he watched one very large intact ship advancing towards his fleet without any visible damage whatsoever, not a single scratch. Laughter went to anger in a heartbeat. "How can that be?" screamed Axon, furious at such defiance of this alien piece of junk, nobody makes a fool out of him. He ordered more of the fleet to commence firing; it would not survive a total onslaught of the Cynturian empire. Axon would be victorious, the alien ship would be sorry it crossed paths with him, it would be destroyed in seconds.

*

The universe watched.

It didn't intervene, but it was not happy, the Cynturians would pay for their trail of destruction later, but the appearance of this lone ship was causing untold chaos of its own. It ripped through from the parallel universe leaving a huge tear in the space time continuum, a gaping hole that would be near impossible to repair.

These aliens were not welcome, both from the parallel universe. The universe blinked furiously thus causing its own problems to worsen across the cosmos.

A huge destructive flux was imminent.

*

Aboard the unknown alien ship confusion was rife, the occupants puzzled why someone would attack them out of the blue. There was no provocation on their part, they were non-violent people from the planet Kangis in the parallel universe. They certainly didn't want trouble; simply came in search of the creations they left behind centuries ago. Kangis-3, a cleverly disguised planet was not where it was supposed to be; the creators surmised it must have entered this universe by mistake.

The Kangans themselves were a unique species, a superior race of beings, half machine, half organic life, a creation evolving over a thousand years. They wanted to improve their kind, so scientists made many advancements in their technology, the ultimate intention was to create a one hundred per cent organic life form in their own image. Eventually achieving success after many failed attempts centuries earlier they were happy with the results and decided to deposit the creations in a spaceship disguised as the planet Kangis-3. This allowed the newly created beings the freedom to live and survive independently. It did work well for hundreds of years but something must have went wrong. The Kangans hadn't heard from their creations for quite some time; requests for updates went unanswered, even the beacon from the ship ceased transmitting. The Kangans had no choice but to trespass into another universe to continue the search, they were concerned they had fallen into the wrong hands. The creations had not been programmed to deal with outsiders even though they were given the ability to think for themselves. The Kangans now feared they may have evolved too far, into something more sinister and maybe overstepped their boundaries.

Experiments of any kind always came with risks, flaws were possible in the genetic make-up of life, so it was imperative they retrieved their property. What they didn't need was barbaric aliens shooting at their ship. It was inconvenient and very annoying.

"Why are they doing that?" asked one of the Kangans, watching the aliens pathetic attempt to destroy them and their ship. He stared out the porthole next to the control section, unable to understand such hostility.

"I really don't know Saron" replied Vissen, also watching the pointless exercise. A third Kangan, almost identical to the other two, joined them. "What is happening now?" enquired Dittos.

"I stopped the ship for now. Are they still being annoying?" he asked.

"Yes, they started firing again" said Saron, thinking how stupid the aliens were to try again. It didn't work the first time. All three Kangans watched on at the futile attempt to destroy their indestructible ship. They showed no emotion, having never acquired sentiment to that extent. It suggested weakness to have feelings, an inferior emotion their robotic brains refused to accept. They stayed watching for some time, taking an identical stance at the portholes; all of them attired in full length blue robes, similar facial features with deathly white faces and long white hair. Their electronic brains, linked by computer inside their heads made it easier to communicate when necessary, speaking not always essential.

Again and again the Kangan ship was hit, each time nothing happened. The aliens could fire on the ship as much as they pleased. Nothing would penetrate the outer hull of their ship. They were safe.

Axon halted the attack once more, eager to inspect the annihilation, he waited impatiently for the dust to clear, but there was the alien ship, still there, still intact, and completely unscathed. Axon was livid with his warriors, *had they not hit the target at all.* This act of incompetence was not acceptable. He was ready to shoot his own crew, he was so mad.

"Perhaps they don't like us in their universe" said Vissen trying to explain the reason for the attack.

"Yes, maybe that is it, they don't like intruders" replied Dittos agreeing with Vissen.

"Well we don't like them" said Saron

"So what are we going to do about them?" asked Dittos, he felt they needed to do something to resolve the situation.

"Should we use the red button?" asked Vissen, "it would solve the problem."

"No, definitely not" said Saron, "We mustn't draw attention to ourselves. It would alert other beings to our presence."

The route the Kangans wanted to take was at present being blocked by the enormous fleet of hostile warships.

They didn't wish to go around.

"We simply push past them, they are insignificant beings, low level intelligence, pretty stupid and certainly not in our class" declared Saron, they had been held up for long enough, it was time to move on.

"And if we hit a few?"

"Minor detail Dittos, we must continue the search for our creations."

"Very well, I will start up the engines" said Dittos departing from the porthole.

"Should we not ask these beings if they have seen anything?" Vissen wanted to know.

"No" said Saron.

"They might have important information" Vissen thought he should at least point out the possibility.

"No Vissen" Saron replied strongly, "I don't think these aliens want a conversation."

"No quite" Vissen had to agree, as the warships began firing again, they would never back down.

The Kangan ship powered up and pushed on towards the fleet with no intention of stopping or going around. Axon was absolutely furious this one ship was giving him so much grief. It was obvious the ship was about to ram his warships, quickly he instructed his own crew to manoeuvre out of the way, this was going to make him look foolish, stupid even that one solitary alien ship had the audacity to attempt such a reckless move.

"Fire again! Don't stop!" he screamed, as his ship was now in a safer position. "Do not let this worthless ship get away from us."

The Kangans had other ideas, ploughing right through the middle of the fleet as they fired at them relentlessly. Several ships were smashed out of the way hitting more of the fleet causing severe damage, some veered off course before exploding. Debris went in every direction, almost a third of the fleet was destroyed or crippled. Axon was safe but feeling pretty small.

"Now that's how you deal with inferior beings Vissen, we merely brush them aside" said Saron, their ship continued its journey.

"We still should have asked the question" said Vissen.

Saron thought not, they had to press on without further delay. He had grave concerns about the whereabouts of Kangis-3, fearing their life's work would all be for nothing.

CHAPTER EIGHT

The Clarizianes continued their lonely journey in the parallel universe in search of their friend Sol; learning more and more about the strange alien ship each day made piloting a little easier, but there was so much more they didn't know about its owners, or how the ship arrived close to their home planet in the first place. That mystery would never be solved. All thoughts of the rightful owners coming after them had to be put to one side for now; the real focus was this awful universe, which seemed to be falling apart at the seams. Voids began opening up in every sector they entered, no way of avoiding them. They had a dreadful notion something sinister was deliberately causing the disturbance, it really made navigation that much more difficult.

Discussions among the pilots cropped up several times as to whether they should enter the voids or simply bypass them. The question on everyone's lips, what would Sol have done? Answers were in short supply. The other concern was the goings on in space itself; mapping the journey so they didn't criss-cross or double back on themselves was proving impossible. Spatial distortions and misalignment of entire constellations put that task of being incorrect from the start. It was assumed this universe behaved this way as normal practice, it was an unusual existence; the pilots only had their own universe to compare. A couple of pilots had doubts they should even stay; this was no way to live. The desire to find Sol proved greater, they pressed on.

*

The rift in the space time continuum was getting larger by the day, with no explanation as to why it was happening. How could anyone expect to understand the dynamics, the natural order of life in the universe was being controlled by outside forces, even a genius would struggle to comprehend the complexity of life on this scale. They, as mere mortals had no chance. Yet the pilots did feel some responsibility as it was their own kind who may have created the chaos. Who knew time travel could mess up the perfect balance and disrupt the physical part of the universe with such devastating consequences.

The Clarizianes certainly didn't.

The pilots entered this universe without fully understanding the importance of their actions. If there had been any other way, they would have taken it.

Time distortions occurred frequently, messing with everyone's own body clock, it wasn't easy to regulate sleep patterns; some were finding it more difficult to deal with. The ship's clock on the control panel never stayed still for long; when it did the pilots had no way of telling the true time, or the date – or even how long they had been travelling. They wrestled with emotions on a daily basis, always thinking, Sol was here somewhere, he had to be. It was hoped he hadn't slipped through one of the voids – or worse, back through the rifts to their universe. They couldn't be sure of anything.

*

Rol made an educated guess they had been in space almost a month, that meant Sol had been without oxygen all that time. That one thought was scary, *were they searching for a dead body?* It wasn't easy to be upbeat, *surely somebody had to have picked him up by now.* That thought was even more scary because until now this universe appeared just as empty as their own. No nearby planets were located, no star systems capable of sustaining life; nothing registering on the long-range monitors, absolutely nothing.

The pilots began to wonder what kind of universe was this, with no life?

*

'It's my universe!'

The universe was furious with the ongoing situation, the integrity of space was beginning to crumble; but it decided these trespassers might actually help at the right time, as long as they didn't make matters worse in the meantime. They made one mistake; it couldn't allow them to make another.

*

Don and Stella felt stronger than ever Sol was still alive, Stella refused to think otherwise; the alternative was not in her vocabulary. Her feeling for her beloved cousin remained steadfastly loyal.

Sol was out there.

Don at least understood Stella, he too refused to believe Sol was dead, he would never give up on his friend. Stella convinced him of that. He had the distinct impression that somewhere along the way Stella bypassed childhood and careered straight into an adult. She managed to get everyone on side, and it was agreed, going on was the only option; Clarizia was no more; and after what Ariel told the pilots, they wanted no part of that life anyway. Going back into one's past in an attempt to put the future right was never a good choice.

The Clariziane hierarchy started a chain reaction of disastrous events that could never be put right. All the spatial discrepancies and timeline lapses were down to their interference. Trying to perfect time travel was a crazy idea; definitely not in the rule book according to the all-powerful ruler of the cosmos – THE UNIVERSE –

Now that universe was angry and started to tear itself apart, getting the first aid box out was not going to be enough.

This was serious shit.

The pilots wanted to fix it, but they were out of their depth, realising it was going to take more than a few pilots and two teenage girls to make amends.

It started to put doubt in some of their minds, they were despondent; time was running away from them – and it wasn't the clock on the control panel going berserk. The ship was on a path to nowhere, no end in sight and no real prospect of finding Sol. It was only Sol driving them on, they had to stay focused, but it wasn't easy.

By some strange force Don began to think something or someone was giving them a helping hand to stay alive. Nothing he could identify as real, just a premonition, something extraordinary, not of this universe maybe. It was unnerving to feel such vivid emotions; he wasn't sure if it gave him hope or not. He would call out to Sol again in his mind.

CHAPTER NINE

With no thought for the other crew members, Hanzon was eating his way through the limited food supply. He couldn't supress his appetite no matter how hard he tried. It seemed his rate of metabolism where food was concerned, was out of control and unregulated. His brain and body remained slightly out of sync, not fully correcting itself when they returned to outer space. The poor man needed reining in, but nobody wanted the job. No one actually realised what state Hanzon was in, he was suffering inside. The food was his only comfort.

Something had to be done, there was now an urgent need to replenish the food supplies before the rest of the crew died of starvation. Strangely the pilots only thought about searching for a nearby planet with sustainable plant life and possible food source, when out of nowhere, a planet was detected on the monitors.

Odd they thought, new worlds until then had been non-existent – another mystery to put on the back burner, Don guessed. Mysteries were beginning to stock up. Could they be lucky enough to actually come across the only planet in this miserable universe to have a possible sustainable food source? Perhaps even fresh drinking water? They could only hope.

Approaching the planet, the early warning siren went off with that awful ear shattering noise. Acknowledging it was the only way to turn it off. Everyone was grateful Rol discovered the right switch promptly. The next task was landing this monster of a ship on solid ground, a task they had yet to perform; no one was sure it was even possible. Piloting a single crewed craft was easy, this alien creation was not in the same league.

Rol and Fisah nominated themselves to give it a try. Rol had more hours at the helm than anyone, he was confident; at least he said he was. With Fisah as co-pilot they were pleased to land safely with only a couple of minor bumps. The ground was firm, the ship settled with little effort. Rol of course congratulated himself; it was easier than he imagined. Fisah dampened his enthusiasm by saying there were two pilots at the helm, he would not be outdone.

Outside, the air quality was remarkably good, pure and fresh. It couldn't have been more perfect. The pilots were eager to rush through the airlock and stand on solid ground. It felt good to be free again, if only for a brief time.

Stepping away from the ship and looking back to get a proper look at their home for the last few weeks; it was soon apparent the immense size, it was overwhelming. They never got a chance back on Clarizia, everyone too busy collapsing with exhaustion, then swiftly ushered aboard without realising the full extent of the alien's ship size.

Now the pilots had more important matters to attend, and they didn't need to go far. It was uncanny to find everything they required close by; so much food stuff growing in abundance. Some of it they had no idea what it was, but it tasted good, and fresh running water readily available. The pilots couldn't believe their luck, it was almost too good to be true. That weird feeling they were being helped resurfaced, just too convenient thought Don. He remained particularly vigilant, having a strange notion they were being watched. He couldn't get it out of his head they were not alone. Such an idyllic world to be uninhabited with so much sustainable food at hand in huge quantities was wrong. A place like this should have life, yet as beautiful as it was, it was empty of life.

Everyone agreed it would be an ideal world to live on, but impossible without Sol. Fisah decided when they were back on board to log the planet's location so they could eventually return with Sol and make it their new home.

Don had words with Hanzon about eating into the reserves again, he had to curb his appetite, or else. He didn't elaborate further.

Back on board, laden with the fresh supplies, the pilots set about continuing their journey. Fisah mapped the sector precisely, logged the star system, putting it all into the computer that he managed to access only days earlier. Now it would be easy to retrace their steps when their mission was complete. He rather liked the idea of this idyllic world; they could be happy here. A different universe wasn't so bad if this was what awaited them.

As the ship sped away, going deeper into this strange universe, the planet they just left suddenly vanished as swiftly as it appeared. There would be nothing to find even if the pilots could retrace their route. With multiple spatial distortions, moving star systems across the universe, logging the planet's location was pointless. In their excitement, the pilots didn't notice the planet disappear.

The universe did.

*

A week on from leaving the unknown planet, the alien ship still held one mystery about it. The pilots were unable to work out what was fuelling the engines – they couldn't even find them for a start. The alien technology was so sophisticated they were completely stumped. The power was there, they just couldn't fathom what it was or how long it would last.

Still no one wanted to touch the red button, that remained out of bounds.

Don was having a quiet moment to himself at the rear of the ship, although peace and quiet to think wasn't really an option when everyone had extra sensitive hearing as all Clarizianes did, useful at times, pain in the arse other times.

Don was feeling low, this journey was taking a lot longer than he first anticipated. He was sure finding Sol would only take days, not weeks. The search was into its second month, enough to drag anyone's spirits down. Don took the weight on his shoulders, he was responsible for everyone, including Stella and Ariel, not a job he wanted but as second-in-command to Sol it was his duty to care for them.

In sheer desperation Don called out to his friend again, hoping Sol would hear him this time; all he wanted was a sign to guide them in the right direction. It was questionable Sol could have travelled so far into the parallel universe; he definitely didn't make it to the planet they left behind. There was no evidence.

Why had they not found him yet?

The one-man reconnaissance ships they had would never have reached outside their own galaxy, Sol couldn't have done it alone. Now here they were, in a stolen ship, outside their own galaxy and in another universe with no idea where to go– or how far.

Don was close to hitting rock bottom, surely it couldn't get any worse?

Stella joined Don for a while, she could see him sat there struggling with his emotions, his anguish written all over his face. He needed comfort, answers even. Stella didn't have answers, but she could offer solace. She had very strong feelings that Sol was alive still and told Don she was more certain than ever after having a weird vision Sol was not alone; although she didn't know who with, but the feeling was getting stronger by the day. Sol had to be close by. He was in this universe somewhere. They had to keep looking, stay strong and they could prevail.

Don thought Stella sounded so grown up, he felt like a pupil in the classroom, her words were reassuring at least. She did however ask Don to speak to the others because doubt was creeping in, the concern was the ship was not enough to search the entire universe. If Sol passed back through one of the rifts into their own universe, how could they hope to search both universes with any degree of success.

Stella also had a sense her cousin was being held somewhere, in a confined space maybe. That thought was scaring her, would aliens treat him well or not?

*

Sitting down together to discuss options it was clear the pilots had none. They couldn't go back, and the way forward was merely more of the same; endless space littered with pitfalls – not a great choice. They did have however agree the most important thing was sticking together whatever was thrown at them. Don and Stella did their best to allay the pilots worries, they would find Sol; it was just going to take a little longer.

Stella had a premonition Sol was reaching out, calling for help; with the vision she had strengthened her belief further. Telling the pilots didn't help, they didn't share her belief at any level, but eventually they did all agree never to give up.

So the journey continued.

*

The universe watched on, noting every detail of the discussion. It would have a significant bearing on the outcome of life in the cosmos. The universe didn't like intruders, it would have to put up with them for now. It stood by its previous decision; they might be useful.

The time to act was soon.

Several time lapses later, with the universe continuing to be twisted out of shape, distorted in every star system, space wasn't exactly the safest place to be. Distant galaxies were feeling the effects of the space time continuum being ripped open, some now on the verge of collapse.

The universe was beginning to crack under the pressure.

Sustaining an equilibrium between the parallel universe and this one was becoming impossible. The natural order of all life had rebelled against itself. It couldn't be fixed. The universe might have to do the unthinkable – ask for help.

The pilots realised they had to find a solution to remedy the dreadful disintegration of the universe before it was too late. If they could put it right, everything could get back to some kind of normality. But again and again they had to kept reminding themselves, they were pilots, not scientists. There seemed no quick solution to the problem. How could they hope to fix a broken universe that wasn't even theirs? And then wondered what was going on in their own.

On top of all their other worries the pilots were about to have company, possible alien contact for the first time. Long range monitoring detected a vessel on a direct collision course; a huge black unmarked ship similar in size to theirs. Fisah and Hanzon sat at the controls oblivious to the monitors, they weren't expecting any action. Space had been quiet for ages, Rol left them to it, he needed a break; staring at a blank screen was nothing short of soul destroying.

Fisah finally looked up at the monitor, on seeing something in the distance zoomed in to check out the image. He didn't like what he saw, spaceship heading in their direction, on closer inspection it was soon apparent it was identical to theirs. Having seen the outer hull of their ship up close when they landed on that planet, there was no doubt. Panic set in, Fisah nudged Hanzon to wake up, he wasn't doing this alone. They had the awful feeling it was the genuine owners, if so the meeting might be a bit awkward to explain.

Fisah was busy on the computer while Hanzon kept close watch on the advancing ship; suddenly the early warning siren went off; that ear piercing noise still as deafening as the first time. The closer the ship got the louder the siren, alerting everyone.

"I didn't do anything, I swear" squealed Hanzon in a pitiful voice, assuming he would get the blame for it. He was getting the blame for everything lately.

"It's okay Hanzon, don't panic" said Fisah as he leaned over Hanzon's control panel and hit the button to kill the siren.

Hanzon hadn't even realised it was that simple, he spent far too much time diving into the food reserves to learn any of the controls.

Now he felt pretty stupid.

On hearing the siren the pilots rushed to the control section to find out what the emergency was. Stella was first being halfway there already when she heard the noise, naturally ready to give Hanzon an earful for meddling with the instrument panel. Nobody else could be so useless she thought. Don was right behind her, the most exercise he had in days.

"Not Hanzon this time" said Fisah coming to his defence for once. "Take a look at the monitors" he pointed to the screen, "we have company."

"Would this be a good time to try out the red button?" asked Hanzon, he was shaking with fear at the prospect of hostile aliens.

"No Hanzon!" Don replied sternly, "we need to know who they are first; they may have information about Sol."

"Well in that case, can I go and get something to eat?" he asked, he'd been at the controls for quite a while and wanted a break – and food.

"NO!" came the reply from several pilots behind him. He needed to stay put, at least for now.

"Just stay with it Hanzon" said Stella in a soft calming voice, she could see he needed reassurance, he was always a bag of nerves. Hanzon felt bullied, no wonder they agreed to give him an extra shift at the helm. He missed his last meal and was incredibly hungry. He didn't realise they were doing it for his benefit.

"What do you think Don?" asked Fisah.

"Well, it's identical for sure" replied Don. That worried him, he felt an eerie presence come over him, this ship was trouble. They had seen nothing for weeks and weeks, then out of the blue a mysterious spaceship in their own image, the coincidence was freaky. He wondered if there was some unnatural force at work, nothing was normal, not since they landed back on Clarizia five years in the future. That was definitely not normal.

Fisah started to calculate the velocity of the alien ship. To his surprise it was slowing down. It meant confrontation, he for one was not looking forward to. As for Hanzon, he wished he wasn't there at all, thinking the twilight zone was a safer option, anywhere but here.

"Fisah, have you managed to work out how to operate that intercom system yet?" asked Don, it was a fair bet they would have to open a dialogue with whoever was aboard. Fisah shook his head, he hadn't managed to work it out at all.

"I can –" said Rol, standing behind Fisah's seat. Fisah was relieved, it was unnerving him watching a mirror image of the alien ship staring back on the monitors.

Rol did his best to concentrate as he sat down, Stella was close by, his heartrate jumped in her presence, if only she knew what she was doing to his emotions. He kept saying to himself, *'focus man.'*

Stella of course knew exactly how he felt, but being lost in space was not the ideal place to start a romance. He was going to have to bottle his emotions a little longer.

"Do you want me to give it a go?" Rol asked Don, who at that moment was doing his best to think on his feet in case a plan B was needed, realistically he needed a plan A first. This was the first real contact with alien life, he had no idea how they should react.

"Okay, play it cautiously Rol, we need to know who they are and what their intentions are."

"What if they're hostile?" questioned Hanzon, still seated next to Rol, absolutely bricking it.

None of them liked the situation one bit, but they had to deal with it.

"We're about to find out one way or another my friend." Don put his hand on Hanzon's shoulder, Stella told him how his confidence was shot right now, he needed a friendly gesture to settle him. He was a damn good pilot, but one with no self-confidence, and that was probably due to getting teased all the time. The poor man wanted out – except he had nowhere to go.

Rol braced himself to speak, first time he'd ever spoke to alien life, it was a nerve-racking experience, his palms were sweating so much; he had to get it right and hoped whoever was on the other ship understood. "Here goes" he said taking a deep breath before flicking the intercom switch. "Hello out there, we are Clarizianes, please acknowledge and identify yourself."

They waited.

"Do you think they understood?" he asked."

"I think so, they just stopped their engines" said Hanzon, checking the monitors and trying to sound efficient, in reality he was scared beyond belief, his stomach was rumbling, he wanted food but too afraid to say so, he would only get teased again.

Everyone was starting to get edgy with the silence. Did they understand or not?

"Ask again Rol," said Don, "be more forceful, it might prompt a reply."Rol obliged, this time the intercom sparked to life.

"Looks like they are ready to talk" said Rol.

It wasn't the reply any of them was expecting.

"We want to know what you are doing with our spaceship?" came a voice through the speaker in a stern brusque manner. Don didn't care for that question, *how could it be their ship, they were mistaken surely, unless these aliens came from the parallel universe as well.* But that didn't make sense he thought, his universe was empty apart from the Clarizianes.

"We want our ship back immediately" said the voice again.

That was going to be a bit tricky, Don thought.

"Also, we want our three-man reconnaissance ship back. We insist you hand over both ships."

"Something tells me they're not messing Don" said Rol, "but what's this other ship? They've got to be kidding, right?"

"I don't think they are" replied Don.

First time they run into aliens, and they get threatening. Whoever they were, they were not getting their ship back.

"First, tell us who you are" Don spoke up, equally firm with his words, no way they were handing over their only means of transport. Another pause on the intercom, the lack of communication was frustrating for the pilots.

"What is their problem?" Rol asked, "even if this ship is theirs, we can't just hand it over, can we?"

Don didn't answer, he was thinking of a solution, something to scare the aliens off. He got the feeling they wouldn't take no for an answer. It was difficult to think straight under pressure, Don was struggling. His crew looking at him, waiting for a reply, but it was Hanzon who spoke first.

"Surely possession is nine tenths of the law, right?" he said rather casually.

"Quite right Hanzon, nice one mate" said Fisah.

Hanzon was pleased someone actually agreed with him for a change.

"Whatever the case guys, this ship is ours" said Fisah.

Everyone was in agreement on that. Hearing the intercom click, the alien spoke again. "My name is Saron; we demand our ship back now. That is an order" he was threatening and more forceful this time, determined to have his property returned. That attitude didn't go down well with the pilots, no one ordered them about, not anymore. The ship may well belong to them once, now it belonged to the Clarizianes. They needed it more than the aliens. As for the other ship they were asking about, the aliens could go and find themselves, they knew nothing about any reconnaissance ship.

"Now what?" asked Fisah, they were in need of a plan urgently, the aliens weren't going away willingly.

"I don't know if it makes any difference, but I swear there are at least two other voices in the background" said Rol, the one-time extra hearing came in handy.

Don finally had an idea; he gestured to Rol to open the intercom again. He wanted to try something and hoped it had the desired result on the aliens.

"We don't know who you are or where you're from, and honestly, we don't care. You are not getting your ship back, it's ours now, so if you don't back off, let me warn you we know what the red button is for and we will use it if necessary" Don signalled to cut the intercom, then took a deep breath, that was a bit harrowing for him, lying through his teeth.

Hanzon looked at Rol bemused, Fisah looked at Don, who then got very strange looks from everyone else. Even Stella right next to him was speechless.

"Are you crazy man?" whispered Fisah, "we have no idea what that red button if for."

Don sort of smiled, "But they don't know that" he said, "and why are you whispering, they can't hear."

Fisah didn't reply, no one did, all stunned by Don's statement. More silence followed before Saron returned to the intercom after discussing the matter with his two associates.

"This could prove interesting" said Hanzon.

"Shut it Hanzon" snapped Fisah.

Saron spoke. "There is no need for violence, I assure you we merely requested our ships back. We can drop you off somewhere" his voice didn't sound quite so convincing.

Rol cut the intercom. "Is he for real? Where the hell can they drop us?"

Everyone thought it was a ludicrous suggestion by the aliens, there was nowhere they wanted to go, besides this universe had nowhere; it was empty.

Don spoke again; he was giving them no choice. "As I said, back off or I will press the red button" he was more forceful now, feeling he had the upper hand. He hoped it was enough to call their bluff.

"No, no, please don't do that" pleaded Saron. He wasn't comfortable having to back down, not used to such an emotion, he was the superior being; no one was as intellectual as they, no one.

*

'You are so wrong.' The universe did not appreciate the arrogance of these beings, they were not superior but the other side of the coin. They would pay dearly for intruding into this universe.

*

With the intercom off Rol spoke, "They're actually scared we might do it. What does that tell us?" He turned round in his seat to face the entire crew, who were standing there, astounded at the aliens response.

"It tells us what we need to know about that red button" said Don with a sigh of relief, realising he got away with that one.

"What's this other ship they're talking about Don?" asked Stella, "it seemed important to them."

"No idea Stella, and frankly I don't care. It doesn't concern us."

If the aliens lost their property, that's tough, they should have been more careful.

"Turn on the intercom" said Don.

"Sure thing" said Rol.

"I have a proposal for you Saron, we won't use the red button in exchange for information, and we still keep this ship. We need it."

They waited again. Saron was not pleased to back down, he realised getting their ships back was not on, a complete disaster in his eyes. He now regretted leaving it unattended on the edge of the universe, the technology inside the ship was far too valuable to fall into alien hands.

How did they know how to operate such advanced engineering?

This universe was not that far advanced. Saron was sure it was too sophisticated for anyone but Kangans to be able to master the controls.

The ship had been left at the edge of the parallel universe in case their creations required it. The Planet Kangis-3, a disguised spaceship was never meant to be permanent. Five hundred years was the maximum, and that time had passed. They wouldn't be here now if the beacon hadn't stopped transmitting. A small three-man spaceship was also deposited in the parallel universe, thinking it would be safe as it too was locked, that also disappeared. The Kangans had seriously underestimated the intelligence of other life. Now their huge spaceship had been stolen by these aliens, their reconnaissance ship was missing. Saron thought it possible these aliens might well have murdered their creations. He and associates now had a dilemma, they might have to bow to these insignificant life forms, but he decided it would be temporary.

"What is it you wish to know?" asked Saron eventually responding to the request, he felt he had no choice for now.

Don was quick to ask, "We are looking for our friend, we want to know if you have seen him. He's six foot tall, dark skinned, shoulder length black hair and raised ridges on his forehead and wearing a white jumpsuit."

Hanzon whispered, "You jammy sod."

"Shh –" said Don.

"We have not seen anyone of that description" said Saron, he was being prompted by Vissen and Dittos; they could be heard in the background eager to hurry along the conversation so they could leave.

"Is there anything else you can tell us about this system?" Don was riding his luck with this alien, but he sensed he knew more than he was saying.

"Only some warlike beings we left behind, rather unsavoury beings actually; only interested in shooting at us."

Don and the others thought that odd because there appeared to be no visible signs of damage to their ship; then they wondered who came out of that encounter with the upper hand. Fisah sitting so close to the intercom heard more prompting in the background, they were holding something back.

"Tell them Saron, about the next system" whispered Vissen.

"Tell us what Saron?" asked Fisah abruptly, which alarmed the Kangans.

How could the aliens hear whispers through the intercom?

"Any information would be useful" said Fisah, "and don't lie to us."

"Nice one Fisah" said Don patting him on the shoulder.

Saron was uncharacteristically rattled; the aliens might have more intelligence than they gave them credit for.

They could possibly be dangerous.

"Tell us where our small spaceship is then, we need it back, it's vital to us" said Saron.

"We have no idea what you're talking about" Don guessed they were playing for time, but it wasn't going to wash with him.

"I'm waiting Saron, my finger is very close to the red button."

"Very well, the next system you come to on your present course, the third planet orbiting it's sun in inhabited, low-level intelligence but they might be able to help you. But be warned, there is trouble there, much upheaval. Those warships we passed, I think they are heading in that direction, what's left of them that is." Saron gave Don everything the Kangans knew, hoping it was enough. They urgently wanted to return to their own universe to re-evaluate their situation; this mission was a failure. Their fear now was the creations were lost forever; secretly they still wanted their ships back, they wouldn't be gone for long.

"One more thing and we'll let you go. Who are you?" Don only asked out of curiosity, it had no bearing on their mission.

"We are Kangans, can we please go now? We have answered all your questions. Please, do not use the red button, ever" pleaded Saron, the fear of being wiped out was immense, he hoped it wasn't used until they left this universe.

"You can go, don't come back" said Don with real conviction, just so they knew he meant it; he signalled to cut the intercom before finally deciding it was safe to relax and breathe; that was one scary moment, their first encounter with alien life and they had to threaten them.

"Like I said Don, you jammy sod" said Hanzon, at least he too could stop sweating, his nerves were shattered with the whole experience.

"I don't know how you got away with that Don but well done my friend" said Fisah.

"Well, we know what the red button is for, I wonder what Saron meant; don't use it ever?" Rol asked, that did seem an odd thing to say.

"We could just have shot them you know, problem solved" said Hanzon, still wiping his sweaty hands on his jumpsuit.

"No Hanzon! That is not our way, we are not murderers" he was adamant violence wasn't the answer. He bluffed his way out of that tricky situation with words, he didn't want blood on their hands. The entire crew standing behind Don applauded his efforts, even Stella was impressed, she did kill guards on Clarizia, that was necessary. Don was different. "Well done Don, you did good, Sol would be proud of you."

Don was proud, it was an achievement just to be alive. Hanzon didn't want to be forgotten. "Now can I go and get something to eat?" he was starving.

"Oh for – go on then Hanzon" said Don, he did deserve a break, "Don't eat everything" he shouted after him.

Too late. Hanzon was gone. Now the pilots were also dispersing, crisis averted for now. Rol and Fisah stayed at the helm, their journey had to continue, in what direction they didn't know. Don hung around for a while with Stella, which didn't help Rol one bit having her so close again. He was going to burst if she didn't say yes soon.

Don wanted to discuss options, mainly what to do next. "So any ideas guys?" he was open to any suggestions.

"We could try that planet in the next system. Sol may have been taken there" suggested Rol, "we have to try something."

Fisah agreed, at least it was better than what they were doing, which was nothing, Stella though was having doubts about the Kangans swift departure. "Do you think they will come back Don?"

"I don't think so Stella, but what do I know" said Don.

"They gave in too easily in my opinion. If their ship is identical to ours, they would also have a red button, right?"

"She has a good point Don" said Rol, thinking it would impress Stella if he agreed with her.

"What about the warships they encountered, they could be a problem?" Fisah asked, worried about another confrontation.

"Let's just concentrate on what we came to this universe for, but just in case I want someone monitoring at all times – if only to turn that siren off."

"Agreed" said Fisah, "That bloody noise could do serious damage to our eardrums" he realised they still had much to learn about the alien ship; he would make it his personal mission to do just that. Then he suddenly had a brilliant idea, something they might possibly need before reaching the next system.

"I've got an idea Don; besides the monitoring, I could try and rig up a listening device, maybe amplify any sounds coming from space, and if that planet is transmitting any data, or anything of interest, it would be useful to know what they're saying before we arrive."

"That my friend is one of your better ideas" said Don, thankful the crew were still willing to carry on.

"I'll need an extra pair of hands then" said Fisah, keen to get started on his plan.

"No problem, I'll send one of the women, they're dying to do something useful" said Stella as she was about to leave. She turned to Rol to give him a smile and a wink. He was going to be putty for the next couple of hours.

Before Don left he asked Fisah a vital question, "Are you sure you can do this Fisah, it's a big job."

"I think so Don, if not I'll just rewire the whole lot – or whatever it is that makes this ship tick."

Don left with a worried look, he didn't like the sound of that; he had a dreadful thought Fisah might end up disconnecting everything and leave them stranded in deep space. On the other hand it was agreed they needed to knuckle down and learn more about the workings of this ship. He had to trust Fisah. Until now the pilots got away with guesses and a lot of luck. Confronting further hostile aliens might not be so easy to overcome without knowing the ships full potential.

*

The Clarizianes were still being observed, their every decision scrutinised. Don made one good judgement call, but it was not enough. More fluctuations in the timeline occurred; the space time continuum was on the verge of collapse. Spatial distortions worsened, violently twisting whole star systems, planets being destroyed as a result. Further rifts were inevitable.

The crack in the universe was growing.

The parallel universe was not helping the situation, it seemed to think it could get away with violating time and space that didn't belong to it. Aliens were coming and going whenever they wished, and with no regard to life on the other side. Now the imbalance between universes was completely out of sync. Beings needed to return to their universe before irreparable damage was done on both sides.

The Clarizianes by being in the wrong universe were not helping the situation, but it was decided they could be useful, they had to stay for now.

The universe was powerless to stop the chaos getting worse, outside forces meddled with the natural order of life. There were still two aliens on the third planet in the next star system who shouldn't be there. They were being held captive, having previously entered from the parallel universe.

They needed to be removed.

CHAPTER TEN

Several Earth federation gunships mercilessly fired on the space rescue hospital ship, Retriever-2. It seemed now they had little chance of coming out of this alive. Panic set in, every deck was in chaos, the crew were being punished with a sentence of certain death for their alleged crimes. On the bridge strange events were occurring, Denny Argent at his station was isolated from the rest of the bridge crew. He started to freak out, screaming for help, but the others were unaware of his plight, they were desperately trying to hang on to their own lives. An invisible barrier prevented Denny leaving the communications station, no one could hear his screams, or see what was happening to him. He yelled so hard his throat was sore, then his body faded away into oblivion, pulled towards a vortex and sucked into a time warp. Suddenly he was gone, trapped between two universes.

Another dimension awaited him.

Cynturian warships would not be robbed of their victory either, they wanted revenge for the death of their illustrious leader Yulan. The assault continued. The men and women of Retriever-2 felt as if the whole universe was against them, determined to wipe them out of existence. Retriever-2 presumed still to be under the command of Captain Valmak, was bombarded from all sides. The gunships carried out their orders received from Mission HQ, no emotion involved, it was just orders.

Now with the ship already missing its tailpiece, blown off in the relentless onslaught, other sections damaged or destroyed and on fire, the outer hull was in danger of losing its integrity. It finally emerged on the other side of the black void. Out of control it plummeted towards a nearby planet that appeared out of nowhere. The crew had no guidance system to operate, the mainframe was in the tail section. Helm controls would not respond, nothing they could do but brace themselves for a violent impact. The unknown planet loomed large, if they survived the crash landing it would be a miracle. They prayed their attackers were not stupid enough to follow into the void. Irreparable damage was done to Retriever-2, they hoped no one came through to finish them off.

The crash would do that.

*

Spending six years in space on the longest tour of duty, working for the benefit of others, giving medical aid to whoever requested it, then through no fault of their own another year going on the run simply for doing their jobs had come down to being hunted down like wild animals, it wasn't what any of the crew signed up for, and yet not one of them regretted the choices they made.

*

The universe was furious at their treatment, these humans were the only beings who had any respect for life. They even tried to put things right, they were the only ones who knew the trauma the universe was going through, and yet they were rewarded with certain death.

This was not the natural order of life; it should not have happened. Intervention was the only option, deemed vital to save the universe from total collapse.

It had to act.

*

Sol staggered along the corridors in a daze, debris hampered his route, stumbling every few yards. He was desperate, dust, smoke and flames made visibility difficult to see his way. Explosions had blown in several bulkhead panels, ceilings crashed down all around him. He was still too groggy from hitting his head earlier. Niko was in trouble; he felt her pain. He had to find the hospital somehow through the chaos.

In all the confusion Sol forgot about the two young strangers who appeared out of nowhere to clear the rubble out of his way. One spoke, but it barely registered at the time. All he could think about was getting to Niko to save her and their unborn baby.

Darryl Harding, a trainee medic, got to Niko moments before she went into premature labour. He stayed at her side, refusing to leave as he was ordered, to try and save himself. He didn't sign up to abandon the doctor in her hour of need, it was obvious she was in a great deal of stress on top of her pain. Two medics lay nearby unconscious or dead, he guessed the latter. Part of the ceiling fell on them, nothing he could do to help them now. All the other medics scrambled for the exit before they were cut off. Darryl couldn't understand their haste, were they in that much of a hurry to die? He knew the ship was out of control but had no idea what was happening. Ideally he wanted to move Niko to a safer place, one more inner bulkhead to go and they would be saying hello to the stars. Niko wasn't going anywhere in her condition. The isolation ward was still intact, they could make it that far.

Sol finally reached the hospital having passed the medics who left earlier, and got hit by a falling bulkhead panel, all dead. Clambering over the broken hospital doors he immediately heard Niko screaming in pain, he assumed she was left behind, alone. Niko was in a bad way, complications and early labour brought on by the trauma of the ship being torn apart; more explosions could be heard on the other decks. The attack had been relentless but thankfully the firing had finally stopped. It didn't help Niko, she was haemorrhaging badly, it was only going to get worse.

Desperate to find his love, Sol called several times as he continued to stumble over the rubble.

Darryl called to him.

"Here Sol" he shouted out.

Sol was quick to find them.

"So glad to see you Sol, I can't do this alone" he said nursing Niko in his arms; anguish written all over her face at the prospect of losing her baby.

"Thank you for staying Darryl, we will do this together." Sol was grateful Niko wasn't alone, he took her hand and looked into her tearful eyes and simply mouthed *'I love you'*. They prepared to deliver the baby just as the ship crashed through the upper atmosphere and plummeted downward at an incredible velocity. Trees were flattened as the battered ship finally hit terra firma with a heavy landing, splitting the hull in two. Bodies were tossed about as it careered out of control. The bow section continued its momentum to rest hundreds of yards away from the stern. Half the crew had already gone in the tail section, mostly engineering personnel. After the smoke, flames and dust died down and the initial shock subsided, one by one injured survivors crawled out the wreckage and sank in the ground, shattered and exhausted, not sure if they were grateful to be alive or not.

How could their own kind do this to them?

The Cynturians cared about no one and gladly shot down anything that moved, but humans firing at them while aboard a hospital ship violated every ethical code in the book. It meant nothing to them; this was blatantly first-degree murder; the very charge brought against Retriever-2 and its crew. How was that going to sit with the authorities? Perhaps they actually ordered the attack. Did they not care about their lives? Was it all for nothing, the last few years of service.

The Avaans faired a lot better; they managed to levitate out the gaping holes, most of them uninjured. The babies carried out to safety, all Avaans accounted for except one. Kanon Garg, their leader was missing. Xander and Ti Glish could not leave him behind and returned inside the mangled wreckage to search for him.

Alec Zymotz and Paul Aztac helped the wounded out, including Adam King and Cal Bartok who were thrown across the bridge and sustained serious internal injuries. Without medical supplies or even a medic to hand, Adam and Cal were set down on the ground, both now critical and not looking good. Paul stayed with them, so they were not alone, while Alec went back inside to help others. He was really concerned about his friend Nely Meki; they got separated when Nely went looking for his pregnant girlfriend. Alec had no idea what part of the ship Nely was in, or even if he made it.

From the rear section of the ship, resting some way back in the flattened forest, emerged Nely carrying Carol, getting out before he too collapsed in a heap. They were lucky, but all Carol could think of was not her unborn baby, but her brother Darryl. *Did he make it out alive?* She hoped so. Nely naturally had thoughts of his best friend Alec; he lost track of his whereabouts when he went looking for Carol. So much confusion followed, nobody knew where anyone was, but it seemed they all were thinking of someone they loved.

Tom Phasner was very gently prompted out the wreckage by Simone Costin, he was reluctant to go outside, scared what he might find. He was still having bouts of depression over Xanders accident; it wasn't something he could forget easily. The attack by his own kind was the last straw, none of it helped his nerves one bit. He wasn't even sure he wanted to carry on at that point, this was no way to live, and the guilt he wasn't sure he could ever get over. For a big guy he had very little self-esteem left, and no faith in the human race for carrying out such a despicable act. Blood poured down his face from a nasty gash on his head from a flying metal panel, he hadn't felt it at the time, but now he had a splitting headache. Simone refused to allow him to give up, he was stronger than that. She stayed with him, giving him words of comfort to reassure him they were alive, and he should be grateful for that at least.

She was.

*

Others made it out of both sides of the wreckage not knowing who else survived in the other section. Everyone collapsed to their knees, none of them really ready to face what may lie ahead. What they left behind was a lifetime of duty dedicated to the service, their payment, to be pursued across the universe and hunted down and shot to pieces.

No refunds.

Did they feel lucky to be alive? No. this was what death felt like, it couldn't get any worse. Everyone lost someone they were close too. Now the worry was how many survived, then, where the hell were they?

*

The universe delivered them to safety, it had to intervene this time to secure their survival. Now it was up to them. The crew of Retriever-2 were the only beings who could help. When the time was right they would repay the debt. The universe needed fixing; the natural order of all existence was completely out of sync with reality. Space was pushed out of shape and misaligned with the physical aspect of all living things, there was no harmony. Time itself was uncontrolled and unregulated, the universe could no longer maintain stability in the cosmos, the events unfolding it could not keep in check, there was too much interference from the parallel universe. This universe was powerless, it blinked so often at the sheer frustration, it merely caused more distortions, ripples in space and time became too much to handle.

The parallel universe needed to be put back in its box, permanently.

*

In the aftermath of the crash, with what the universe perceived as a new beginning for the survivors on a seemingly deserted idyllic world, many of the men and women struggled to face up to the reality of what just happened to them. Looking at the huge wreckage towering over them, this had been their home for the last seven years. It made coming to terms with their ordeal all the more difficult to accept; to face death in such a violent and barbaric act was not something they would forget easily.

Was it over? They didn't know.

Retriever-2 was torn apart in a callous act of brutality on defenceless people that left parts of the ship floating in space along with so many crew still in the tail section. They didn't stand a chance. It meant only one thing; the survivors were stranded. On the upside they had been searching for a world where they could live together in peace, away from the authorities and without prying eyes. No one would ever think of looking for them in a black void, wherever this black void was. Strange how the mysterious planet just appeared out of nowhere at a very opportune time. Not one survivor believed it was a coincidence, destiny had a hand in their fate, who was controlling that destiny was not clear.

Neither the federation police nor the Cynturians entered the void to pursue the onslaught. It was assumed Retriever-2 with no tailpiece and on fire was doomed, and would eventually break up altogether, mission complete. Federation gunships retreated swiftly before the warships turned on them, an immediate return to Earth essential now to report their success and hopefully collect a lucrative bonus.

The surviving crew were grateful the attack was over and the federation police and Cynturians didn't follow, they had more than enough grief to handle, they had nothing left to fight back with, the stuffing was well and truly knocked out of them. When the grief subsided a little, anger began to boil over at the way Earth treated them like criminals. First and foremost they were just pilots and medical staff aboard a rescue ship;

intergalactic law meant they should have been safe, and besides they were only trying to do the right thing, put the universe right and get space back where it should be. Unfortunately outside forces and faceless bureaucratic Earth authorities prevented them from completing their mission. In the end they were pursued to the ends of the universe as murderers, renegades of Earth; a charge they couldn't defend, of course they were angry, had every right to be, but that anger had to go, the survivors could not build a new life hanging onto bitterness. That one emotion was not enough to move on with their lives.

So many lives were lost in the initial attack, many more in the crash, that sadness and the sight of the wreckage scarring the landscape in such a brutal fashion would forever be a painful reminder.

Laid out on the ground in the huge trench caused by Retriever-2 and stretching all the way to where the bow section broke away, the survivors nursed their injuries in silence. No one wanted to speak, or even get to their feet, they were exhausted, wounded and bleeding, their very soul had been wrenched away. *Where could they go anyway?* Each crew member tried to collect their personal thoughts and feelings but would not speak of them. Everything was still very raw, wondering, *did that really just happen?*

They were really there, but it felt so surreal. The sadness worsened when it became known Cal had suddenly slipped away following his head trauma and internal injuries. Moments later he was followed by Adam with injuries too severe to survive. With no medical care they had little chance of pulling through. It was a huge loss, Adam was a good leader who led the crew through a terrible time, and Cal, a brilliant science officer. Their deaths hit the others real hard.

The heartache got worse when Xander and Ti Glish finally re-emerged to announce Kanon Garg had also died. The Avaans took his passing with great sorrow, he didn't get to see this new world with all its splendour. It was believed Kanon

Garg died of extreme old age rather than through injury, though it couldn't be certain stress had a hand in his death or not. Ti Glish said he had no idea of his exact age but from the many stories he heard over the years back on Avaa, he surmised he was probably a hundred and twenty years plus. To the Avaans, it was their greatest loss.

Eventually the survivors one by one began to sit up, those who could; then to take stock of their lives and try to clear their heads. They needed to regroup to see who survived and who sadly didn't make it. That task was not an easy one to face up to. Eyes stared left to see the rear section close by, then right to see the bow in the distance where it finally came to rest. Retriever-2 continued to smoulder, the flames slowly dying out, a lifeless shell broken in half, a giant metal coffin for some.

How did they manage to crawl out of that carnage?

Survivors slowly got up and made their way along the deep grooves where they soon spotted more survivors coming towards them, it was good to see each other. Many trees were uprooted viciously in the devastating crash, the plant life would at least regenerate over time, not so for human life. They realised the extent of their own mortality, the sight of the wreckage would always be there as a reminder how some of them cheated death, but it would also be a memorial to those who didn't make it. Many were unaccounted for; greeting friends brought some relief, the survivors thankful for that. It would be a painful process but sooner or later they had to go back inside the mangled mess to search for anyone alive. They needed to know how many made it to the new world. At first glance the numbers were low, that was depressing for anyone to deal with.

*

Inside what was left of the hospital Sol and Darryl battled to save Niko's life; she was barely hanging on having haemorrhaged so much blood giving birth to her premature baby. She slipped into unconsciousness and was critically ill. Sol refused to let her go without a fight, even though there was no equipment left intact, the machines all smashed. He would have to do the unthinkable, a difficult decision to make, there was no choice. All the blood supplies were damaged and unusable. Darryl begged him not to do it, mixing his alien blood with hers might actually kill her. He knew he wasn't a match for Niko, still he offered instead, at least she had a slim chance of pulling through.

Sol refused to let Darryl do it and prepared the procedure himself, he found needles and tubes that would do the job. He told Darryl he could assist or leave, go while he had the chance. The hospital was crumbling all around them, the isolation ward about the only room standing, except the ceiling looked like it was about to fall down. Working in semi-darkness didn't help, lights flickered on and off, the power was draining fast.Darryl stayed. He would not abandon his duty.

Sol carefully set up the arm-to-arm transfusion; blood was soon flowing along the tube into Niko's arm. She lay motionless, totally out of it; just as well Sol thought, she would probably refuse to let him do it. Now he hoped his blood with its unique DNA properties would mix favourably with human blood. It was something he would explain to Darryl later – if it worked.

The procedure itself was something Sol had never attempted before, but he did recall his doctor father did once to save a life. His father Janus Nussar wanted Sol to become a doctor also, instead he chose to be a space pilot. Now he was sure his father would be so proud of him. Niko had to survive, he could not live without her, and he would not let his father down, this was in his memory.

Darryl tended to the newborn, he went in search of a usable oxygen cylinder, thinking it could only help the little guy, and blankets maybe. He was determined to be a good medic right to the end. Actually the baby was doing remarkably better than his mother. Maybe he wasn't early after all. Being half alien might have made a difference, how was he to know. He wrapped him up in the blanket and put him in a crib left over from the Avaan babies. Darryl couldn't help noticing he had two quite distinctive ridges on his little forehead, Sol had three and though he was dark skinned with jet black hair like his father, he had enchanting blue eyes like Niko. It certainly made him unique.

Baby was comfortable, quiet for now, but Darryl knew he would need feeding soon, he wasn't sure what to do about it; for the time being he found a chair to sit at the bedside opposite Sol who maintained his vigil, holding Niko's hand and with one eye on the blood supply in the tube, the other eye watching his love for any sign of life. Darryl needed to keep an eye on Sol as well, he had no idea just how much blood he intended to donate, he had an awful feeling he might have to deal with three patients. It did worry him; he wasn't actually a qualified doctor yet. He never got the chance to take the exams Niko promised him.

The walls continued to crumble around the hospital, bulkhead panels crashing to the floor, the ceiling panels hanging down close by; wires dangling with the odd spark of life soon to be extinguished. The hospital doors that were blown inwards left broken glass and debris in the entrance. Darryl glanced round at the destruction in and around the isolation ward, if the rest of the hospital was as bad as this, he couldn't help thinking if Niko was awake, she'd be furious at the mess. She was very particular about her hospital. Nothing he could do about it. He suddenly remembered seeing some intact saline pouches, maybe he could rig up a drip, it could only help Niko's condition and went to get it. This time he told Sol not to interfere, he was going to help her anyway. Sol said nothing, he was getting very tired.

After setting up the drip Darryl sat back down at the bedside, knocking off pieces of ceiling from earlier, it wasn't the most hygienic of environments but better than nothing. He could see Sol needed to stay awake, this could be quick or a long-drawn-out process, it didn't matter, they weren't going anywhere. It would take as long as it takes. He decided to engage in conversation, that at least would keep them both awake.

"What are going to call your son Sol?" he asked.

Sol, still holding Niko's hand firmly, like she once did to bring him back from the brink. He looked up.

"Nicolas, she wanted him called Nicolas if it was a boy."

"That's a good strong name, Nicolas Nussar, got a nice ring to it I think."

Sol nodded, they weren't married yet, if she pulled through, it would be the first thing he would do.

"You know my sister is pregnant."

"Yes I did know Darryl" his eyes went back to watch Niko for that one flicker of eye movement, anything to tell him she was fighting all the way.

"I hope she made it out, Nely is a bit of a prat sometimes, but Carol adores him. No idea what she sees him really."

Sol smiled, he understood what Darryl meant, you can't choose the person you fall in love with.

"You know, when we Clariziane men find love, it's for life, I can never love anyone else now."

"I understand why you won't let her go now."

Sol loved Niko from the very first moment he set eyes on her, he knew she felt the same, they were destined to be together. She had to pull through.

"She often said how much she loved you Sol, you're a very lucky man."

Sol was happy to know that; it felt good to talk and he was grateful for the company. It eased his burden a little, Darryl was a good human, staying to care for Niko when he could have left to save himself, although the other medics that fled didn't get far. He passed their bodies under the rubble outside the hospital, it did give him grave concerns about finding Niko alive.

Suddenly the baby started to cry, a definite hungry cry, Sol wondered how he was going to feed him, Niko couldn't. there was nothing aboard the ship to give him.

"What can I do Darryl? he will be hungry." He knew his son would need nourishment, and soon, he started to worry.

"Don't know mate, you can't exactly pop out for baby formula, can you?" said Darryl in a jokey way, he tried to lighten the mood with humour. He wasn't sure Sol would even get the joke.

"Baby formula? What is that?"

"Doesn't matter Sol, it's a human thing" Darryl went to pick up the baby to soothe him, little else he could do but hold him for a while.

"I like you humans; you have a sense of humour I find very perplexing but refreshing."

Darryl turn to nod in appreciation, he wasn't that bad for an alien.

Sol watched Niko for quite a while, her eyes flickered for a second, she was maybe in a light sleep, or at least he hoped so. It was hard to tell how she was, no instruments available to monitor her condition, nothing to say she was improving.

"Don't you think you've given enough blood Sol, you look pale; I think you should stop, you've done all you can" said Darryl, still doing his best to pacify the baby.

"Stop now, before it's too late and you kill yourself."

For once Sol had to agree, he might well have given too much already, he felt weak. Fumbling with the needles he managed to detach them, his blood would replenish itself soon enough, he just needed time to rest.

Darryl continued the conversation to keep both of them awake, it seemed like they had been there hours, he lost all track of time.

"You know Niko had faith in me, she said I would make a good medic, she is a very good teacher."

"She has that quality to bring out the best in people, and besides, after today I have faith in you."

"Thank you Sol. That means a lot to me" Darryl was pleased with his efforts; it had been tough going for a while. Now it was all up to Niko to pull through. He also had a unique talent with the baby, he was quiet for now, asleep again, albeit sucking on Darryl's little finger. Sol was happy for him to care for his son, he had a soft side to him Sol never realised. Men on Clarizia didn't normally get involved or even emotional with babies, especially other mens. He was determined to be different; to be a good father, not the typical Clariziane male.

Time ticked by slowly, both had been silent for a while, resting. Eventually Sol broke the silence.

"Where do you suppose we are?" he asked, it was quite clear the attack stopped some time ago, hours he guessed, even he couldn't judge the time.

"Don't know, but I think we landed on solid ground, it got very bumpy at one point. We must have crash landed somewhere, and we're still breathing the air. That's got to be a good sign" replied Darryl, who then wasn't sure if landed was the right word. For all he knew they might have crashed on an asteroid or something, but that didn't explain the air they were breathing.

"I hate your people Darryl, they did this, they tried to kill us all" Sol didn't want to sound vindictive, but the humans were not nice people in his eyes.

"Well Sol, I hate your people for messing with the universe in the first place, they put us in this predicament."

"I guess I asked for that one" said Sol, "sorry."

Darryl smiled, it didn't matter anymore, nothing did. It was a good possibility they were the only ones left alive, not something to look forward to, wherever they were.

"I don't hate you Darryl. you're a good guy."

"And you my friend are also a good guy." For an alien from another universe he wasn't too bad.

"Will you two shut up, you're giving me a headache."

Neither of them realised Niko had woken up and all she wanted was peace and quiet.

"Niko! You're awake, thank goodness my darling" Sol shot to his feet and abruptly fell straight back in his seat, light-headed, lack of blood gave him a weird sense of dizziness, he felt nauseous for a second. Niko, too weak to move looked alarmed, worried something happened to him. Darryl put a hand on her shoulder. "It's ok Niko, Sol will be fine. Look, you have a beautiful baby son." He showed her baby Nicolas as Sol slowly recovered from the dizzy spell, this time rose to his feet slowly to sit on the bed close to Niko.

"Darryl, thank you for staying" she said, as Darryl handed the baby over so they could both look at him. For Sol it was an unforgettable moment, for Niko it was everything she ever wanted, a baby with the man she loved.

"My pleasure, you didn't think I was going to run out on you, did you?" he was pleased he succeeded in his first real live medical emergency, as daunting at it was, he reckoned he nailed it.

Niko and Sol stared at their baby. "He's beautiful Sol, he looks just like you."

Sol of course was beaming with pride, Nicolas had a bit of both of them, jet black hair and lots of it, and those piercing blue eyes like Niko.

"He only has two ridges on his forehead." Niko couldn't help notice the small details, especially the eyes. Sol's were black.

"I did see that. Makes him special, don't you think." Sol was so happy to have his family at long last, nothing could compare with this feeling, nothing else mattered, not even the dizzy head, that would pass in time.

"You two are very lucky people" said Darryl, seeing them together so happy made him feel a little envious, he had no one.

"So what else has been happening?" asked Niko, "this place looks like it needs more than a feather duster." Looking up she saw there wasn't much of a ceiling left, never mind the walls. Sol looked puzzled by her comment; he would have to get used to this human humour if he was going to fit in. *And what is a feather duster?*

"Don't concern yourself my darling" Sol didn't want her stressing over anything, they were alive and that was enough. He gave Darryl a sideward look, the bit about the blood transfusion he would explain later. Now was not the time. Darryl understood.

Suddenly a sound was heard in the background. "I hear voices" announced Niko, "someone is coming."

Darryl hadn't heard a thing; *how did she hear before Sol?* He too was puzzled, but moments later, a familiar voice called out.

"Hello, anyone in here?"

"I know that voice anywhere" said Niko.

Then scrambling over the hospital doors and crunching broken glass in came Nely and Alec.

"Over here" called out Darryl.

Nely and Alec headed straight for the voice, pleased to hear someone alive.

"Hi guys" said Alec, so glad to see survivors at last, then he suddenly realised Niko had given birth, which came as a total shock, she wasn't due. "Wow! I wasn't expecting that, congrats Niko, Sol."

"Thank you Alec" said Niko, "where's that cheeky face Nely?"

"Is everyone alright?" asked Nely as he walked in, trying to step over the broken ceiling panels without stumbling over. "Niko, hi, I think it's about time you got the decorators in, don't you." Nely was his usual self, but really it a was how he dealt with stress, he always made light of adversity to get through life.

Sol looked across to Darryl, confusion written all over his face. "Human humour?" he said.

Darryl grinned and simply nodded.

"Nely, I've missed you" said Niko, she loved his silly sense of humour, and hoped he never changed.

Darryl wanted to know about his sister. "Is Carol alright?"

"She is fine, so is the baby" announced Nely happily.

Without warning the power finally gave out, lights gone completely, then shafts of natural light gleamed in a couple of gaping holes that were ripped open on impact.

"We better move out before the ship collapses round us altogether, and while we still have daylight." Alec was keen to get everyone out the wreckage as soon as possible. Sol wasn't so eager to move Niko yet, but he realised they would probably be safer outside, wherever that was.

"Where are we?" he asked.

"Not sure yet, we do have survivors, not many but some." Alec was sad it was only a few. It was fortunate anyone got out alive.

"We might need a little help guys, Niko has been through a lot, and Sol isn't feeling quite fit" said Darryl finally getting to his feet, it would be good to leave this hellhole. His comment sent alarm bells ringing in Niko's head, *what was wrong with Sol, he looked fine, a little pale maybe, and he was lightheaded.* There was obviously more to it, she left it for now, but she would find out sooner or later.

"Don't worry, Nely and I got this" said Alec, prepared to carry out every last survivor.

"Ready to go then Doctor Summers?" said Darryl.

"As ready as I'll ever be Doctor Harding" she replied.

Sol was about to say something when Darryl butted in rather abruptly.

"Whoa, just a second, did you just say Doctor Harding?" he wanted to make sure he heard right, and Niko wasn't delirious.

"Yes I did Doctor Harding. After what you've done I'm giving all your exams a pass. Congratulations Darryl."Sol nodded in full agreement; he deserved it.

"Do you hear that guys –" he said to Nely and Alec, excitement written all over his face, "I'm a doctor" he was ecstatic, this meant everything to him.

"We heard, now that we got the academic degrees sorted, can we go?" said Nely, he wasn't comfortable staying in this coffin box a moment longer. Creaking noises suggested the whole lot was about to collapse on top of them.

"I take it we are on solid ground then" asked Sol, it was a minor detail, he had to ask all the same.

"Yes my friend, we just don't know where. Be warned though, it's not a pretty sight out there, a lot of bodies" Alec thought it best to warn them.

*

The right people survived, they were the chosen ones, the ones who would heal the universe when the time was right. The universe had no choice but to bide its time, even though time itself was completely screwed, out of alignment with space. Life was now on the verge of collapse, the rifts were bad enough, but huge cracks in space needed to be fixed. The natural order of all existence was compromised by the outside interference. The universe just had to hold it together a bit longer.

It had to wait.

CHAPTER ELEVEN

The recent events of the federation attack was slowly sinking in, the survivors struggled coming to terms with what their own kind did to them. That feeling of horror would haunt them for the rest of their days. The trauma was difficult to deal with; physical injuries would heal in time, mentally they weren't so sure. Some would never forgive Earth, they lost so many friends and loved ones. Only twenty-three crew survived the attack and subsequent crash. A doubt hung over the whereabouts of Denny, or his body, he was on the bridge at the time the ship passed through the void, or at least he was supposed to be. No one remembered him leaving his station. He had to be listed as missing, presumed dead. All the Avaans, except Kanon Garg survived, it was enough to make an existence, a small colony they could grow in time.

Getting used to the mysterious planet was another matter, strange how it seemed to have everything they needed to survive, edible plant life, fresh running water. It all appeared too convenient to be real. That feeling they had someone directing their destiny came up again, they were alone, yet they were not alone. For now they let it go. The healing process took precedence over their suspicions that someone was controlling their future. In a strange way they got their wish, a world hidden away from any authority, the federation would never find them.

At last they could live their lives in peace.

Knowing exactly where they landed was a mystery not to be solved, best not to ask too many questions.

All instruments on Retriever-2 were smashed, computers non-operational, nothing of any scientific value could be salvaged, and even if it could there was no power, no possibility of pinpointing their location in space, if indeed they were in space. Some of the survivors had serious reservations about the black void and surmised they might have left the universe altogether. In the end decided it didn't matter where they were.

*

Some weeks passed before a decision was made on what to call this piece of rock they now called home. An idyllic paradise world the survivors couldn't believe was theirs, and theirs alone. It was a deserted planet just waiting for life to appear. Planet Utopia seemed appropriate given the beautiful surroundings, the ambient temperature and the bountiful flora. Everyone settled on that; then settled into a life without technology, without any kind of modern structure. Everything they needed would have to made by hand, and whatever materials were available. That proved to be the hardest adjustment to make, something they all had to get to grips with pretty damn quick if they wanted to survive.This was the new beginning.

The Avaans decided not to stray too far from their human friends, they were so happy to survive and not live in fear of being hunted to extinction. They would always be close at hand if needed. Not a day went by without several Avaan children floating about as they passed through the village playing their games, sometimes playing tricks on the humans by doing it invisible. It's what they did for entertainment, natural mischief makers. Xander would never forget his friend Just Tom, they had a very special unbreakable bond, a friendship to last a lifetime. He vowed to always be there if ever Just Tom called him.

The Avaans had the world they were looking for, after so many years travelling the universe in search of such a place. Now they had so much space to float around in the air in complete safety. The young ones could thrive in the lush environment. The humans delivered on their promise in the end. What more could they ask for, to them this was heaven on steroids – extra strength.

*

The universe was pleased.

*

Niko recovered from her baby's traumatic birth extremely well, much to everyone's surprise and delight. Niko herself was astounded, as a doctor she knew it could have gone either way, she felt incredibly lucky. Now she was feeling different, strange in fact, but in a good way. Her body bounced back in remarkable fashion, she was full of revitalised energy, more than ever before. Her hair felt stronger and smoother. It wasn't until Sol noticed her beautiful blonde hair had black streaks beginning to show, that he realised it was time to come clean. He was still regaining his strength having given Niko more blood than he should have. Luckily her body accepted his alien blood so well she began showing signs of his DNA. The black hair was just the start, her hearing had definitely improved along with a fiery temper, typical of a Clariziane woman. More astonishing her left eye had changed colour; it was now black.

Niko had wondered how she managed to survive the birth; human women would never have pulled through after such dramatic blood loss, and it did account for Sol's weakness lately. When he told her everything she really wanted to swing for him for putting both their lives in danger, her inner temper was close to erupting for the first time. But how could she be angry when he only acted out of love, they were meant to grow old together, and now they were finally married. There was still the question of Sol's age, he said he was twenty-eight. That of course was in his universe that had a timeline differential of about a thousand years. Who knows how old he really was? Then again being married to a much younger man rather appealed to Niko, it wasn't something really to dwell on, they were happy, and baby Nicolas was thriving. Niko was okay about it – as long as she didn't turn into a Clariziane woman completely.

What Niko didn't realise, she was already halfway to transformation, Sol's DNA was taking over. She would soon be aware her body was aging differently, in sync with Sol.

Tom finally snapped out of his depression after having a heart-to-heart talk with Xander, who never once blamed him for the accident that caused his wonky eye. Xander refused to hold a grudge, life was for living, not dwelling on the past. They were friends for life said Xander, nothing would ever change that. Now Tom had a wonderful supportive shoulder to lean on with Simone Costin by his side. All he needed was a few kind words of encouragement in his ear, not direct orders to pull himself together. He remembered being angry at Adam for giving him the order. Now he wished he could say sorry for being such a pain in the arse, because Adam meant well. Now he was gone, that hurt would always be there. In time he hoped it would fade. Simone really helped him to move on with his life, something all the survivors had to do. Tom was grateful to Simone for all her kindness and love.

Nely and Carol were waiting for the birth of their baby with excitement, secretly Nely was absolutely bricking it, he was terrified at the thought of fatherhood. It carried a lot of responsibility; he didn't want to screw it up, worried he wasn't ready for it. His friend Alec, always at his side, assured him he would be a great dad, the making of him. Trouble was big brother Darryl was there constantly in the background, watching out for his sister, at the same time keeping an eye on Nely, waiting for him to make a mistake. He was getting paranoid, not an admirer of Nely's antics. He was though, looking forward to being a good uncle, the second baby to be born on Utopia. He just couldn't see Nely changing his idiotic ways.

Every survivor considered themselves very fortunate to be alive to enjoy this idyllic new world, they had no complaints.

Life was good to them, having everything they could possibly need handed to them on a plate. But, and it was a big but, it seemed too good to be true. There was that nagging doubt, could this world be real or not, could it suddenly be taken away without warning? For the time being they had to accept Utopia for what it was, their home.

*

Tom made a big decision on his future and decided to take a time out from the usual routine of daily life and take Simone for a walk. He had something very important to ask her and wanted complete privacy to do it.

The lush flora was fragrant as ever, and colourful. It would make the ideal walk, Tom thought. He took Simone along the edge of the forest where the trees stopped, and the undergrowth took over. Hand in hand they strolled along the narrow pathway. The warm sunshine felt pleasant on their faces, neither of them had a care in the world it seemed, Tom was biding his time, waiting for the right moment, especially the one where he could get his tongue untied.

Much of the plant life they passed was found to be edible, although no one was actually sure who first tried any of it to know that, but Nely was getting the blame. A rumour Nely suspected Darryl of putting about. It was a rumour he didn't mind taking credit for. Nely decided it was one-nil to him.

Trees were a useful commodity, many of the fallen caused by the crash came in handy for building shelters, proper homes would come later. Tools were fashioned out of anything that could be salvaged from the wreckage of Retriever-2, which for now remained a blot on the landscape. It was a painful reminder of the ordeal, eventually it was hoped the forest would claim it and shield it from sight.

Utopia was a gift; the survivors were determined never to abuse it.

Tom found the ideal spot, a small clearing just inside the forest, complete privacy. The sun glinted through the treetops, the perfect place for what he had in mind. He was still holding Simone's hand when he stopped suddenly, this was it, now or never. Turning to face her he wanted to say it there and then, but he couldn't, he was a bag of nerves. Simone looked startled for a second, thinking something was wrong.

"Tom, you okay?" she asked.

He smiled. "Of course, I just wanted to stop and admire the surroundings." Tom was playing for time, struggling to get the right words out.

"I know what you mean, it's lovely Tom, thank you for bringing me here. We're so lucky to have all this beauty around us."

Tom thought he was the lucky one, Simone was kind, thoughtful and very beautiful. On the ship he never realised just how attractive she was, he was always so wrapped up in his work to notice anyone. Now all he could think about was Simone, he loved her smooth dark complexion, her tight frizzy curls, her button nose, but really, he loved her whole nature. She adapted to this life easily, her outlook on the future was always upbeat, she radiated so much warmth, Tom fell in love instantly.

"Simone, I have something to ask you."

She couldn't help but notice he went all serious on her. The fact was, Tom was really shaking inside, this was a one-time question.

"Simone Costin, will you marry me?" he blurted it out quickly because if he didn't do it now, he'd never get it said. Simone for a second was stunned, she didn't see that coming.

Out of nowhere, JT, Xander's eldest son appeared right there, floating at eye level to Simone, almost in her face, his eyes swinging in all directions with sheer excitement. Tom standing over them, almost a foot taller than Simone looking just as shocked as Simone.

"Say yes Simone" squealed JT, buzzing with enthusiasm. Once Tom got over the initial shock of not being entirely alone, he got mad, angry with his namesake. The little guy must have been with them the whole time staying invisible, the devious, sneaky little sod, Tom thought. All the same JT ruined his special moment, Simone would never agree to marry him if one of the Avaans popped up any time they pleased.

"JT, what the hell do you think you're doing?" bellowed Tom in his ear, if anything he was embarrassed at the intrusion.

"I'm doing as I was told, my dad said to keep an eye on you, but he didn't say which one, he's still worried about you. I was only trying to help Just Tom."

"Well you don't do it by sneaking about like that, no more JT. You go and tell Xander I don't need looking after. Now go away." Tom waved his hand in his face, while Simone simply stood there grinning at JT's antics. It was actually funny even if it wasn't the done thing. Tom was right to tell him off. JT swiftly left; he had news to tell the villagers.

"Sorry Simone, I had no idea he was there, or that Xander would pull a stunt like that" said Tom, he felt that special moment had gone, Simone wasn't angry at the little guy, she reached up on her toes and kissed Tom.

"Well, if we are going to get married you better sort JT and Xander out, there are certain boundaries not to be crossed. I don't want one of these guys in my marital bed."

Tom agreed as they continued their walk, then it dawned on him what Simone said.

"Sorry, did you just agree to marry me?" he asked.

Simone shook her head with a tut under her breath in total disbelief.

"For a one-time science officer, you're a bit slow on the uptake Thomas Phasner."

Tom couldn't believe his luck, after JT ruining the moment she still wanted to marry him. He scooped her up in his arms and swung her around before kissing her warmly, his life was sorted at last. He couldn't wait to tell everyone the good news, although he suspected JT was already back in the village spilling the beans. He also guessed it was the end of a quiet life.

Xander would see to that.

CHAPTER TWELVE

The Clariziane pilots, weary from the long journey had finally negotiated the last, they hoped, of the distorted sectors of space. It had been arduous and stressful at times. As for the multiple rifts in their path, they barely managed to dodge them, but did so, mainly with some great piloting from Rol. It was also a worrying thought where the rifts led to if anywhere, the pilots didn't want to find out what was on the other side, for all they knew it was certain death. And besides, they still hadn't finished their mission in this barren universe, because up to that point the Kangans were the only other life they encountered. Now they had reached the edge of the next system, where they were informed by the Kangans, the third planet orbiting its sun was indeed inhabited. The long-range monitors had indicated that fact. The pilots hoped to gain information concerning Sol's whereabouts. Someone had to have seen him by now. They had no idea if the Kangans visited this planet or not, they didn't say, but if they did what did they find?

Many questions needed answers, and now, not later because it was becoming obvious something was seriously wrong with the universe. A disturbance in the natural cycle of life in the cosmos was affecting every system, it was being manipulated by some unseen force, natural or otherwise, it was suspected the latter. It needed correcting but the pilots were not the ones to do it, they were after all in the wrong universe, and not by choice. The plan was, find Sol and get the hell out of there. After that who knows, in reality they had no bloody idea what to do.

Right now the pilots hoped the occupants of the third planet were in some way intelligent beings and able to assist in their quest. This was the first colonised world they found, so hopes were high. As vast as this universe was it was odd no other life was found, other than the Kangans, they hoped never to meet them again, and glad they weren't neighbours, they weren't very likable beings.

The past few months were put behind them to concentrate on the beings on that planet ahead and pray they were not hostile. A confrontation they did not want, everyone was tired, not used to the prolonged space travel into other star systems, and the problems thrown at them along the way. It was the first time Clarizianes had ventured outside their own system, they had no idea what to expect, a parallel universe was not even on the list. The technology was available for intergalactic travel, yet Clariziane leaders chose to waste it on secretive projects like attempting time travel, and look where that got them, a fractured universe.

Still the pilots were unable to work out the driving force of the alien ship, something was powering it, some unknown energy source they had yet to fathom, except the fact it appeared to be an endless power source. Most of the instruments and dials like the guidance system, the long-range monitoring and air quality filters were all reconfigured to their own specifications. It made controlling the ship much easier. The red button at least for the time being was out of bounds. Still no one dared to touch it.

What was not expected was the continual timeline disruptions the pilots had to endure. Outside Clariziane space was unknown territory, they had no idea what to expect, experiencing strange spatial phenomena and weird timeline fluctuations had never entered their minds before. Not knowing the true time zone the pilots were travelling in, made it difficult to calculate if the ship was going back in time or forward into the future. The past they would rather forget, shooting into the future was unnerving because the pilots weren't sure if they went back over and over, could the future be changed, or even did they want it to. None of it relevant to the search, yet it played on their minds.

There were times when one or two of the pilots questioned if they even had the right universe. Had they perhaps negotiated a course through a spatial rift by mistake. Star charts were useless, the universe kept twisting space out of shape and even moving entire systems. Not even the alien ship could help them with that problem.

This had to be the right galaxy, the long-range monitors pinpointed the third planet, the pilots proceeded with caution, it was still unknown space, they had to stay alert. Bizarrely Don suddenly had a suspicion there might be more than two universes in existence. Something was telling him so. Was there life beyond the realms of normal? A question he asked himself over and over, nothing felt real anymore. He couldn't find the answers; whatever lie ahead, there was no going back. They had no home, possibly no universe anymore, effectively they were homeless drifters in space. With Clarizia having destroyed itself, the only mission left was to find Sol, and even that was starting to stretch their resolve.

Stella was beginning to lose faith in her belief that Sol was still alive, she maintained he was out there, lost in the depths of space, but deep in her heart she started to have doubts. She had a vision and questioned that so much she also questioned her commitment to the mission. This endless journey was draining all their strength, physically and mentally. It looked less and less likely Stella would ever see her beloved cousin again, he was her only family, having been orphaned at an early age.

Perhaps it was a foolhardy mission from the start. Stella and Ariel risked their own lives for this quest, did the unthinkable at spaceport to save the pilots from certain death just so they could go on this idiotic adventure. At the time Stella was sure it was the right thing to do but chasing a lost cause across the universe and beyond was possibly the worst decision she ever made. Now she felt guilty about the whole situation she and Ariel put the pilots in, because she knew they would never give up.

Don was more driven, his friend was everything to him, he privately continued to call out to Sol, this time he had a strange stirring in his mind and wondered if his pleas were reaching across space finally. He was certain more than ever he was alive. He experienced a weird vision in his mind's eye, of an unknown planet, but it was vague, he didn't know where it was, only that it definitely wasn't the planet in the next galaxy. *Was it the same vision Stella had?* he wondered. Don still had hopes the people on that third planet might have good news, they were all running out of ideas.

In the meantime Don continued to wrestle with the uninvited visions in his head, for a split second he thought he saw Sol, but the image was out of focus, too hazy for him to be certain who he was seeing. It disturbed him greatly, the visions were random but always shortly after he called out to his friend, he felt it was an omen. For now he hoped and prayed Sol would hear his call and give him a sign. The pilots were getting desperate, this might well be their last chance of finding Sol.

Don tried harder to reach out, if it meant calling to Sol across two universes, then he would.

*

A slight problem standing in the pilots path as they headed for the third planet was a small fleet of spaceships that entered the system ahead of them. Surmising these were the menacing warlike ships the Kangans mentioned, they held back to monitor the situation. If these warrior ships favourite pastime was shooting at anyone who got in their way, the pilots didn't want to get involved. They still needed to know what their intentions were.

From a safe distance, the newly acquired tracking system rigged up by Fisah had seven ships advancing towards the third planet in perfect formation. Modifying the alien technology aboard their own ship gave the pilots an insight to what was happening out there. Listening to conversations aboard the alien ships didn't make for good news, but picking up the occasional transmission from the planet surface wasn't good news either. The approaching alien ships merely wanted to annihilate the people, wipe out the entire planet from existence. The Clarizianes had a dilemma, should they intervene, or not? It wasn't in their plans to engage in war, or involve themselves with other beings, or their business.

It was hard to imagine how seven ships could possibly hope to decimate an entire planet and its inhabitants, the aliens had a lot of guts – or stupidity.

One thing was certain, a space battle was not on the cards for the pilots, they were not soldiers of war and wanted no part of the confrontation. They did however question their own conscience as to whether they could stand back and do nothing to stop the destruction of an entire race of beings. Then again if they allowed it to happen they would not get the chance to speak with the inhabitants.

It was a choice no one wanted to make.

Don took a time out again; he had to call to Sol one last time. He was sure deep-down Sol would hear eventually. Maybe this time he would have success. Sol would know what to do, he was a born leader. With the vision Don experienced, there was a chance Sol was close by, he felt a strong connection like never before. He had to be here.

Further conversations picked up from the planet surface were very disturbing, it appeared two aliens from another world were being held prisoner and about to be tried for multiple crimes, including murder. That wasn't good news, whatever the crime it didn't sit right with Fisah who was monitoring the transmissions. He was appalled at the attitude of these people. Did one planet have the right to hold aliens for trial in this manner? He wasn't happy with what he was hearing, and continued to listen in.

Rol was seated next to Fisah, his job, keeping an eye on the fleet of ships closing in on the inner planets, he started to wonder what they got themselves into, this was out of the Clarizianes comfort zone, they really didn't prepare themselves for this mission. The events unfolding no one bargained for. Rol realised they were all so naïve to think it would be easy to find Sol. *Who did they think they were kidding?*

The conversations Fisah was picking up were brutal to listen to, the more he heard, the angrier he got. Something major happened on this planet a while back, he couldn't work out exactly what precipitated it, but he was starting to dislike these aliens even before he met them. Apparently there was enormous civil unrest, a failed government, a collapse of an important organisation, and the worse, he heard the planet was once the leading intergalactic force across the universe. Now it seemed they were social outcasts, other planets shunned them. Fisah thought that strange, *where were these other worlds?* They never came across a single colonised planet in the three months they were in space, and what could these people on the third planet have done so wrong to be ostracised in such a brutal fashion. He discovered the only important thing to these people was making two aliens possible scapegoats for their own shortcomings. It definitely wasn't right, Fisah informed the other pilots everything he heard. Something told them they would not get the answers they wanted from these aliens. They didn't come across as very friendly and possibly very likely to be hostile to aliens from other worlds.

The discussion now, were the fleet of ships wanting to destroy everything in their path, any better? Fisah thought not, and he was not alone. Could they allow the ships to open fire on the planet and wipe out a world that probably didn't deserve to live anyway? Or should they intervene with the red button?Neither option was great.

Another option Fisah suggested, rescue the two alien prisoners and then get the hell out of there fast. Nice idea the others thought, but Don said it wasn't feasible, they wouldn't get past the ships for one, he then pointed out it wasn't their war, and they had to remember that. None of them knew the circumstances, and quite frankly Don was adamant he didn't want to know. Still the pilots debated the pros and cons of the situation, a decision had to be made what they should do.

Hiding behind one of the outer planets for safety, staying undetected seemed the best option, the pilots couldn't agree on their next course of action. They all had different opinions. Hanzon said just use the red button and be done with it. He was promptly told to shut it if he couldn't come up with something more constructive, so he decided to retreat from the argument in favour of food, that usually solved his problems.

Without a decision coming, time was dragging on, they were getting nowhere. Suddenly out of the blue another spatial shift occurred, the planet they were hiding behind moved out of its orbit and veered off.

Their cover was blown.

Space itself was now in a state of upheaval, it twisted out of shape, the monitors were showing a misalignment of space and stars that looked blurred on the screens, as if the monitors were malfunctioning, except they weren't.

Fisah and Rol rushed back to their seats in a panic, unsure what they should do, Rol cursed himself for only keeping one eye on the monitors while discussions were going on. He watched as the planet careered out of control, its many natural satellites pulled in opposite directions, one collided with their ship, shattering into hundreds of pieces of rock before drifting away, heading on course for the inner planets. No damage was done to the hull, the alien outer casing totally impenetrable. The pilots were safe for now at least.

The fleet of ships were also displaced in the spatial shift, strange forces controlled the ships in an unnatural manner, one entered the upper atmosphere of the third planet, others scattered further afield, but one abruptly appeared at the bow of the pilots ship which had mysteriously maintained its position, albeit exposed. Panic set in, now they had to act. The pilots crowded round the monitors waiting for a response from the alien ship, certain they would try something. *Would they fire first?* The tension was making everyone nervous, the situation couldn't get any worse, except Hanzon was back, he heard the commotion and decided he should sit close to the red button, if all-out war was about to happen, he wasn't hanging around to be blown up. He did actually want to stay with the food he'd prepared, on this occasion his brain kicked in instead of his stomach.

"Don't even think about it Hanzon!" snapped Rol, knowing full well why he sat himself down close by.

"I wasn't going to do anything" pleaded Hanzon, trying his best to sound innocent even he if wasn't.

"Okay Don, what do we do now?" asked Stella, who came up behind Rol, loitering with her hand very conveniently on his shoulder. Rol was again putty at that point; he hadn't got around to telling her how he really felt. Stella knew of course, it was obvious from the start, and besides she was warming to his personality and demeanour, but she would keep him hanging on a while longer. It still wasn't the time for romance. Don didn't reply, he was stunned for words, *what could he say?* Stella decided to leave the men to it, she realised it was the only way to snap Rol out of his dreamlike state, she wasn't helping the poor man to concentrate on his job. Don and Fisah kept an eye on the monitors, wondering why the alien ship hadn't made a move, it was quite clearly aware of their presence, both ships motionless, bow to bow. *So why didn't they shoot?*

"Do we shoot first, ask questions later – or what?" asked Kat, wandering into the control section, and possibly hoping for some action. She felt they had to do something other than standing around looking at the small screen, it was worse than watching paint dry, frustrating. The women pilots wanted the men to stop dithering and make a decision.

"I don't know –" said Don, "if we shoot first, the people on that planet are going to rightly assume we're the hostile ones." He had a valid point; it still didn't get them anywhere.

"From what I've learned from that planet, they're in no position to make any assumptions" said Fisah, "and I'm more concerned why these alien ships moved position like that, it shouldn't be happening" he added.

"It doesn't help our problem whatever we do" said Rol, doing his best to come to his senses. If Stella didn't commit soon he was going to burst a blood vessel. Don couldn't think of anything to say, the others had no suggestions either.

"We're screwed, aren't we?" said a defeated Fisah.

Don had done all he could, Sol was the only one who could help the pilots now.

Where the hell was he?

CHAPTER THIRTEEN

Three Utopian men, Mike, Tom, and Nely sat on the wooden step of Mikes home in complete silence, waiting for two of their sons to return to the village. They had been sent on a very important life or death mission. They were late, the men began to worry for their safety. It had been hours; the boys should have returned a while ago. *What was keeping them?* Panic was setting in, the men questioned their decision to send the boys on this secret mission, they were still teenagers after all, very young for such an important job. The boys knew of no other life but Utopia, this was their home, the only one they had ever known.

Stepping back into the universe on a risky undertaking was a tough ask for anyone, risky because the men couldn't be sure the boys calculated the right time period in history and the right sector of space to appear. It had to be spot on, because if not they might well cause major repercussions for life itself. If the two boys, Tom's son Calum and Nely's son Josef, aged fourteen and fifteen respectively, were not accurate in the calculations it might cause an imbalance in the universe just by being there. It wasn't their place of birth, but re-entering the universe was supposed to be brief, at least that was the plan. It was always going to be a big risk simply because it had never been attempted before. And then had to be done in secret because Sol couldn't know what was going on, not until the time was right. He couldn't know the circumstances in case the events created a paradox, the universe had enough problems of its own, it didn't need further complications.

So Mike agreed to help Tom and Nely with the plan which involved the boys, there was no other choice.

They remained sat on the solid wooden step, fidgeting about every now and then, the hard step made the prolonged sitting uncomfortable, but they stayed, refusing to budge until Calum and Josef returned safely. The time dragged on agonisingly slow to the point of mental torture.

Calum, who Tom named after his friend Cal Bartok, who sadly died in the crash fifteen years ago, was in Tom's eyes, a sensible level-headed and grown-up lad for his age, but still young. Nely's lad Josef had a lot of his father in him, Tom deemed him adult enough to accompany Calum on the mission. It didn't stop them worrying about sending teenagers to do a man's job. The decision was made that no one else could do the task for fear of being recognised in the process. Then again if anything did go wrong, it would most certainly cause an overlap of time and space, and the two boys lost out of their time, and that would definitely cause a paradox in the universe, something they had to avoid at all costs.

The situation as bad as it was, the men didn't want it to escalate, they couldn't allow past events to jeopardise future events that had already happened. It would surely create a catastrophe the universe would not be able to correct; plus Tom and Nely might lose their sons in the past, in a universe they knew nothing about. That one thought really scared them, how were they going to explain it to their mothers, who knew of the mission but sworn to secrecy. Nely for sure knew he'd be dead meat, and it wasn't Carol he was worried about. Darryl would pulverise him.

The hardest part of this secret mission was keeping it away from the Avaans, naturally nosy, inquisitive beings who would pop up anywhere without warning, and they were no good at keeping secrets. They were told time and again boundaries had to be respected, most of the time they took no notice. Invisibility was a unique trait they liked to exploit at every opportunity.

Many, many times over the years they mischievously disobeyed the rules, yet again and again they had to be told there was a time and place when it was acceptable and when not. They did eventually agree to abide by the rules, but it wasn't any fun for them, and keeping their offspring in check was never easy.

The mission had to take place without Sol's knowledge, his son Nicolas couldn't know either, so that meant keeping it from Niko which really hurt Mike to do. He hated the idea of keeping secrets from his best friend, he always told her everything going on in his life, they had a very special unbreakable bond. That was something he didn't want to lose. But this was the biggie, a mission too important as it involved Sol, who was in danger, he needed help. Niko was also in serious trouble with her unborn baby. As much as it hurt Mike to stay quiet, they had to intervene to save one of their own. If someone didn't go back into the universe in the past to help Sol, injured, groggy and trapped in a corridor on Retriever-2, he might not be alive today. It would most definitely change the future, then young Nicolas would not be born alive, and worse, Niko would not survive the birth. It was a huge undertaking; it had to succeed. Mike couldn't lose his one true friend.

The Utopians didn't want disruption in their paradise world, living all this time outside the universe in perfect harmony; they thrived beyond all expectations. The children grew up content, healthy and knowledgeable of their idyllic environment. They learnt so much about life, the adults were quite happy to keep it that way. Life on Utopia had been good to them, but now it seemed fate took a wrong turn, pushing them away from the peaceful surroundings. The villagers had long suspected their destiny was in the hands of some unseen supernatural force, something or someone controlled their future, compelling them to act.

It was payback time.

The universe gave the Utopians the ability to live productive lives, grow their community, now it gave them the one tool to complete the cycle of life. The rest was up to them.

The universe hoped they would get it right.

*

It all began when arriving back home from a day out with the menfolk, Tom was immediately drawn to something on the top step of his log cabin, a strange wooden object was placed there. It was clearly old and had a mystical aura about it. At first Tom had no idea what it was or who put it there, but he felt an overwhelming emotion his life was about to change, he wasn't sure for the better or not, in fact that feeling gave him a terrifying foreboding about the whole village and its future.

Tom's wife Simone, son Calum and daughter Annie were inside, they knew nothing about it, heard nothing and initially thought he was playing games with them. They didn't bite. He went outside again, almost afraid to pick up the object, there was something about its presence. He sat on the step studying it, an ancient looking artefact if he had to describe it, round, with symbols and odd lettering on the outer part, and what appeared to be some sort of hieroglyphics carved in the centre. It was puzzling but also intriguing. Tom knew straightaway it had been put there for a reason.

But why him?

Where did it come from?

More baffling, *how did it get to his doorstep?* Tom realised it had a specific purpose, he just had to work out what it was.

The artefact was ancient, that much was certain, old dried out wood, a relic from long ago, at least a thousand years Tom surmised. *But what was it doing on this planet?* At that point he was extremely worried they might not be alone in their beautiful sanctuary.

Did someone else live here?

In the fifteen years the survivors lived on Utopia they found no evidence of any other life, so it was hardly likely, but was it possible beings lived there before they arrived? It still didn't answer the question of how the object found its way to his doorstep in the first place, or why no one else noticed it.

Tom had to force himself to pick it up, the only way perhaps to discover its origin, then find out its purpose, because he was certain it had one. A strange sense of awe swept over Tom, something almost supernatural was the only way to describe the artefact. When he eventually picked it up, found it was uncannily lightweight for a chunk of wood. Almost immediately an eerie green glow emanated from the centre, startled, Tom almost dropped it, he had to compose himself, his hands wouldn't stop shaking as he carried it inside. Simone was waiting for him having dispensed the kids to their rooms, she had a notion Tom might be serious this time, just a feeling she had. Placing the wooden artefact on the table in front of Simone, it continued with the strange glow, activating itself was unnerving to both of them. The centre began to rotate clockwise, aligning with the outer symbols. They didn't know what it meant or what they were supposed to do, the only real thing about the carved object, was that it was definitely manmade, and that thought really scared them.

Tom and Simone kept the artefact a secret from the other villagers, at least until Tom could work out what it was, and what the symbols represented, then he would make a decision. At first he found it incredibly hard, not having a clue where to begin. Clearly the symbols resembled ancient hieroglyphics from Earths history, but that wasn't possible he thought. They were thousands of light years from Earth and a universe apart.

The study of such hieroglyphics died out hundreds of years ago in schools, it wasn't deemed important or even necessary to hang on to the past anymore, but Tom recalled reading about such a subject once, before those ancient books his father gave him were taken away and destroyed. Not many survived, it seemed the human race had stringent views on the past staying where it was. Leaders of Earth did their upmost to wipe out history completely, it didn't go down well with diehard historians. Tom never forgot those books; he found it astonishing he could still remember that far back. Earth was another lifetime ago; he hadn't thought about his home planet in a very long time. Suddenly after all these years he was homesick, but only momentarily. He could never go back, nor did he want to. Earth was now an alien concept to him. The people there were no better than savage murderers, he like the others considered themselves Utopians – not humans, not anymore.

For many days Tom worked on the artefact in secret, slowly he began to understand what the symbols referred to, but not how it actually worked, at times it seemed to have a mind of its own, which he thought a bit freaky. Then he reached the conclusion that it was he who activated it just by holding it, he had a distinct connection to the artefact, now he had to find out why.

After many hours working late into the night Tom now hoped by pressing the correct sequence of symbols, something would eventually happen to give him a clue he was on the right track. He was right, but also surprised, the centre of the artefact activated itself again by turning anticlockwise this time and glowed in a blue haze rather than green. He triggered something, strange thoughts and images projected into his head out of nowhere. He had to decipher what he was seeing in his mind's eye.

*

The universe knew the artefact was in the right hands, Thomas Phasner was indeed the true guardian of the ancient symbols, his son Calum would be too. One more was needed to complete the cycle.

The time had come.

The universe needed the Utopians to begin devising a strategy, it was imperative they succeed.

*

Tom sat there in the dark, disturbed by everything in his head, no way could he sleep knowing what had to be done. A plan was needed, that was the part he hadn't managed to work out yet. *Who could he involve? Who would understand the seriousness of the matter and still be able to maintain the secret?* He struggled with his conscience for hours, with no solution in sight. His mind drifted away in deep meditation, trying to piece together any sort of plan, when silently two soft arms curled round his neck. Simone was there wondering why he hadn't come to bed. She had been aware he was finding the artefact a huge burden on his shoulders, and the fact he had to keep it a secret from the villagers, it was hard on him, but it was just as hard for Simone not to say anything. For now it was Tom who needed comfort and support. They sat together until morning talking.

Tom told Simone everything, about the visions he was having, and why he had to involve Calum, who at that point knew very little about what was going on. He hadn't even shown Calum the artefact, still Tom had an inkling the boy would be able to fill some of the gaps he was struggling with.

Simone naturally was hesitant about her son getting involved, he was still a boy, it was a big ask for him. She however understood why it had to be done, but she didn't have to like it. What Tom had in mind was dangerous, far-fetched and downright unbelievable. The only thing Simone had faith in was her husband, he was adamant it had to be done. The artefact gave them the means to complete the mission, as dangerous as it was, but in the right hands Tom was confident they would succeed.

It had to.

Simone went along with it.

The next part of the plan was down to Mike, he had no family to keep secrets from and he was close to Niko. He had to convince Sol, Niko and son Nicolas to take time away from the village for a couple of days, they couldn't get wind of the plan, it was after all in their best interest – and their survival.

Mike was regarded as honorary uncle to Nicolas, he loved that kid to bits, so his idea would not come as anything but a friendly gesture. Niko was all for it.

The very next day Sol, Niko and Nicolas packed a few supplies and headed off into uncharted land, to explore parts of the planet not seen before. It was an adventure, especially for young Nicolas who thought it would be great fun. Sol didn't really get the whole camping thing, Niko would simply say it was a human custom, that was her answer to everything. Sol had never got used to human ways, and wondered if he ever would, but he was willing to please and go along with the idea, if only for a quiet life. Besides with alien DNA permanently running through Niko's veins he wasn't about to argue with his feisty wife. Clariziane women were naturally that way, Sol got used to it over the years, it was what was expected of the men. He might have once saved her life, something he would never regret as long as he lived, having a feisty, spirited and passionate wife with a fiery temper, he gladly took on the chin, then he thought she still looked incredibly sexy even after all these years. Sol loved the jet-black streaks in her hair, even when her blond started to show grey, she would always be the love of his life.

Niko said she wanted to teach Nicolas some real-life skills now he was fifteen years old, already towering above his mum. It was time he learnt to do certain things for himself. This trip was a good opportunity, Niko thanked Mike for suggesting the idea. They would be gone for days, time for Tom to proceed with the mission. He had to rope in Nely and Carol, he needed Josef on the mission, two strong boys would do the job a lot easier than one.

Nely naturally was reluctant, apprehensive about sending his son on a ludicrous and crazy assignment. '*What was Tom thinking about?*' fortunately young Josef was not like his dad, he was adventurous, brave and totally fearless. He was actually jealous of Nicolas going off exploring. When Tom explained everything to Josef, he fully understood the consequences, he insisted he could do it. If Calum was going then so was he. They would succeed to help their friend Nicolas.

Carol realised the seriousness of the mission, she didn't like it but convinced Nely their son should go, but they could not say a word to Darryl, he wouldn't agree to it and the less people who knew the mission the better.

*

The minutes and hours ticked by as the men impatiently waited for Calum and Josef to return home. The tension was getting unbearable, it was difficult for all three. They had so much to lose if the mission went wrong, explaining it to the villagers would be impossible, never mind the boys mothers. They chatted awhile to pass the time, it wasn't easy to concentrate on anything, they just wanted their boys back safe. Tom had a question for Mike, something he wanted to ask for a long time, although he wasn't sure if this was the appropriate time, but he asked anyway.

"Mike, you and Niko, you and she have been close friends for a very long time, right?"

"Yes" he replied, he was actually thinking about her at that moment, wondering what his life would be like without her in it, and the way things were going that was a very real possibility.

"Well, how come you two never got together, I mean you know, get married."

Mike knew the answer to that without a doubt.

"She's my best friend, that's it really" replied Mike.

"Yeh, and? –" asked Nely, sat in the middle of them.

"You don't marry your best friend." That was the only thing he was sure about in his life, Niko was the only constant he had, she had always been his rock.

"So you never married, why?" asked Tom.

"I don't know, never found the right woman I guess, I just think I'm better off on my own, besides, Nicolas is a great kid to have around. I love being uncle to all the kids." Mike was happy with his life the way it was, no need to change a single aspect of it – except wish for the boys to come home.

“That’s really intense mate” said Nely, he was so lucky Carol, and the kids were in his life. Besides Josef he had eleven-year-old Maria, who was growing more beautiful by the day to mirror her mother. He couldn’t imagine a life without them now.

“So how much longer do we wait guys?” asked Mike, deciding to change the subject away from his personal life.

“As long as it takes my friend, we wait for the boys to come home” said Tom. If he went home without Calum he could guarantee of being in the doghouse for an eternity. Silently he was now beginning to regret letting his son go, but apart from Calum and Josef, none of the other children on Utopia were old enough to understand the importance of the mission or even have the physical strength to do the job. It had to be Calum once he picked up the artefact and activated it, then Tom knew his son was part of the equation, it responded to the boy with immense power. Tom realised the artefact was presented to him to do a specific job; he had a duty to perform but Calum had a much stronger connection. Coupled with the night visions he experienced, knew Calum was the chosen one for this mission, he had to fulfil his destiny given to him by unknown, unseen forces.

The light was fading as the sun slipped behind the trees, worry was also setting in, six hours was too long. The boys should have been back, something must have gone wrong. Nely stood up to stretch his legs, his own anxiety levels had hit the top step ages ago. He paced around in circles, kicking the dust up in frustration.

“You know, if we had a pub, I’d go and get drunk, or something.”

“Sit down Nely,” said Tom “this is not the time for your flippant jokes, we’re all worried, okay.”

It made no difference; Nely was trying to deal with his stress the best way he knew. The truth was his nerves were shot.

"You do realise Carol is going to kill me when I get home, that's if that brother of hers doesn't get me first." He was angry, more with himself for agreeing with the stupid idea that a piece of wood would keep his son safe. Whichever way he looked at it, he was screwed, he wasn't getting out of this with his balls intact. Darryl would see to that.

*

Coming out of the darkness two happy figures emerged through the gaping hole in the trees created by the time portal opening up. Calum and Josef fought their way through the undergrowth not understanding why it was dark, they had only been gone a few minutes, having left when the sun was at its highest point. They pushed on, heading for Uncle Mike's home, the agreed meeting place on their return. They just hoped they were going the right way, the faint moon was no help, the much brighter moon had yet to appear in the night sky.

A sudden wave of relief swept over the men as they heard the boys voices giggling in the dark as they approached. They all jumped up and ran towards them. Tom was first to recognise his son in the shadows, he quickly grabbed him and hugged him, the emotion he felt right then was sheer ecstasy, so pleased to have him home safe and well, then he couldn't help but get a little angry with the lad.

"What the hell happened Calum, what took you so long?"

"We completed our mission dad; we did everything right. It was exciting." Calum was full of pride he and Josef succeeded.

"You should have been back hours ago." Tom really wanted to tell him off, but how could he.

Nely was holding his son tight with deep affection; he too was relieved.

"Dad, let go, we're okay honestly, we did complete the mission."

Nely decided that was the first and last time he was letting Josef out of his sight, he was never going through that anguish again.

"Really dad, let me go, I can't breathe" said Josef, trying to free himself. As much as he loved his dad this was too much for a fifteen-year-old boy. Nely let go but he had words to say.

"You don't know what you two put us through, it's been unbearable" he said, his stressed-out brain was all over the place, but deep down, he was so happy.

"But we were only gone a few minutes" said Calum, "Hi Uncle Mike" he added, just about making out Mike hovering in the shadows. Mike sort of waved, nobody was more relieved than him, he didn't want to explain his part to Niko if it all had gone wrong, then again if it had, she wouldn't be alive today to tear him off a strip. His brain cells were running riot, he'd gladly settle for a good telling off, so long as Niko and Sol came home.

"So tell us what happened" Tom wanted all the details.

"Like we said dad, we did everything like you told us. We saved Sol and sent him on his way. Honestly dad, I thought we were only gone a few minutes. Why is it night-time?"

"Try about seven hours son" said Tom.

The boys were astounded, surely that was not possible, nothing went wrong.

Mike stepped forward. "It seems you were only gone minutes through the portal, but hours passed here, maybe you entered the wrong sequence and returned in a slightly different time zone." Mike didn't actually understand the mechanics of the artefact, but he surmised that was the only logical conclusion.

"I told you Calum, you screwed up the correct time for our return" said Josef.

"I did not!" said Calum quite indignantly, then again Josef was right. "Well maybe a slight miscalculation, I did rush it a bit" he admitted, a bit sheepish. He was so eager to get back, and he was the one in charge of the artefact, he couldn't blame Josef.

"Sorry dad, but we did good, yes?"

"Yes son."

"How about we all go home" said Nely.

"Yeh dad, I'm starving" said Josef.

"Me too, wonder what mum has got for us" said Calum.

"Probably a good telling off for being so late, let's go" said Tom, "next time we better practice a little more restraint with the artefact" he added, clutching Calum as they headed home, he had some explaining to do himself, telling Simone they would be home within the hour.

"Just letting you know Tom, if there is a next time, count me out. I'm not going through that ever again. Goodnight guys" said Nely, walking off into the dark, he decided this was a one-time thing never to be repeated.

*

The universe was less grumpy now. The first part of the mission was a complete success. The humans did well, now it was up to the Clarizianes to get involved, the universe could help no more. It was out of options, and out of favours.

They were on their own.

CHAPTER FOURTEEN

Several nights in a row Sol had restless disturbed sleep. He couldn't switch off his troubled mind to relax properly. Sleep was getting further and further away each night. Something was wrong. He experienced strange dreams even though he was awake most of the time. Visions appeared in his head, but he couldn't understand what they meant, nor had he any control over the emotional turmoil he was feeling. His head was all over the place, the fatigue wasn't helping. It all started on his return to the village after his family camping trip. Sol didn't enjoy it one bit but never said.

Watching his son embrace life out in the open, and his mother so happy, how could he spoil that moment. They were so carefree, sharing a special mother and son bond, it warmed his heart. Niko was more Clariziane than human now, probably even more than Nicolas; she still had so many human traits that made her unique. Sol couldn't have been happier to see his son so grown up, it made him think of the past. He and Niko never had more children, it being the only downside in his life. Niko miscarried a second baby and refused to try again, her age and the fact she nearly died having Nicolas meant she wouldn't consider it. Sol had to live with it.

Now back home in the village everything changed for Sol, it wasn't the camping trip that troubled him, he was sure of that. There was an eerie presence in the village, nothing he could put his finger on, but it made him feel nervous, unsettled and it worried him deeply. Then suddenly he had a premonition he was needed; someone was calling to him, wanting his help, he didn't know who, it scared him not knowing, and why now?

Clarizia popped into his head, but it couldn't possibly be that causing so much anguish; his home planet was destroyed a long time ago. The memories of his past life had long since faded. His pilot friends then entered his thoughts, *why?* He had no answer; it was the one thing keeping him awake at night. The pilots would all be dead now and no help to him in this crisis. *So why did he keep thinking about them?*

Sol was afraid to say anything, it wasn't something he could put into words, he felt so alone, isolated from his surroundings. He knew he wasn't ill, so it couldn't be his well-being; besides he never got sick on Utopia, life it seemed had no expiry date. The Utopians enjoyed a good healthy life. Nevertheless Sol's mind was being tortured by some supernatural force, he was terrified what might be happening to him. Lack of sleep didn't help, the night visions got worse, and he just didn't know what to do about them. He became afraid of his inner soul, but even more afraid to think it might all be real. And it wasn't the first time he lost his mind. How could he explain what was in his head, when he didn't know himself.

Niko realised something was deeply troubling her husband because his constant restless nights were disturbing her also. She was fearful for him, still Sol said nothing. It wasn't like him to clam up, he had finally learnt to be more laid back in his approach to life, even trying to learn human ways at one point. He never got far, so stopped and decided it best just to be himself.

Niko actually thought he enjoyed the camping out, though he never said. She could only guess what was wrong with him, it certainly wasn't easy to read him. He was stressed out and she couldn't let it carry on and say nothing. It was time for a serious heart to heart. Sol needed to open up, let out his feelings.

After another sleepless night Sol was up early sitting outside his home in the warm air; he wished the wooden steps he built many years ago were a little more comfortable, but they weren't. his mind had been racing throughout the night, disturbing him yet again. This time he heard messages calling for help, at least that's what he thought he heard. He couldn't quite make out the exact words or who it might be. It was all a blur. That started him stressing again, making his anxiety worse; his brain going completely haywire, now unable to make a rational decision as to what he should do.

Sol couldn't handle his emotions out of control; he felt he was losing his grip on his sanity, so he got up and sat on the steps outside for what seemed like hours. The sun started to rise over the trees in the distance, still nothing was making sense to him; he spent the night asking the same questions over and over, getting an answer wasn't as easy.

A short while later a soft loving arm slipped over Sol's shoulder, Niko didn't get much sleep either with him tossing and turning all night. Nicolas would not be up for ages being a typical teenager, so Niko thought it would be a good time to talk, and she wasn't taking silence for an answer.

"Talk to me Sol" she said calmly but in a way that made it clear he needed to open up, offload what was on his mind. It really hurt her to see the man she loved in such mental pain; his anguish was causing him a great deal of torment, it was hurting both of them. He needed to unburden his problem, she couldn't take secrets, it wasn't what they were about. Sol didn't know where to start, *would his beloved wife even believe him?* It was hard, the premonitions were torture, and the last few nights had completely drained him. How could he put into words that his worst fear was the fact he might be having a nervous breakdown. It had been over a week since the first distressing dreams, he hoped it would pass, but it just got worse.

"I think someone is calling me Niko, but I don't know who."

Sol blurted it out finally, it sounded stupid out loud. He was sure Niko would assume he was crazy, and maybe he was and didn't realise it. Niko didn't think that at all, she actually believed him, it did explain his odd behaviour, his anxiety was genuine. She had no doubt the poor man was fretting about something. Touching his tired looking face, a few stress lines were appearing, the ridges on his forehead more prominent than usual, a clear sign of stress. She pushed back his long black hair off his shoulders, as she often did. He was beginning to age now, that much was evident with the odd grey hair. She still had no idea of his true age, *how would she ever know?*

Niko had a few grey hairs herself, yet the jet-black streaks, curtesy of her husband's blood transfusion were very much still there. Turning her into an alien almost, was not exactly in her plans for life, but staying alive to live with the one true love of her life made it bearable. He still needed to talk.

"Is it voices you hear my darling?" she asked.

"No, no I don't think so, I don't know what I hear. Its just – just a feeling I have, someone is telling me I have to go, but we can never leave this place." Sol was so overwhelmed with emotion, he didn't know what he was saying, nothing felt real anymore. Tears started to roll down his cheeks, something he never did before.

"I'm sorry Niko, I'm scared, really scared for the future. What's happening to me? Help me understand what's going on in my head. Please, tell me I'm not crazy." Sol was desperate, drained of energy, physically and mentally, his sleepless tortured nights erupted into thoughts of uncertainty. He felt lost, he put his head on Niko's shoulder and wept uncontrollably, the only way to release all the built-up tension in his body. Niko held him tight and allowed him to get it all out.

Suddenly Niko began to have her own worries as she held her sobbing husband. She had a feeling this day might come. Their happiness was going to be ripped away without a moment's notice. Maybe it was time to leave Utopia.

The question was, how?

There was no transport off this world, how would they ever be able to leave. She began to question what this planet was all about, *was it really a planet?* It was all too convenient when they first arrived, everything handed to them on a plate. Then Niko had the stupid thought they were all in the afterlife, maybe none of them survived the crash. She soon put that out of her head, she had Nicolas, he was definitely real, and suffering from the pain of his birth and the agony of her miscarriage, this wasn't a dream, or the afterlife.

Niko did have a secret yearning of her own, something she felt was very important to her and Nicolas but for years dismissed it as sheer fantasy. She had always thought there was a faint hope she could take her son to Earth to show him the home of her birth. He was after all half human, although he was looking more and more like his father every day, then she thought, so was she. *How could she explain that?*

Having spent seven long years aboard the ship travelling through space, before settling on Utopia for the last fifteen years, *could they really go back?* Earth was a lifetime ago; everything would have changed. *Was it possible that all past sins would be forgiven?* Maybe not, it was just a silly pipedream. They could never go back. Besides, most of the time Niko thought Earth authorities were idiots to the point of stupidity. No, it was unlikely she would ever see home again. Utopia was home now, still it was hard to believe it was theirs, *did it really belong to them? Or were they merely borrowing it?* Niko wished for her own answers, they would never come, and none of it was helping Sol with his problems. She found it impossible to help him if he didn't open up.

"Come inside Sol, have something to eat."

"Not hungry" he said, lifting his head and wiping tears off his face.

"Now look here my darling, you will come inside, and we will work something out over breakfast. Maybe you could talk to one of the men, you get on well with Tom, Darryl perhaps, Alec, Paul, hell, even Nely could listen to you, although I'm not sure you'd get a lot of sense out of him. You have to try Sol."

He felt silly now, crying like a baby; of course Niko was right, she always was. He now realised he couldn't go on night after night being tormented by voices he didn't know or understand, he had to find a solution to his torture before he had a complete mental breakdown.

"Yes, voices!" Sol suddenly blurted out.

"What?" said Niko, puzzled by his words.

"Voices, I do hear voices, or at least one voice" he said.

"What is this voice saying to you?" Niko urged him to unlock his mind for the answer, it was there somewhere, she was sure of it.

"I don't know, things are still a bit hazy at the moment."

Niko could see he was behaving much calmer now, maybe with a little more prompting he would understand what the voice was saying.

"Time for breakfast Sol, I hear Nicolas finally moving about." She helped him to his feet, and they headed inside.

"And you will eat" said Niko firmly, and in a way Sol knew not to argue with.

"Yes dear" he said, he learnt that bit from humans, the men said it a lot. Niko was a good caring wife and mother; he trusted her instincts and would go along with whatever she decided.

*

Wanting to arrange a get together for later in the day, Niko spoke to the one person she knew she could rely on, Mike. Firstly she told him of her worries, and she wanted to organise a meeting with the villagers. She said Sol was suffering, struggling mentally since returning to the village.

Alarm bells went off in Mike's head.

Niko thought the men perhaps could help Sol to unburden his problem, talk to him to reassure him, listen to what he had to say. Mike knew Niko didn't ask this lightly, it was serious, and he guessed why. He had a bad feeling about it, dreaded the moment. He of course agreed, he had no choice and left with a worried look, realising the men involved were going to have to come clean and confess what they did while Niko and Sol were away. This was no coincidence so soon after their return. *Maybe the mission didn't go quite as planned, how could he know?*

No one mentioned the artefact or its purpose, because when they came home from the camping trip happy and relaxed, it simply meant the mission had been a success, they survived the ordeal, so little point in saying anything. Calum and Josef did a good job, Mike now realised he was in deep trouble with his best friend, Niko wasn't going to like it. She hated secrets.

Tom had hidden the artefact away, believing they had no further use for it, although he was never one hundred percent certain about that. There was always a niggling doubt at the back of his mind their future was in the hands of and unknown entity, a thought Tom harboured for years but never spoke of it. He didn't want to upset the happiness the survivors finally achieved. Now it looked like it was coming back to bite them in the bum. Mike on the other hand knew he was in deep trouble, speaking to Niko every single day and saying nothing about what happened, it was sure to set off her fiery temper, which was well known now. After the crash everyone was glad she survived, Sol too, who sometime later did mention how Clariziane women were prone to temper outbursts, especially after becoming mothers. Niko was no exception. It seemed with Sol's DNA running through her veins, the villagers had to get used to it.

Mike was now more scared of losing his special friendship with Niko than anything else in his life. She probably wouldn't forgive him for the deceit. He developed a close bond with Nicolas, he was like family. In turn all the village children regarded him as 'uncle', a title he cherished, he didn't want to lose that closeness. The meeting was going to be a bombshell moment. Mike didn't actually lie to Niko, but not saying anything was worse, she was going to explode.

Unsure if it would help Sol or not, Mike told Tom and Nely they had to come clean about the artefact, tell Niko everything. He could not keep the secret any longer, it was killing him to stay quiet. They did agree, reluctantly. They didn't seem to have a choice.

Tom knew deep down this day would come; he didn't expect it so soon. Mike was right, guessing it was about time to bring out the artefact and explain themselves. He wasn't sure how to handle the situation, it would be a lot for some to take in.

*

Inside Tom's home, he and Simone along with Calum sat quietly waiting for everyone to arrive, Mike was already there, dreading the fireworks later. Simone wasn't too happy it had come to this; she felt a mixture of anger and sadness. She said all along Tom should have spoken out at the time, but she always stood by him. Her sadness was because she had kept the secret from Niko who she liked and admired very much. It was a difficult time for her. Calum sat with his mum, telling her it would be fine, it would work out in the end. He had complete faith in his dad, and the artefact. He had only activated it that one time to do the mission with Josef. It was the right thing to do, and he was proud of it; he found travelling across time and space in a blink of an eye exciting and wished he could try it again. A typical response from a fourteen-year-old who was all about having fun. His dad was adamant that would never happen, it was wrong to meddle with space outside their boundaries, the universe was not to be messed with. Tom knew from previous experience, although now he had a strange feeling it was all coming back to haunt them, the truth would be brutal. They had to prepare for the backlash.

It was coming.

Calum's sister Annie was packed off to keep Nely's daughter Maria company, they were too young to understand the circumstances. Simone wasn't happy about that either, more secrets to deal with; the kids would find out sooner of later. She still couldn't believe how Tom and managed to keep it from the Avaans, Xander especially, he was usually in and out of their home all the time, mainly for food but also to be with his friend. Keeping secrets from the Avaans was nothing short of a miracle.

Nely, Carol and son Josef arrived, with Darryl in tow, who at that precise moment had no idea what the meeting was about. He'd been left in the dark from the beginning, by Carol; she knew what he was like, always having a dig at Nely, it was unwarranted, and she told him so many times. He never listened. Carol didn't like the situation any more than Simone, but they both realised the importance of saving the life of one of their own. Nely on the other hand was already quaking in his boots, expecting a right mouthful from his brother-in-law for keeping him at arm's length, if he knew about the mission that involved his beloved nephew he would have tried to stop it. Darryl had his suspicions about Nely, acting the fool, always up to some kind of scheme; he couldn't understand why his sister ever got tangled up with such a jerk. It was decided at the time, the fewer people who knew about the artefact, the better. But nothing stopped Darryl, the overbearing brother, keeping an eye on Nely waiting for him to slip up. He never knew whether to have words with his sister, or strangle Nely, he was waiting for the right moment, maybe after he found out what this meeting was about.

Tom was getting edgy with the wait; he had an awful thought anarchy would rear its ugly head if suddenly everyone wanted to go off time travelling. He couldn't allow it, that wasn't why the artefact was given to him for safe keeping. The universe put it in the right hands. Tom fully intended to uphold the promise to himself to keep the artefact safe. If there was to be another task, he was sure a sign would appear to him.

Next to arrive at the gathering, came Paul and Alec, as mere observers they said, but as it involved one of their own, they were always on hand to support them. Alec hoped his childhood friend Nely had not been up to his antics again, but then he guessed not, this meeting sounded more serious than that. The rest of the others stayed away, they had chosen to live on the outer limits of the village, wanting as much privacy as possible. Adjusting to life cut off from the rest of the universe didn't come easy for them, even after all this time. They dealt with the trauma in their own way, isolating themselves from the villagers, that isolation was to be their sanctuary. It had to be respected. Some still harboured deep animosity against the bridge crew for not taking them home to Earth when they had the chance. The years on Utopia hadn't helped those feelings. The outsiders stayed away, raising their children their own way, shunning all contact with the villagers.

Finally Sol, Niko and Nicolas arrived, greeted by Tom who waved them inside to be met by a crowded room. Now Sol wasn't so sure he wanted to be there, he felt intimidated, overwhelmed, and maybe a bit silly if he was honest with himself. Everyone was standing or sitting around the room, all eyes focused on him, he turned to head straight back out the door, Niko stopped him, grabbing his arm and pulling him inside. His strange behaviour had to be sorted; the meeting was the best way for the villagers to air any problems and get help and support from the others; something they had done many times when one of them was struggling. Talking things through was a great way to deal with matters.

Niko was sure of getting the help Sol needed.

Without any prior announcement, Xander, JT and Po teleported through the door seconds after Tom had just closed it. They had somehow heard about the meeting taking place, and Xander decided they should be represented.

"You guys didn't need to come, it doesn't concern you Xander" said Tom, he hadn't planned on the Avaans gatecrashing the meeting. He had a feeling things were going to erupt later, the Avaans would make it worse, they were a bit full on at times, and Tom wasn't even going to ask how they got wind of it.

“I disagree Just Tom, are we not all Utopians. Any business to discuss, I believe we should be here. By the way Ti Glish sends his apologises, Ke Tegan is very pregnant again. He won’t leave her at the moment” said Xander robustly, hoovering mid-air at eye level with his friend, he was not going to be left out. Tom nodded, he didn’t want to start the meeting on an argument, besides it was always good to see his little buddy again. It was weeks since his last visit.

“Well, we’re all here I guess, shall I start?” said Niko anxiously, “like what is that wooden piece of junk doing on the table?”

Everyone had eyes on it, obviously put there for a reason, yet Niko couldn’t see any relevance to it being there.

What was Tom up to?

It definitely wasn’t what she had in mind when speaking to Mike earlier. She hoped the men weren’t playing games with her, because right now it wasn’t funny.

Tom stepped forward towards the table, he nervously spoke to explain about the artefact.

“This object Niko, found its way to my home, please don’t ask how or why because I don’t have the answer, it just appeared.”

Sol reached for Niko’s hand for support, he suddenly had a weird sensation run down his spine, this strange object did concern him, he felt a supernatural presence emanating from it, he was scared, the eerie presence was similar to how he felt round the village when he returned home. He was sure it had a connection to his visions.

“Go on Tom” said Niko sharply, feeling Sol tightening his grip on her hand, he was anxious, she felt his tension, but more so she feared there was strange goings on in the room. Now she was feeling a deep sensation building up, her Clariziane blood was beginning to erupt into a full-blown temper. She tried to contain it, but the others weren’t making it easy.

She dreaded what might come next.“Okay, well it took me a while to discover what this carving was, what it represented.

To cut a long story short, it's an ancient artefact that when activated it opens a portal in time and space – to travel through." Tom paused, to allow everyone to take in what he said, a few puzzled looks around the room with the odd gasp of disbelief from the ones not in the know. To them, Tom was talking complete and utter nonsense. Sol said nothing, but he had a suspicion Tom had more to say, but he struggled to continue, had he done the right thing?Niko wasn't happy, her cheeks already glowing red with anger, *why was she left out in the cold?*

At that point Xander floated over to his friend and sat on his shoulder, he sensed Tom needed moral support. Tom just wished Xander wouldn't grab his ear so tight, still he was glad the little guy was with him. Taking a deep breath, Tom announced the bombshell.

"We did actually use it, just once" he said nervously, almost shaking.

"What? –" bellowed Darryl rather loudly and looking directly at Nely, who declined to make eye contact. Now he knew the little jerk was involved.

"How, why, and more importantly, when?" asked Niko, she was livid, *how could something so startling as this be kept secret from the rest of the villagers? How could Tom keep her in the dark after everything they had been through?*

Niko's glare made Tom feel bad, but he had to continue now. He didn't answer Niko, instead looked at Sol, who at that moment was still trying to take it in, he was as confused as the others.

"Do you remember back on the ship Sol, when we were being attacked?" Tom asked.

Sol vaguely recalled the events, not that he wanted to, he didn't wish to dwell on the past. He nodded to Tom. Niko wasn't happy and showed it, her temper was almost at boiling point.

"Are you mad Tom, trying to traumatise us all over again. This is not what we came for, I expected better judgement from you."

"I'm sorry Niko, it wasn't my intention to deceive you, but this is important."

Darryl was about to step in and give Nely a piece of his mind, before ripping his head off. Tom shut him down.

"You can listen Darryl, but say nothing" Tom was firm, he couldn't let things get out of control. Xander didn't help by waving his finger at Darryl to warn him who was in charge.

"Let him finish Niko" said Sol quietly, he wanted to hear every little detail. He was being pulled towards the artefact, it was as if it was calling to him, drawing out his inner feelings. It had a purpose, and Sol knew he as part of it.

"Do you remember the two strangers coming to help you when you were injured, you hit your head" Tom tried to stay calm in his words, this was a revelation in their lives. He was fearful of the reactions of one or two of in the room, too many bad vibes already floating about.

Again, Sol nodded.

Niko turned to him, surprised. He never mentioned that before, although she did recall Darryl saying he had hit his head. She couldn't remember much else about that time; she was out of it for a while. Sol had actually forgotten the incident until now, it brought back bad memories of that fateful day, he was feeling uncomfortable having to relive it over again.

"Well my friend, the two strangers who helped you that day were Calum and Josef" declared Tom; gasps sounded round the room, then Darryl jumped to his feet.

"Now you're talking absolute rubbish, how can that be? They weren't even born fifteen years ago, and I was with Sol in the hospital, he would have said." Darryl was fuming, he was so pumped up, he hadn't really grasped what Tom was saying. This meeting in his opinion was turning into a complete farce before it got going. He started to wonder why he bothered to show up. Then again maybe it was to see Nely finally get his comeuppance.

"Darryl, shut up and sit down, you know nothing" said Mike, he thought the man was making a fool of himself, he wasn't getting the whole picture.

Then Niko stared across the room at Mike, "Were you in on this conspiracy Mike? That's if I believe what Tom is saying, which I don't at the moment."

She knew the answer straightaway by the look on Mike's face, he couldn't hide the fact.

"Why didn't you say something, did our friendship mean nothing to you?"

"I'm sorry Niko, we thought it best at the time, someone had to go back into the past to save you and Sol, and you're here now alive, that's what counts." He was very apologetic, he never meant to hurt her, now he guessed he may have to grovel for her forgiveness until the end of time.

"When did this alleged farce happen?" Darryl demanded to know, he wasn't going to keep quiet where his nephew was concerned. It was all he could do to stop himself flying across the room to strangle Nely; he was in on the secret for sure, then he wondered about his sister, how could Carol keep that from him, he wasn't going to back down.

"As for you Nely, how dare you involve Josef, I ought to take you outside right now and kick the shit out of you. You are one big loser, a total waste of space."Without warning Darryl got one hell of a slap across his face, enough to leave finger marks. Carol had heard enough.

"Don't you ever speak about my husband like that again. Now sit DOWN!" she yelled.

Darryl did so, but he would get hold of that idiot later for sure, he wasn't getting away with this.

"Nice one Carol, if you hadn't done that, I would have" said Alec, nobody calls his friend a loser, Nely didn't deserve that. For his part Nely kept a dignified silence, holding Carol's hand.

"It's ok Uncle Darryl, really" said Josef, he loved his uncle, but not necessarily his behaviour. He had to understand why they acted in secret.

"Calum and I had to do the mission to help, Nicolas is our friend."

Carol put her arm round her son, he was indeed a brave lad, perhaps turning into a good man before his time. Utopia seemed to influence the way the children grew up, all with intelligence and adult perspective on life. Nicolas smiled at Calum and Josef, he felt humbled by them, they were good friends.

"It was something that had to be done to save you" said Tom, he did his best to keep it calm and civilised. He wasn't sure everyone was agreeable and getting the gist of their actions. Darryl was most certainly losing the plot. Paul and Alec said nothing for now, but Alec kept an eye on the seething Darryl, he was a ticking timebomb.

"Sorry Niko, we couldn't tell you what we were doing, we couldn't risk jeopardising the outcome. It's because we love you we had to do it" said Mike, he was desperate to redeem himself.

"Is that why you suggested the camping trip, to get us out of the way? Was that when this took place?" Niko was trying to stay calm for Sol's sake, she was struggling to contain her temper, Sol was just struggling.

"Yes" answered Mike meekly.

"Uncle Mike?" Nicolas was perplexed by his surrogate uncle; *how could he deceive them like that?*

"Quiet Nicolas" said Niko, she didn't need her son to get involved.

"Michael B. Dyland, you and I will have words later about friendship and loyalty."Mike hung his head in shame, what could he say, she was going to tear him to shreds, worse than a wallpaper stripper, he was dead meat.

Niko turned back to Tom, she hadn't finished with him, Nely she could forgive, he was easily led.

"Why Tom, just tell me why, and what or where does this piece of wood come into it? Why have you got it?"

"That's what I want to know" said Darryl, who just didn't know when to keep his mouth shut. His face was still stinging from Carol's slap, he was sure a tooth got dislodged, it felt loose anyway.

"You were told to shut it Darryl, best it stays that way" said Tom.

"Well who made you leader all of a sudden?"

"The artefact did, okay, and if you don't like it, go and live with the others." Tom hated being heavy handed, but Darryl was being disruptive, he wasn't helping himself. Carol gave him a dig in the ribs and a glare to melt the icecaps. He got the message.

Tom pressed on to explain.

"I have no idea how the artefact came to me Niko, but I soon found out it was to save you and Sol, in turn save Nicolas. Only Calum and I have managed to activate it so far, I am certain there is more to come. We learnt barely enough to send Calum and Josef back into the universe, and back in time at the precise moment you needed help."

Xander moved from his comfortable position on Tom's shoulder to hover in front of him, now he had words to say; he looked Tom straight in the eye, or at least he tried to, his wonky eye drooped down, staring at Tom's feet, his good eye swinging in all directions.

"You deceived me too Just Tom, I'm your friend, I was best man at your wedding, you should have trusted me. I could have helped."

"Sorry Xander but you can't keep secrets, it's not in your nature, besides, it was for Sol and Niko, you couldn't go back in case you were recognised. None of us could, that's why it had to be the boys. We couldn't risk running into our other selves in the past, the artefact might have failed if a paradox occurred, and the timeline was disrupted."

"I understand" said Xander, "but I'm not happy about it" he felt put out being excluded from the mission. Tom should have trusted him. Tom continued to explain, hoping it would at least ease the animosity he felt going about the room.

"I also believe there is more going on that we have yet to discover, an unknown entity, a supernatural force may be guiding our destiny through the artefact. Please Niko, believe me when I say we are truly sorry for not telling you. We came clean because Sol's behaviour might have some bearing on our future. Everything changed after the boys returned to Utopia, it must have started a chain reaction. We're all here for Sol."

Silence crept across the room, everyone trying to take stock of the severity of the situation, no one could anticipate the circumstances when they arrived. Darryl still wanted to punch Nely's lights out, how could he involve his nephew in this escapade, across a universe that could well have lost the lad in the wrong time zone, although he wasn't entirely buying the story of a space and time portal, this ancient artefact thing, he really didn't get it.

Alec walked across the room to join Nely, who he thought was a prat at times, but if Darryl wanted a piece of him, then he'd have to go through him first. Nobody touches his childhood friend. He did want words with him all the same.

"You did a bloody stupid, idiotic, foolhardy thing with your son Nely, but also a very brave decision to take, that took guts my friend. I for one am very proud of you and what you did for Niko and Sol." Alec was almost in tears with such emotion, his admiration for Nely had rocketed in that one split second. Nely threw his arms round Alec, those words meant more to him than anything in the past, he was a true friend. Alec hugged him back, watched by Carol, proud of her husband, and even more so her son Josef, he showed a great deal of maturity in all this.

Niko had for a moment calmed down, but seeing the men hugging like that, she shook her head in disbelief.

"Oh, for goodness sake you two, get a room." Their affection for each other was never in doubt, but it wasn't helping Sol's problem.

"Get a room?" whispered Sol in Niko's ear, "is that a human saying again?"Niko thought even after all these years he still didn't get it; he was so naïve to human ways. She looked to him with a smile that said, *'let it go'*. She loved him just the way he was and hoped he'd never change.

"How does this help Sol?" asked Simone, finally deciding to speak out, this was after all her home, she should have a say.

“Well, that’s why we’re here, isn’t it?”Carol nodded in agreement; the two boys were pivotal in the rescue mission, somehow it had to be tied into Sol’s erratic behaviour. None of it was going down too well in Darryl’s eyes, he just kept tutting under his breath but loud enough for everyone to hear. He wanted to leave, the meeting was pointless, one more glare from Carol said, *‘don’t you dare move.’* He had little choice but to sit it out. He was still festering under the surface.

Tom spoke, “I’m not exactly sure how the artefact will help Sol, not yet anyway. I do believe there is a connection here, we have to find out what it is. Rest assured Sol, we will do everything we can to make things right.” Tom meant it sincerely, but he wasn’t sure at that point how. Sol listened to the debate going on around him, putting forward their views, he did appreciate it, but he couldn’t see how it was going to stop the voices in his head. Thinking about how it all came about, he could see in his mind’s eye the two strangers coming towards him back on the ship, through solid walls, he now clearly recalled. He was on the ground having been thrown against a bulkhead after another huge explosion ripped through the hull, he was bleeding from a head wound, dazed and the corridor was blocked with debris.

“Was it really Calum and Josef who came to my rescue?” he asked.

“Yes” said Calum, “we were the only ones who could help you.”

“We couldn’t risk you recognising any of the crew” added Josef.

Sol went silent for a moment, going over it in his head, it was beginning to make sense now, *were they the voices in his head?*

“I believe them” he finally said, glancing over to both boys.

“You saved my life; in turn I was able to save my wife and baby. I can never repay you, thank you.” Sol smiled at them, so did Niko, the boys risked their lives to save theirs.

They felt humbled.

"We did it Sol, because it was the right thing to do, and we couldn't see our lives without Nicolas in it" said Calum.

Nicolas too was humbled now; to have such devoted friends, he had no words to express his gratitude, just a nod to say, *'thank you'*.

Still holding on to Niko for moral support, Sol realised how lucky he was, he had his family and amazing friends, willing to put their lives on the line. He hadn't regarded any of them as aliens in a long time, in turn he never felt the odd one out, Niko was now half alien like his son. The Utopians were one family, that's what counted. The others, thirteen of them at the time still lived on the edge of the village making no contact in the last fifteen years, were still part of the Utopian family, if they wanted to be – maybe one day that would happen, but nobody was holding their breath waiting for that day.

"They did this to help us Niko, don't be too angry" said Sol, he didn't like her losing her temper, he was the only one able to calm her down. This episode might take more energy than he had to give.

Niko looked at Sol, then her beautiful son, she was angry, yes, and still wanted answers, but she was calming down.

"So what now Tom?" she asked, Sol needed answers desperately, and he needed them now. Sol answered the question by approaching the table, wanting to take a closer look at the strange object. He felt drawn to it like a magnet, he thought it was beautifully carved, very intricate and the symbols weirdly mystical. He had never seen anything like it before and yet he felt a real connection to it.

"Someone is calling to me" he suddenly announced, "I don't know who, but I think whoever it is needs my help. Is this object the answer?"

One or two in the room were baffled for a second, stunned by Sol's words, not sure what he meant, or how to answer him. It was hard to know how to handle the situation because no one knew what the problem was. Sol couldn't tell them, he didn't know either.

"How does the object, an artefact you call it Tom, how does it actually work?" Niko asked, she was sceptical this dried up chunk of wood held the solution to Sol's problem, it surely couldn't be that simple.

Making the decision to handle the artefact, Sol got a huge shock when it lit up, gleaming strongly from the centre which then rotated half a turn. Tom moved closer to the table, he was surprised, Sol was able to activate the artefact simply by picking it up meant only one thing, he had to be involved, he would complete the connection.

"Tom, what is this? What does it mean?" asked Sol, his voice was shaking, it made him nervous, but he couldn't put it down if he wanted to; unknown forces compelled him to keep a hold of it. Niko stood with him, putting an arm round him for support, letting him know they would do this together, if necessary.

Tom was quick to reply. "Not totally sure yet Sol, it does appear only certain people can activate the artefact, me for one, Calum but not Josef, now it seems you can. It has to mean something, maybe it is all connected to your trouble mind."

Sol continued to study the strange markings; he had no idea what they meant. "So how does it actually work then?"

"Not sure Sol, even I haven't worked that out, I'm guessing there is some kind of mechanism inside. I really don't know my friend" said Tom, sorry he didn't have more answers.

"And you risked the boys lives on a totally not sure idea, how stupid is that? What kind of father are you?" yelled Darryl across the room, he'd heard enough, his temper just hit the top floor, he was fuming at the thought of losing his nephew in this bizarre quest. Simone jumped to her feet, furious at Darryl's outburst, he wasn't getting away with that. Tom gently put a hand on her shoulder.

"It's ok Simone" he strode over to stare Darryl in the face. "Talk like that again in my home and I'll deck you. No more warnings Darryl, now bloody well sit down and shut up."

"Not before I do this Tom." Alec said coming up behind Tom, he launched a fist at Darryl, who then fell back in his seat with a bloody nose.

"There was no need for that Alec, I don't want a fight in my home." Simone was up on her feet again, scared there was going to be a free-for-all. Niko was worried for Darryl, he had completely lost the plot, this wasn't the man she knew, a kind gentle compassionate human being. He had changed over the years, and not for the better. Her own temper hadn't yet disappeared completely, it was rising again, and she was struggling to contain her emotions. The atmosphere in the room wasn't helping, the men really needed to calm down, Tom included. Josef stepped in.

"You okay Uncle Darryl? You shouldn't worry you know, Calum and I knew what we were doing, the mission was a cinch." He didn't like his uncle being so mean to everyone, especially his dad. Carol was embarrassed by his behaviour and wanted to yank his arse outside, Darryl said nothing, he was finally bullied into silence – for now.

Niko wasn't finished with the men; she needed to put them under no illusions how she felt. "Look you men, I maybe can understand why you did what you did, but you should still have trusted Sol and me with the information. I'm warning you all now. Pull a stunt like that again without discussing it first, I will string every one of you up by your balls, and that's just for starters. Do I make myself clear?" she was red in the face, they knew she was angry.

"Mum –"

"Quiet Nicolas" she snapped.

Xander, now back on Tom's shoulder, leaned in, to whisper in his ear. "I hope she doesn't mean me Just Tom; I didn't do anything." He was worried he was getting roped in with the rest. JT and Po edged their way to the back of the room, wishing to stay out of it. If Niko's temper erupted they would vanish through the wall if necessary.

Sol heard Xander's whispers as did Niko, he simply thought, *'another human saying'*. At the same time he had never seen his wife vent so much anger towards the villagers, her alien DNA over the years had not diminished, in fact it seemed to get stronger. He wasn't sure if it was a good thing or not. He would have to let it go. He had to get back to the artefact, he felt it important, even if Niko didn't.

"Niko, I believe this will help me, I am sure of it" said Sol, he was less stressed now. The artefact suddenly gave him an air of confidence he never felt before, he felt normal, the best he felt since the bad dreams started.

"Okay my darling, if you think so." Niko wasn't as optimistic as Sol, but she could see in his eyes he had a positive attitude to the situation.

"Well, Tom. What does it mean? What's the next step?" she asked.

"I wish I could give you definitive answer Niko, I can't. the artefact has a purpose for sure, one we may well have to act on" replied Tom.

"I'm not understanding how it will help Sol, he needs answers now, before another sleepless night" Niko said, worried they weren't getting anywhere. Tom couldn't give her the answers she wanted. Sol though had a different view, he recognised the artefact had some hidden secret that would benefit them all, not just him. He now knew it was up to him to discover the secret locked inside, then the true purpose would reveal itself.

"I guess we wait for a sign Sol, those with a connection to the artefact will know what to do, when the time is right" said Tom. Airing his own theory. Using the artefact that one time didn't make them experts by any means, but he worried they had bitten off more than they could chew.

"What if we just get rid of it, problem solved" mumbled Darryl, still angry, still unable to keep his mouth shut, and still refusing to accept the artefact as anything but a useless chunk of wood causing a heap load of trouble. He didn't want to believe his sister voluntarily allowed her son to get involved with such lunacy. He hated everything about the meeting, his anger clouded his judgment from the start. He couldn't even see the irrational mood he was in, all it got him was a hefty slap, a broken tooth and a bloodied face.

"No Darryl! That is not an option, we can't discard it just because you don't like or understand it" said Tom, now wishing he'd thrown him out earlier, the man was a complete nutcase.

The artefact was vitally important to their continuing existence on Utopia, it had to be kept safe. Tom addressed the entire room.

"The first part was to save Sol and Niko in the past to ensure their survival. I know there is more to come, we must be prepared for whatever lies ahead. We are all in this together." He said the last bit staring at Darryl, simply to warn him. But Tom was afraid of the future, there was even the possibility they might have to return to the past again, he decided not to mention that yet. The villagers had to be patient, and Darryl given time to calm down, although Tom surmised that might take longer with his attitude.

*

The universe watched on.

The plan was almost in place, Tom was indeed a worthy leader, wise, rational, and with Sol by his side they would lead their people on a mission to save all life in the cosmos. The mission was time critical, Sol had to learn the secrets of the artefact, and soon. The Utopians had a huge task ahead of them, to put the universe right and every being back in its rightful place, in the right universe, seal the rifts and stop the spatial distortions from reoccurring that had displaced entire galaxies. The space time continuum would be restored and the timeline returned to its natural cycle. The universe couldn't tell them how to do it, they had to work that one out for themselves, but it had to be now, and it had to succeed. There were no other options. The Utopians had to work swiftly, a huge crack had opened up in space, they would be affected soon, they had no choice but to act.

The universe hoped it had not left it too late to save itself.

*

Tom decided it was time to wrap things up for the day, everyone was tired, hungry and irritable in some cases. Nothing more could be achieved this day.

"I'm sorry guys that we haven't managed to resolve the problem for Sol, but believe me, we will. I have a strong feeling the artefact is going to help, and sooner than you think. Sol my friend, take the artefact with you, study it, learn its secrets. Whatever is going on in your head that object you're holding is the key. The answers will come."

Sol thanked Tom for believing in him, it meant a lot, and he promised not to let Tom down. Everyone suddenly stared round the room at each other, a realisation the unknown was about to descend on them. They had a simple life on Utopia, one that had been very good to them, now there seemed a real possibility it was about to get ripped out from underneath them.

Only Calum and Josef had the experience of the journey through the portal into the past, for their young years they possessed a great awareness, and they truly believed the artefact had a purpose for them all. Calum spoke to Sol before he left.

"Sol, I believe in the artefact, I also believe you can do this. It was me who helped you to your feet and then Josef and I cleared the debris out of the way. We did it because we believe, you should too."

"My son is right, you have to trust us Sol, trust in your own ability" said Tom, proud of his son for speaking up. Nicolas stood by his dad at the door.

"You have to try pops; you will be successful," he put a hand on Sol's shoulder. "You're my father, you can do this."

Tom was confident now; the boys were indeed old enough to understand the importance of all their lives. He knew they all had a date with destiny, unfinished business.

It was coming soon.

CHAPTER FIFTEEN

With so much to think about, Sol shut himself away for a few days so he could concentrate on his task, studying the artefact was a priority, it was very important to him. He had to learn the symbols, discover what they meant, what they represented and finally unlock the secrets, if he was to complete the circle he had to know as much as Tom and Calum, and after the first day he was making progress, establishing what some of the symbols were. He thought that was the easy part, but not all of them were so simple, still it gave him the confidence to persevere. He found certain characters round the outer part of the artefact related to positions in the universe, although at that point he wasn't entirely sure if that was significant or not, nor did he understand how he knew. *Maybe that was how Calum calculated the precise position and time in history to journey to?* He would enquire about it later with Calum and Tom.

There were things going on in Sol's head he couldn't decipher. The universe was a lifetime ago, and it wasn't even his universe, yet the star systems appeared in his mind that he could relate to, that was fine he thought, but the worry was everything in the universe might have changed – if of course it was still there, where they left it.

Some of the inner symbols Sol had no idea about, he couldn't grasp their meaning, it was proving a sticking point in his quest for knowledge. Tom and Calum would have to assist with solving those. What he really wanted to know was where this strange ancient piece of wood came from, and how it found its way its way to the village. The others couldn't have put it on Tom's step, they never ventured outside their small commune. The artefact and its origin remained a mystery, even to Tom, who said it best not to ask too many questions, they might not like the answers.

Tom realised from the beginning there were unknown powers at work, but no way did he want to meddle with mystical forces, unnatural goings on happened that had no explanation; to get involved with that was playing with fire. He did however suspect they had a guardian angel watching over them, it was just a gut feeling, but Tom hung onto that one thought, any help would be appreciated.

Several times Tom paid a visit to Sol, wanting to know how he was doing, time was of the essence. He experienced a strange premonition this was now a matter of urgency. He couldn't explain his inner thoughts; it wasn't something he was able to put into words. All he knew was, action was needed, now not later; but he had no clue as to what action they were to take, only that it was urgent, and Sol was needed to complete the circle. As Tom sat with Sol he observed how well he handled the artefact, it was clear he had a stronger connection to it than him, even Calum was more adept than Tom, the glow from the centre was more vivid, more intense when either Sol or Calum held it. Tom knew they could crack the code; it was just a case of when. That time had to be now, Tom urged Sol on in spirit, he had to do it. Calum had one of two suggestions for Sol, but only when he could drag himself away from the other village kids, which seemed more fun to him, he was still a kid at heart.

Unable to date the artefact with any degree of accuracy, Tom surmised it could be hundreds, if not thousands of years old, the wood was showing signs of age, dried out and cracks round the outer rim did suggest that. The one sure thing Tom and Sol did agree on, it was obviously created by far superior beings than them. The artefact's origin was immaterial for the time being. Sol and Tom were still struggling to crack the final sequence to unlock the mystery. They were hoping something would simply jump out at them, but that would have been too easy. Calum and Josef did their mission without needing to decode all the symbols, they got lucky. This time was different, every single symbol had to be solved before knowing what the mission would be. It was the one fact Tom was certain of, that there would be another mission. He always knew the destiny of all the villagers, including the others depended on completion of this unknown mission. But not knowing what they had to do was beginning to bug him. Sol needed to concentrate harder, Calum too had to assist, Tom exhausted all his theories about the artefact; he was out of ideas, and it was frustrating to think the mission might fail before it started.

Many more hours passed before Sol realised Tom's theory of an important task to undertake could actually be more than a theory, he still had no details of what it entailed. The artefact was not giving up its secrets easily.

Tom suspected they would need to leave Utopia to complete this task whatever it was. The very idea frightened him to think he and his family might have to leave their safe haven. What little information they did discover they agreed to keep to themselves until the final piece of the jigsaw revealed itself. It was going to be one hell of a bombshell for the villagers, Tom guessing some would be unable to accept their findings, there would be no way of breaking the news to them gently.

*

On the fourth day everything changed for Sol, the voice in his head was suddenly clear and explicit, he was shocked to recognise the voice – a voice from his past life, his one-time good friend and fellow pilot Don Kant was calling to him, asking for help. It was a strong unmistakable message. Sol was unnerved to hear his voice again especially now after all these years. He assumed Don, along with the rest of the fleet returned home to Clarizia and perished when the planet was destroyed. He sat back in his chair to think; *did he really hear Don's voice? Or was it what he wanted to hear?*

Sol questioned his own thoughts, he had so many unanswered questions rattling in his head. He wondered about his home, long forgotten lives; this wasn't what he expected to happen, the artefact gave him more to think about than he wanted. But once he acknowledged it had to be real, strange new clues emanated from the artefact straight into his head, symbols he and Tom once struggled to connect now beginning to make sense.

Whatever the symbols were saying, Sol couldn't understand why a voice from the past came into his head without warning, a dead voice stretching across two universes from so long ago. It deeply troubled him because he feared losing control of himself, he suffered so much mental anguish in his other life, he didn't want to go through that awful torment again, that was one place he never wished to revisit.

Tom did his best to ease Sol's worries, telling him his mind was as sharp as ever. He had to trust his inner feelings, believe his gut instinct. Sol didn't know what Tom really meant, but it was good to know he had his back. What Tom told him about the artefact sort of made sense, it was still hard to believe they held in their hands a gateway back into the universe, across time and space, directly into history. Sol wondered if he really wanted to return to the past, his people tried that and paid for their mistakes with their lives. It was a daunting thought.

How they used the artefact was up to them, but it had to be for the right reasons, it wasn't a plaything. Tom knew he had a lot of responsibility on his shoulders, he would use the artefact wisely and only when it was necessary, that time was now. Sol had to complete his task to link everything together. He had already worked out it didn't lead into the future, only the past and back to the original entry point. He wasn't sure he wanted to lead his people into the future anyway, scared what he might discover; besides they had enough dealing with history catching up with them.

The future could wait.

Sol thought more and more about his friend Don, it was hard to tie him into this mystery. *Was he part of the equation?* The artefact wasn't giving away any clues – not yet anyway. Deciphering each symbol was timely, the right combination wasn't forthcoming, especially with Tom interrupting his concentration by calling round every hour and asking how he was doing, it was distracting but Tom felt an urgency about the mission. Something was telling him they were running out of time. Sol was doing his best, still that voice remained in his head, he had to find the connection between the artefact and his own past, and soon, or his head was going to explode.

After the first mission back into the universe, back into the past by Calum and Josef, Tom was confident whatever this new mission was, it would be successful, at least that is what he told Sol. Tom could see he was struggling with self-doubt, but he assured him the answers were there and there was no danger involved. He had complete faith in the artefact or else he would never had allowed his own son to go. Sol needed that same belief, because it sounded very much like his friend was in trouble and that's why he was calling out for help. This had to be what the mission was about, one of their own needed help, it didn't matter which universe his friend was in, or what time in history, Tom said they would all help if necessary.

Sol was grateful his friend believed in him, it urged him on to find the final calculation to tell them when and where to go on their journey into the past. It was clear they had to act, and act now, if Sol's friends were in danger, time was short. Tom began to worry about what perils lie ahead in the universe, who knows what happened after they left. He feared going back, there was every chance of encountering the federation police who so nearly wiped them all out. The Utopians had no defence against their enemies, until now they didn't need it. The thought of another space battle brought Tom out in a sweat. He kept his suspicions to himself, not wanting to alarm the villagers especially as he told Sol there was no danger. He knew this mission had to happen; it had to succeed for life to continue across the universe and not just to save humans but all beings. It was a tall order, Tom felt the hand of destiny pulling at him, he knew he was chosen to do this, he couldn't back out. He just wished he knew what part of history they had to save. He had to keep pressing Sol to finish his task.

Tom's thoughts were beginning to run riot in his head, he sat at the table opposite Sol, watching him work on the artefact. It was a difficult time for both of them. Tom tried to help but his mind kept wandering back to the universe, the place he was forced to leave; his worry now, if the space time continuum had been disrupted again, it meant beings had broken through from the parallel universe and most probably causing havoc on an epic scale. He did point out if Sol's friends were looking for him then they had already violated the natural order of the universe by coming through the rift between the universes. If that was the case it was going to be hard to negotiate space safely, the imbalance would cause further rifts in space to open up, and this time would be far worse than before. The damage might be irreparable and timeline fluctuations would start affecting their world. It was vital to act to save their idyllic life.

Sol finally accepted in his heart it was Don calling to him, the message was the same over and over, it had to be genuine. It pushed him to try harder with the artefact, to learn all the symbols and the correct sequence to activate it in order to know its true meaning. Only then will it tell them what they had to do.

Sol didn't find it as easy as Tom and Calum, he was new to this strange technology. Calum never used every symbol, but he had to; the thought of his friends in trouble urged him on. Now he knew it was Don calling him for sure, he could not fail, he said he would complete the task or die in the attempt. Tom told him not to be so drastic. He had all the villagers behind him, willing him to succeed. Everyone wanted to know their fate, would Utopia survive the outcome? Sol promised not to let them down.

*

The mission seemed crystal clear now, putting the artefact in Tom's possession was just one part of the equation; putting it in Sol's hands reaffirmed Tom's belief they were the chosen ones, designated to fulfil their destiny; aided by a mysterious unseen force. Someone or something supernatural deemed it necessary for the Utopians to get involved.

The universe was in trouble.

Tom believed this was the time to repay the debt for their lives on Utopia. All along he had a suspicion at the back of his mind, they were there, not by chance, but placed on this planet for some future purpose. That time had come. He also believed the artefact had complete control over their destiny; their very future depended on how they used the artefact. Then Tom thought, *why couldn't more of the ship's crew have survived?* They would have a much better community now.

Was it fate only a few survived? Was that the intention? Tom thought so.

While working alongside Sol for the last couple of hours, Tom continued to give him encouragement to seek the answers they needed to finish the task. One particular symbol baffled both of them, it was the same one Tom and Calum didn't use because it seemed irrelevant at the time, but they never managed to solve its purpose. Now it appeared to be the most important symbol of all, the vital piece of the jigsaw, and it was missing. They sat in silence staring at the artefact, hoping for a clue to jump out, when Tom suddenly felt a weight come down on both his shoulders, he knew it had to be Xander and JT, they materialised but stayed unseen, and sat themselves down in their favourite position. They were so quiet Sol never heard a sound.

"Okay guys, make yourselves visible, I know you're there" said Tom, shaking his head at their sneaky entrance.

"Why do they do that Tom?" asked Sol.

"Because they can my friend" replied Tom with a wry smile.

"Hello Just Tom, Sol" said Xander.

"Hello" added JT.

"Hi" said Sol, as the two of them appeared on Tom's shoulders, cross-legged, arms folded, JT with his eyes swinging about non-stop, surveying the room. Xander being more sedate but hanging on to Toms ear as usual. Tom did wonder if subconsciously his friend was still scared of falling off and having another accident, he didn't need two wonky eyes staring down at his own feet. Even after all these years he still insisted holding onto Tom, JT simply copied his dad.

"Has Ke Tegan had her babies yet?" asked Tom, he actually lost count how many she had now, Xander himself had twenty offspring, his eldest son JT normally stayed close to his father, but the rumour was he now had a girlfriend and Xander was possibly about to be a grandfather for the first time. Tom doubted if that would stop Xander's mischievous antics, he loved playing tricks on Tom, it was part and parcel of their long friendship.

"No, any day now Just Tom."

"So, why are you here then?"

"Because I feel a dreadful foreboding emerging, there is much danger ahead Just Tom. You must tread carefully" said Xander, sounding very concerned, it wasn't like him to be so serious.

"How do you know this?" Sol wanted to know.

"You forget I inherited Kanon Garg's sixth sense, his wisdom, I have the ability to sense when something is going to happen. Why didn't you feel it Sol? You did before many years ago on the ship."

Sol accepted he had a point, but the truth was he had been so wrapped up working on the artefact, he felt nothing – only his friend Don calling. He was angry with himself now, for not sensing there were more lives at stake, his mental state was not at full capacity.

"I know we have a mission to do, so let's get started" said Xander, still with his legs crossed, arms folded and with a look of determination.

"No Xander, you can't possibly think you are going anywhere with us, it could be dangerous and even Sol and I are not sure yet what the mission entails."

Tom used his sternest voice to make his point, he didn't want Xander involved.

"Firstly Just Tom, don't lie to me, you know damn well what the mission is, and thirdly, I've told you before, where you go, I go, no question. My wife will understand. Sol is my friend too; JT and I will assist any way we can. You might need more help than you realise, extra eyes and brains." Xander was just as firm with his words.

"We are partners, yes?" he added.

"Yes Just Tom, we will assist," butted in JT. "Even if my dad had a wonky eye you will need both of us."

"Xander, you still can't count, and I'm not lying, Sol and I haven't figured it out yet."

"He talks more and more like a human everyday Tom" said Sol. For once he saw the funny side of Xander. He had a great mind, intellectual beyond his size and still he couldn't count. He was certain though the Avaans should have been scientists.

Tom had to admit the Avaans would be quite useful at times, he wasn't so sure about his namesake JT, he was a bigger handful than Xander ever was. Sol decided to add his point of view.

"He might be right Tom, I get the feeling whatever this mission is, we will need extra help. Xander might prove invaluable."

"Thank you Sol" said Xander, at least someone in the room had seen sense. "So how long have we got Just Tom? Have you and Sol worked it out yet?" It was the obvious question Xander thought, he felt it in his bones they hadn't got long, there was an air of urgency descending on them.

Before Tom or Sol had a chance to answer JT interrupted. "Have you any food Sol? I'm very hungry" he asked.

"Help yourself, Niko is in the kitchen I believe" replied Sol. JT floated off swiftly, he missed his breakfast doing chores for his mum, he was late up again.

"Right, down to business" declared Xander, eager to help in any way he could, moving from Tom's shoulder and onto the table next to the artefact which had gone quiet now. Nothing was working on it; Sol was at a loss to know his next move. He looked at Tom for help, that didn't do any good, Tom was distracted with Xander attempting to get the artefact to light up.

"It won't work Xander, so don't touch it" said Tom.

"So how can I help Just Tom?" asked Xander, whatever they had to do he was eager to get the mission under way. He was full of excitement at the impending journey he knew they had to take. It would be an adventure.

"You can help by not touching the artefact and staying out of the way, and by the way I've told you countless times not to materialise without warning, it's rude." Tom sounded stern, Xander hung his head in shame, he was sorry his friend was cross, but he couldn't help himself, it was his nature. In the end Tom smiled.

"It's ok my friend, Sol and I are under pressure at the moment" he admired the little guys enthusiasm, but every now and then, he could be such a pain in the backside.

"Please Just Tom, let me help" he pleaded, he insisted his insight could be beneficial to the mission. Tom thought it pointless to deny him. Xander would always be there at his side and just maybe he was right, he might actually be useful.

Sol slid the artefact across the table to Xander and pointed to the one symbol he was unable to decipher, both he and Tom had tried to explain the complexities but as he had no prior knowledge of such intricate markings, even his scientific brain failed him this time, not that he would ever admit to it. Tom told him they had to solve the meaning of the symbol, or the artefact wouldn't fully light up with the correct sequence; without the proper activation, it was useless. They couldn't afford any mistakes, space, time, even the date line were all relevant in the mission, which they now knew to be a rescue mission, the final symbol would tell them where and when, and if they didn't get it right they were all effectively screwed, as Tom put it bluntly. This one symbol was the sticking point, Tom regarded himself to be of above average intelligence, his years as a science officer on the ship counted for nothing now.

Why couldn't he solve this symbol? He felt the answer was locked in his brain somewhere. Nothing jumped out at him.

The three of them stared at the artefact for ages, trying to come up with a solution. For now it had shut down, no glowing lights coming from it, no movement, nothing. Xander leaned in for a closer look, he always wanted to appear smart, he didn't let on that he was as clueless as Sol and Tom. He put his tiny fingers on Tom's hand, sensing he was anxious, he looked stressed. Time was running out, he heard a voice in his head telling him the clock was ticking, and they were no nearer to solving the mystery.

Niko entered the room and sat down at the table seeing the men staring at the artefact, deep in concentration, and Xander sitting on the table leaning over, almost on top of the artefact. They were never going to work it out at this rate. She deliberately allowed Sol time alone to work on it. He was so uptight at times she thought it best to leave him in peace. A clatter from the kitchen sent Niko rushing back, worried JT was wreaking the place. She was back in seconds, guessing the men needed her more, maybe someone with no connection to the artefact.

Sol was now getting agitated to the point he thought, *how could he be worthy of the responsibility? How could he be if he couldn't solve a simple puzzle.*

"Who told JT he could raid my kitchen?" asked Niko, breaking the silence finally.

"I did, sorry my darling" said Sol, lifting his head, "he was hungry."

"He was up late again and missed his breakfast" said Xander, making an excuse for him.

"Typical teenager, he should join Nicolas, they'd make a great pair" said Niko, she wasn't entirely happy with JT eating everything in sight.

"Except Avaans years are a bit different to humans Niko" replied Xander.

"Oh whatever" Niko said with a sigh, it made no difference to her, they were all kids still.

"Anyway, what are you three up to? Staring at that chunk of wood won't make it come alive." She stood behind Sol and put her arms round him as she leaned over to see what the problem was.

"Well, it seems we have one problematic symbol we can't identify" said Tom.

"It's different to all the others" added Sol, "we don't know what it represents."

"I knew that" said Xander, he was just trying to impress Niko, even if he was none the wiser.

Niko sat back down just as she heard more clattering coming from the kitchen.

"If he wrecks my kitchen Xander, he'll have more chores to do. Now, which symbol is it?"

Sol immediately pushed the artefact over to his wife and pointed to the mystery symbol. "This one Niko, we can't see how it connects to any of the others, it's different and we just aren't able to activate it."

Niko studied it for a minute or so, she thought it looked familiar for some reason, but that didn't make sense because none of the other symbols appeared to represent letters, and then there was no evidence to suggest the artefact was of human origin. It was impossible to think humans reached this far anyway.

"What are you thinking Niko?" asked Tom, he saw a glint of recognition in her eyes, she knew something.

"Well, if I had to make a guess, I'd say it looks very similar to ancient written texts from thousands of years ago in Earth's history."

Tom was suddenly wide-eyed, had Niko stumbled on something he missed. Sol and Xander merely looked at each other, puzzled.

"What do you mean?" asked Tom, he hadn't seen any connection.

"Tom, you must remember the ancient writings, before the books were all destroyed. I think this symbol resembles an old-fashioned letter Ɛ, after all, you did say the artefact is ancient, is it possible it came from Earth?"

Tom's face suddenly lit up with sheer excitement. *Why didn't he see that?* He did after all recognise the hieroglyphics, but this one symbol had him really stumped. Once Niko made the connection he knew it had to be a letter and not just any symbol, he wasn't sure about the artefact originating from Earth, still Niko had a valid point.

"Niko, I could kiss you" he said jubilantly, this was the missing piece of the puzzle, he was certain.

"Tom –" said Sol sternly, "don't kiss my wife."

"It's just a saying Sol, just a saying" said Tom, smiling as he looked at Niko shaking her head, as she always did when Sol didn't get the joke.

"You humans, I will never understand your language" said Sol. In his heart he really wanted to be like the humans, living with them all these years should have rubbed off on him. It hadn't.

Niko leaned over and kissed Sol. "I love you the way you are my darling."

"I'd like to kiss you too Niko" said Xander, he didn't want to miss out on the fun.

"Xander!?" Niko didn't quite know how to take his remark, she gave him one of her stares, her black eye bearing down on him menacingly, her blue eye, he was even more afraid of. She looked scary, really scary.

"Okay, okay, just a saying" he said jokingly, he didn't want Niko getting angry and throwing something at him, or worse still, throw him across the room. He slid his backside nearer to Tom for protection.

"I'll pretend I didn't hear that Xander, the only alien I will ever kiss is my husband, you got that?"

"Right, now will you shut it pintpot before you put both feet in your mouth." Tom told him, he could see Sol was looking puzzled again, but enough, they were straying from the business in hand. He reached for the artefact to take another look at it, he had to know what this letter meant. *What did it mean to their mission? Could it really represent Earth? Was it to be their final destination?* His mind was racing, it had to be connected to their home planet, but it was one hell of a stretch of the imagination to think Earth had any link to Utopia.

Tom realised long ago they weren't in the universe, although he had no idea where they were, it didn't matter. The truth was Earth people could never have travelled this far and not leave their mark, the authorities on Earth had a habit of leaving a trail of destruction in their wake. This land of theirs was completely unadulterated.

"Tom, what are you thinking?" asked Niko, he had been quiet for a few minutes.

"Just thinking Niko, about Earth and what we left behind, family, friends." Tom's heart sank at that moment, why he didn't know. The people back there never gave them a chance in the end, but after all was said and done, it was still home.

"Does this mean we have to go there?" asked Xander, now standing on the table putting a hand on Tom's shoulder, he needed comfort and reassurance.

"You have us Just Tom, we're your family, and we'll always be friends." Tom smiled, Xander was indeed a true friend. Then they looked round at each other and realised this was the mission, or at least part of it. Tom wasn't that happy about the future, Niko felt worse. The mention of Earth brought back bad memories; she wasn't sure how Earth would react if they returned out of the blue. She was certain they would never accept her as human now, her mind most definitely was, her body and physical appearance said otherwise. *How would that go down with the so-called authorities?* No, going back to Earth would only end in disaster. None of them wanted to end their peaceful life on Utopia, this land was theirs and it had been good to them. Yet Tom knew he had to go; he had no choice.

"Is that where I will find my friends?" Sol asked, he was desperate to know their whereabouts.

"Don't know Sol, maybe" said Tom, he couldn't be one hundred percent certain it was their destination, only that Earth featured prominently in the mission. He had a bad feeling about it. Going back to Earth was one thing, Earth in the past where the federation police would still be looking for them was a daunting prospect. They tried to kill every last one of the crew, and very nearly succeeded.

"So what's next Tom, how are you going to handle this?" asked Niko, they had a big decision to make about their lives, it wasn't going to be easy. Everyone was happy on Utopia, but she feared not all would agree with what they were doing. She hoped the others were happy in their own way. She remembered training some of them as medics in the hospital. Now they shunned the villagers, all because they were part of the bridge crew who made the decisions on their behalf. The villagers had no contact with the others in the fifteen years they lived on Utopia. Nothing would ever change that.

The Avaan population grew at an alarming rate, they would prosper, their existence secured. They would never leave. They had everything they ever wanted in life, and that was simply to survive.

Tom couldn't make a decision for now, they still had a lot more to learn about the artefact, as it stood they knew nothing. The artefact had not activated itself in hours, even after they decided what the last symbol represented. Tom knew there was more to come, but for now, "I'll tell you what's next –" he said, "how about a cup of that leaf tea of yours, I'm gasping."

Niko smiled and got to her feet. "You can if JT hasn't completely demolished my kitchen."

Then they heard the sound of more clattering of pottery, followed by something smashing as it hit the floor.

"Sorry" came the plaintive voice of JT.

Tom and Sol sat back to relax, it appeared all the symbols had a meaning they both understood, everything was coming together. They now had to wait for a sign, something to say what the next stage was. Sol quite frankly had enough of the strange thoughts rolling around in his head, but he'd gladly take one more if it meant finding his friends finally.

*

The universe was satisfied with the Utopians, they finally solved the ancient puzzle. The doctor was an integral part of the equation, that had not been foreseen by the universe. It mattered not. The next stage would commence.It was time.

*

Without warning Nicolas and Calum came rushing home, looking dishevelled, completely out of breath from running almost two miles back to the village. They both tried to speak at the same time, neither could get a word out until they stopped gasping for air; their lungs were just about bursting. They had urgent news that couldn't wait, and their parents were not going to like it. Playing near the edge of the forest, close to the wreckage of Retriever-2, now almost hidden by the undergrowth taking over, the boys saw a strange phenomenon. They knew the forest was a no-go area, banned by their parents, they also knew they were in real trouble, but what they witnessed was far more important than a reprimand. It took several minutes before they regained their breath, watched by the adults bemused by the state they were in, then both boys tried to explain what they saw, both at the same time, it came out garbled and no one understood a single word. Tom and Sol had to shut them up for a second, they needed to calm down.

"Right, slowly and one at a time. Nicolas, what's the problem?" asked Sol.Xander sat down on the table and folded his arms. "This could be interesting" he said.

"Shut up Xander, just listen" said Tom.

"Dad, there's a strange green light glowing out in the forest, we saw it through the trees."Calum nodded in agreement.

"Where?" asked Tom, alarm bells were ringing in his head, this was it, the next stage, he was sure of it.

"In the forest, like I said."

"Yes son, but where exactly?" asked Sol, already thinking what punishment he could dish out for going anywhere near the forest unsupervised.

"Near the wreckage of that ship, the stern I think, I'm really sorry dad. We were just playing" said Nicolas.

"And it was only at the perimeter, not in the forest, honest" added Calum, pleading to his dad not to be too harsh on them. Tom gave his son a stern look, he thought better of Calum, it was expressly forbidden to be anywhere near the wreckage.

"But dad please, we didn't go into the forest, it's just, well that weird green glow, it was really spooky" said Calum. Nicolas backed him up, but looking at his mum, he knew he was in deep shit. He waited for his dad to tear him off a strip. Nothing came. Sol just glared at him, he was the eldest of the children, he should have known better.

"What do you think Tom?" Sol asked, much more concerned what was in the forest than lecturing the boys right then.

"I think I better cancel my tea order. I have a feeling we just reached the next level of our mission. We will have to investigate I suppose" replied Tom. He was reluctant to go anywhere near the wreckage, it was not a good place, memories started to flood back. Suddenly he saw himself being helped out of the ship aided by Simone, bodies lay on the ground, his mental health down in the depths of despair, he could smell burning hanging in the air. He wasn't sure he could do this. *Did he have a choice?* A strange uncanny force urged his inner being to make the right decision, lead his people to succeed to the next level. Yes, he did have a choice, succeed in the mission and repay the debt or die a failure.

Sol nodded; they had to investigate what the boys saw. It happened too conveniently, just after they solved the last symbol, destiny was calling again.

"Good!" jumped up Xander, "Action at last" he got so excited, his one good eye was swinging out of control, it was hard to tell where he was looking, and he nearly made himself go dizzy. But Xander needed to focus, he felt a more powerful force emerging, his sixth sense warned of a dreadful time ahead, they had to tread carefully, or it would not end well. His friends were in danger if they didn't get it right.

Xander had to protect his friend Just Tom, he made a promise to himself. "I will come too Just Tom, we will search for the answers together.

Tom wasn't about to argue, Xander was right, he always trusted his intuition, if not for his antics. For now he had to pull himself together, he was part of the link to the artefact, his son needed him, Sol needed him, he could not break the circle now.

Sol sensed the fear in Tom and took charge of the situation until he gathered his thoughts.

"Okay boys, I guess you better show us exactly where this strange light is coming from" said Sol, getting him up from the table. Niko was apprehensive about them going, it was late in the day.

"Be careful my darling, and make sure you're all back before dark." She had her own concerns about the forest, it was as if evil lurked there, it was much more than bad memories, for now she had to keep her worries to herself, the men had to go in search of answers.

"Right then, it's you me and the boys Tom, let's go" said Sol, he suddenly felt revitalised, having all the symbols in his head and knowing what they meant was a big boost to his confidence, the sleepless nights forgotten now. Tom was wavering, he had deep reservations about returning to the forest. It may have swallowed up most of the wreckage, but the fact remained it was still there, a huge memorial to the dead.

"Come Tom, whatever happens, we do it together, yes"

"Okay Sol" said Tom just about managing to get his words out, he was choked with emotion. Xander went to sit on his shoulder. Tom needed comfort.

"You can do this Just Tom, I'll protect you, we will succeed – have faith."Tom had to smile, the little guy was a real confidence booster, his small stature meant nothing, his heart was bigger than any being in the universe, he was a great comfort to Tom.

"Okay, I'm ready little buddy, let's do this" said Tom.

"Me too, don't forget me" said JT floating back into the room swiftly, landing on the table next to the artefact. He was just about finishing his last mouthful of food. No way did he want to get left behind, if his dad and the others were going on an adventure, then so was he.

Niko had other ideas. "You get back in that kitchen and clean up your mess."JT looked at Xander thinking his dad would rescue him.

"Dad –"

"No JT, do as you're told" said Xander, knowing he would be in trouble with Niko if he didn't back her up.

"Oh drat." JT floated off to the kitchen, miserable now he was going to miss the excitement.

"And mind your language" shouted Xander.

*

Ready to leave they stepped outside to be greeted by the luminous green glow in the distance. Though the forest was nearly two miles away, the eerie glow was clearly visible through the trees, and it was getting stronger by the minute.

"See dad, I told you" said Calum, "something is out there and its scary."

"What do you think it is Sol?" asked Tom, worried their peaceful existence was about to be shattered. For a second he wasn't even sure the glowing light was connected to the artefact, how could it be?

"I don't know, but I'm guessing it isn't good news." As he spoke, Niko grabbed his arm, she didn't want him to go, or Nicolas, she was afraid for their safety. This wasn't supposed to happen to their idyllic lives, she felt they had all paid their debt to the outside. Fear started to rise up, everyone felt a chill run down their spines.

"No, it bloody well isn't good news" said Tom, it wasn't what he expected, and he was sure the others would have spotted it and blamed the villagers no matter what.

"Calum, go and get the artefact, I have a feeling we may need it" said Sol, still taking charge; Tom was now alert, focused and very anxious. This could be more than they could handle but he couldn't back out now.

"Well, are we going or not?" asked Xander, eager as ever, he was probably the only one excited about it; he looked on danger differently to the humans, it was more of an adventure for him. It was the Avaan way. He floated off at full speed, not bothering to wait for anyone. Tom dashed after him if only to keep him in check, so much for Xander promising to look after him.

"Foolhardy bloody pintpot, will he ever learn?" muttered Tom as he ran. He was quickly followed by Sol and the boys.

"We'll see you later Niko, don't worry about a thing" Sol shouted back.

But she was worried, standing in her doorway, she caught a glimpse of Simone looking out, then Carol as she watched Nely in hot pursuit. Suddenly her alien blood ran cold. She felt fear like she hadn't since Nicolas was born, and she didn't like it. Now getting JT to clean up after his mess didn't seem quite so important. She shouted at him to go and follow his dad, JT didn't need telling twice, whizzing past her like a gust of wind at top speed.

"Thank you Niko" he called back.

*

Sitting alone in the semi-darkness, Niko was feeling immense anxiety, her stress levels were running out of control. Her alien DNA was not helping her cope with the loneliness of the night. The men were late, full darkness would come soon making it hard to find their way home safely.

Niko learnt over the years how to cope with being turned into half alien, it wasn't so bad, as long as she had the man she loved by her side. Clariziane women were naturally strong-willed, forceful, fearless even, her volatile temperament was well known in the village. Sol explained all women on his world were like that, it was in their genetic make-up, and the stronger the woman the more appealing she was. Now Niko was suffering the dreadful experience of a vulnerable and very frightened human being. It wasn't the best feeling to have, sitting alone in the dark, afraid of her own shadow. She was worried, something must have happened to Sol and Nicolas. *Why was it taking so long?* Niko chose not to go to the forest, as soon as the wreckage of Retriever-2 was mentioned, her heart sank to new depths. Now she was all alone, having nightmarish flashbacks of being on the ship while under attack as she was giving birth, her mind was tormenting her to the extreme; bringing to the surface long dead memories that knotted her stomach, then she realised the pain was real, as if she was giving birth again, and she couldn't stop it.

Niko nearly died that day, going back to the site would only make her feel worse, then she wondered, *could she feel any worse right now?* Frightening thoughts came into her head, *what if Sol and Nicolas never returned? What if none of them returned? What would she do without them?* She desperately wanted her family home safe. Tears began streaming down her cheeks, a feeling of utter helplessness weighed heavily on her shoulders, this could be the end of her perfect life. All she could do for now was curl up and sob her heart out, eventually falling asleep, exhausted.

Bad dreams didn't let Niko rest for long, her sleep repeatedly disturbed by the flashbacks. That fateful day fifteen years ago felt like it happened yesterday.

*

It was late into the night when Sol and Nicolas stumbled home, dishevelled and scratched all over, the dense undergrowth in the forest was unforgiving in the darkness. They were both relieved to find their way back to the village and their home. Going out at night was not to be recommended in normal circumstances, they never anticipated being so long. The moons didn't appear for some reason. Now they and the rest of their party were finally back, tired and exhausted by the trek, having to blindly feel their way home, but satisfied they discovered the answers they were looking for. Reaching the source of the mysterious green glow was not anything like they expected. It was emanating from inside the rear section of the ship, at least what was left of it after the federation blew off the tailpiece in the attack.

Sol was aware Niko had fallen asleep in a chair; he could hear her breathing. She was restless, he left her alone, it was best to leave her until morning. She would be more understanding then to listen to what he and Tom had to say. What they discovered was crazy, mind-blowing at the very least. Sol was ecstatic to learn not only was his friend Don still alive, but also the other pilots as well, he was heartened to learn that; then he thought, *okay, they're alive, but only in the past.* The big question was how were they going to rescue them and more importantly, *what to do with them afterwards?*

Tom pointed out that Sol's friends couldn't stay in that universe, it was the wrong one, then again they couldn't go home either. Sol wondered how he would explain that to his friends. For now he just wanted to sleep, but how could he when he had so much going on in his head, which was at the point of bursting with information, symbols, letters, sequences, all of which he had to commit to memory. It was good to know the pilots never gave up looking for him, that was one consolation Sol had.

On the downside, in the wreckage of Retriever-2, Sol saw his own spaceship for the first time in years. It was rusting away, every bit of circuitry crumbled to dust when he touched it. It was a sad sight for him, he didn't think he could feel anything for the ship. But he did, it held a lot of memories, some good, some not so good. He had been close to losing his sanity, if that didn't happen he was a dead man, and it wouldn't have mattered. Then Retriever-2 picked him up, barely alive, dehydrated and unconscious, halfway to losing his mind.

How could he ever forget that time?

Recovering in the hospital he opened his eyes to see a vision of beauty, and she still was. He was eternally grateful for that. Now, it was time to leave his ship to be reclaimed by the forest, he had no more use for it.

There were more urgent matters to attend.

The strange unknown black alien spaceship the late Captain Valmak instructed his crew to recover while en route to their next mission, was still alongside. No one managed at the time to discover its origin, or who the owner might be; so it was left in the hangar deck undisturbed. How, it and Sol's ship never floated off in space when the ship lost the tail section was nothing short of a miracle. Here it sat all this time, forgotten about alien technology. But like everything else aboard the broken ship – too many bad memories to deal with, the reason the few survivors had to get up and walk away, Retriever-2 meant nothing to them anymore.

Now the mystery alien ship stood before them in all it's glory, intact, in pristine condition; the smooth black outer casing reflecting the sunlight back in their faces. It was late afternoon, light still glinting through the trees, they had to be quick to complete whatever it was they had to do in order to get home before dark.

The alien ship appeared to be fully functional, and the source of the fluorescent green glow coming directly from the controls like a beacon calling out to them.

Well, it got their attention.

The computer system lit up inexplicably, activating itself when Tom and Sol climbed into the three-man ship; Calum then occupied the third seat. Xander and JT sat on Tom's shoulders, it was a bit cramped, but they refused to be left outside with Nely and Nicolas. Seconds later Mike managed to catch up with them when he heard what was happening. He was just as eager to know the truth.

It was no coincidence the ship coming to life after all these years sitting inside the wreckage. It had been waiting for the right time. It had to be connected to the artefact, which also lit up being in close proximity to the ships computer system, now Tom was certain someone was definitely guiding them to their destiny. They were meant to be there, he didn't question who or why, but he had his suspicions.

Strange they all thought, how the vegetation hadn't grown over the alien ship, unlike Sol's; he had to pull away the thick undergrowth to get inside his. The plant life growing inside engulfed every single bit of his past. The alien ship on the other hand had an aura of an ancient mystical power shrouding it, almost the same aura surrounding the artefact, it was assumed the two were of the same origin, no other explanation.

Sol, once a highly skilled space pilot and knew his way round the workings of a spaceship, and Tom a first-class science officer, and Xander with high intellect, all sat looking at the controls for a few minutes, completely clueless and thinking '*what do we do now?*' Calum sat there clutching the artefact as if his life depended on it. The far superior technology staring back at them was complex, unreadable, nothing made sense. Tom didn't want to touch anything until he was sure of its function.

Nely put his head in to see what the problem was, the silence was killing him. "Well Tom, are we screwed or what?" he said in his usual manner. Not really helpful, Mike gave him a dig in the ribs.

"Why do you have no faith in my dad?" Nicolas said, he was hurt by Nely's comment. His dad, with Tom and Calum would solve the mystery, he was certain of that.

"Keep quiet Nely, watch and learn" said Mike.

Without anyone touching the controls, things started to happen, dials registered strange readouts, the instruments clicked into action, lights flashed right across the control panel, slowly everything was realigning with each other. Being dormant for so long had little effect to the system. The artefact was communicating with the ships mainframe, Calum was spooked by the artefact's movement, it didn't do that the first time. He gripped it harder; he couldn't let it go. The onboard computer system was coming back to life, they had no idea where the power was coming from, it just happened. The computer began to reveal long dead files, important data they needed to know for the mission. That was the moment they realised lives were about to change forever.

Everything was making sense now.

Xander had his part to play, he and Sol had connected once again with telepathic thoughts, they had knowledge to exchange and this way was faster. Now Xander knew he had a big role to perform on the mission, but details were patchy, Sol unable to elaborate at the present time, the little guy would know when the time was right. For Sol, having that feeling of being inside each other heads was frightening, he'd had enough of voices in his head, and Xanders was full of clutter. But Sol had to admit his scientific brain and unique sixth sense was a bonus. Xander could always allay his fears and said so with one word. "We're a team."

Sol looked at him, he still couldn't count.

Having all the details they required, all the symbols on the artefact now solved and aligned with the ships onboard computer, they had their mission, and then agreed it was time to go home. The hours had passed by without any of them realising it was pitch-black outside the ship. Getting home might take a little longer than they first thought. They would also have a lot of explain to do in the morning.

It was time to leave Utopia.

Tom had serious reservations about the mission, Earth was not his favourite place to visit. He still harboured hatred for what the authorities tried to do to them, and they very nearly succeeded. But the fact remained the vital data locked away in the alien ship confirmed Earth was their final destination, after they picked up Sol's friends on the way. The mission to Earth still wasn't clear to Tom, and he didn't want to second guess at this stage. At least Niko was right about the letter on the artefact. She was going to love that.

Stumbling along in the dark, Tom took one last look back at the ship, flashing lights still lighting up inside. He had many questions about its origin. It sure as hell didn't come from Earth, far too sophisticated for one thing.

'How the hell did it look like it just come out of the showroom?' Tom shook his head and left.

In reality, all the data they recovered happened fifteen years ago, when the universe was in turmoil. Going back in time could be more trouble than they could handle. It also appeared the problematic spatial rifts in the universe only escalated in their absence. Tom guessed it was up to the Utopians to save the universe again. He prayed they would be in time. He was more certain than ever the ancient artefact and the alien ship were given to them for this one specific purpose. Outside forces were at work again. That bit he learnt not to question; he would never understand it anyway. He was chosen for the mission because of his strong leadership. The universe was a complete and utter mystery, he still couldn't work out why there were two in the first place.

*

'Don't question it Tom.'

The universe itself had a major part in controlling the outcome. It thought 'clever boy Tom, but don't question the existence of life.'But they would succeed in their mission, the parallel universe will be stopped – the chosen ones will do well.

CHAPTER SIXTEEN

Night slowly broke into morning over the village; for some it had been a late-night trekking back from the forest. They fell into bed exhausted. No one was keen on rising as early as normal. Tom and Sol had a lot to think about, and a lot of explaining to do. Tom was in two minds whether he should approach the others to speak with them. None of the villagers went near their commune in the last fifteen years. He thought they might want to know if their future was in doubt. Utopia was at risk, yet Tom didn't know why, when or how; the only certain thing he knew was some of the villagers had to leave on a mission, Tom included. He also knew the others probably still couldn't forgive the decisions the crew made on the bridge od Retriever-2.

It was a long time to hold a grudge.

Tom eventually fell asleep thinking of the others, unable to make up his mind what to do; some of them were close friends once, it was a hard choice.

One by one the Utopians rose from their slumber; it was soon apparent all was not well; the light was different. The sun was up as normal, but not as bright as it should be. It hadn't gone unnoticed for long, several villagers stepped outside to be greeted by a strange unnatural sight in the sky. A sight that sent shivers down their spines, this could not be happening to their perfect world;they began to question *how it could happen? Why now? Why would Utopia do this to them?*

*

After a restless night in the chair, Niko stirred, woken abruptly by loud voices outside, that wasn't normal. She hadn't heard Sol or Nicolas come home; fear suddenly began to take over again. Something must have happened to them. *Had they not made it back in the dark?* Niko was scared of being left alone, not something she cared for, except someone was making an awful bloody racket outside her home. She was getting cross, forgetting about her sadness of being alone, and her aching bones from being in the chair all night. Her eyes were sore and puffed up from crying half the night. Now her extra sensitive hearing disturbed what little sleep she had managed. Wearily she got up and went to investigate the commotion. As she opened the door Sol and Nicolas emerged, bleary eyed and a bit annoyed they were woken up so early. Nicolas was grumpy, his sensitive hearing was one trait he wished he didn't possess.

Niko turned back so relieved to see them. "Sol!" She rushed across the room and threw her arms round his neck, never again would she let him go off without her. She couldn't take another night of mental torture; life without Sol was unthinkable.

"It's alright my darling" said Sol, "you can stop strangling me now." He appreciated her love and devotion, but right then he needed to breathe, and he too wanted to know what was going on outside.

"What's up pops? Is someone having a row out there?" asked Nicolas, still rubbing his eyes and yawning his head off.

Outside, the villagers were gathering around, all trying to speak at the same time, looking skyward in total disbelief. A cloudless sky like most mornings, but this day was not most mornings. Now the villagers were looking at a strange anomaly so unnatural; a huge black mile long jagged void, directly above the village had opened up. The sunlight was half strength even for that early in the day.

The sky had been ripped opened.

Nely and Carol held their children tight, fearing for all their lives, not knowing what to expect or even realise the enormity of what it meant for Utopia. Tom held his family close also, he at least knew what it was immediately, and it wasn't good news. He rushed over to Sol and Niko, standing in their doorway.

"We have big trouble guys" he announced.

"What is it Tom?" asked Niko almost in a panic now she's seen the sky. "What does it all mean?" She clutched Sol's arm for support, she had a crazy idea it was because of something they did when they went to the forest.

'Had they caused this strange void in the sky?'

It certainly didn't look repairable.

"That's one hell of a crack in the universe Sol, whatever is going on out there, is now affecting Utopia" said Tom, he didn't want to admit to himself, let alone the others, but the sky was in danger of cracking up completely.

"We have to act Sol, like now." There was an urgency in his voice, he was scared, it was quite obvious their world was no longer a safe haven.

"Best say your goodbyes Niko, we leave right away." Tom spoke with a saddened heart, he knew there was no other choice, they had to go, he didn't expect it to happen quite so soon. He had hoped for more time to prepare for the mission, now they would have to wing it.

The villagers could stand by no longer and do nothing, not now it was affecting their world. If Sol's friends needed help the decision was made. It was highly likely they were the cause of the disruption in the universe, although Tom surmised it was something more than that, something he hadn't anticipated, and something more sinister than he could ever imagine. The scariest part was the unknown factor. *How could they prepare for that?*

For now the villagers had to go with what they knew, rescue Sol's friends from whatever danger they were in – then destination EARTH.

Tom felt a heavy burden on his shoulders, he was worried Utopia might not survive this upheaval, what could they do about the Avaans, they were happy and thriving, this latest episode might be the final straw in their existence. The responsibility was his alone, he was leading his people into the unknown.

Paul and Alec arrived soon after, followed by Mike and Darryl, who then immediately questioned their motives. Darryl wanted assurances that going back in time would actually solve their problem, or would it make it worse? They were probably all doomed anyway. This crack in the sky merely escalated the problem. He so wanted to blame it on Nely, he must have done something bad. His sister was there with Nely, he kept his mouth shut for now, not wishing to embarrass himself in front of his niece and nephew.

Whatever the villagers thought, Tom was adamant they had to try. They could go, or they could stay.

Nothing was stopping the mission.

Sol went inside to collect the artefact, he'd heard a faint whirring sound coming from it, as if it was alive. It never made a noise before. As he grabbed it an incredible surge of energy coursed through his body, heightening every one of his senses. It was apparent now he had the strongest connection, each symbol locked inside his head. Calum had done the same for the first mission, solving the clues except the one symbol Niko solved. That one wasn't necessary at the time. Now it featured heavily in the new mission.

Sol took on the responsibility of the artefact, relieving some of the burden from Tom's shoulders. He couldn't argue with that, he was grateful. He made the decision Calum and Sol would be perfect guardians of the artefact; the success of the mission depended on them. Calum promised his dad that with Sol's help he could do this, he did it once before, that was a piece of cake. It gave him the confidence he needed, he felt man enough to stand shoulder to shoulder with Sol. He dad would co-ordinate with them.

Simone, although very proud of her son, feared this would be too much for him to take on. She worried about the role placed on such young shoulders. It was a huge risk; he was only a kid in her eyes. Her love and faith in Tom never once wavered, she went along with the plan because it was important, she had to trust them, but her heart was breaking.

Getting the re-entry point back into the universe at the precise time and location in history left no margin for error. No one wanted to pass through the portal into outer space. They all knew the risk, all knew their lives were in the hands of a higher power, there was always the possibility they weren't coming back. Some decided not to try it, they would stay in the village and pray for survival.

The others watched on from a distance, still unable to bring themselves into contact with the villagers, still harbouring animosity even after all this time. They had no idea what was going on, they guessed it had a lot to do with the huge black void stretching over their commune. They initially wanted to lay blame with the villagers for it, *but then would they be that stupid to jeopardise their idyllic world? Yes.* The others thought so, they were capable of anything. The villagers had the last say in everything aboard the ship, no discussions, no choices, no debate. The bridge crew made all the decisions without consultation.

No. They couldn't bring themselves to speak with them and ask what was going on. *What would be the point?*

*

Sol was ready to go, Calum stood with him beside his friend Nicolas, and Niko who refused to be left behind. She would not be separated from Sol ever again. Sol had all the symbols memorised in his head, he simply had to press them in the right order. His main problem now was the wife to contend with, all he needed was Xander with his telepathic thoughts and it was standing room only. Xander at that moment was nowhere to be seen, maybe he had a change of heart about going, which was fine with Sol. He had to concentrate. They were ready to leave, the chosen entry point selected, all that was left to do were the goodbyes. For some it was a painful decision, especially for Tom. He was leaving Simone behind, the woman who was his whole world, who saved him from the brink, and his beloved daughter Annie. Simone wanted to stay, she understood why Tom and Calum had to leave, they were the chosen ones. It didn't make parting any easier to bear. Many tears were shed.

Nely reluctantly agreed to go, he too struggled to leave his wife and children. Carol said he could contribute to the mission and support his friends. She always had complete and utter faith in his abilities, never once doubting his commitment. She even liked his silly antics and his quirky outlook on life. It made him who he was. At the same time she insisted on staying. Alec then said he had to go, if only to keep an eye on his friend. He had no one to leave behind anyway, but he was going to miss Josef and Maria, he adored those kids. Nely was a very lucky man to have two great kids and a loving wife.

Darryl was adamant he couldn't go as he was the only doctor left. That was his excuse, he still wanted to punch Nely's lights out for leaving Carol behind with the kids. It was her idea Nely should go, but Darryl was having none of it. He thought the useless wimp couldn't face up to his responsibilities. Carol warned her brother he needed to change his attitude if he was staying, she needed him to help care for his niece and nephew and that he had to stop bad mouthing their father. She loved her brother, but he was such a pain in the arse, a slap in the face days earlier had little effect on his manner.

Mike decided to stay also even if it meant saying goodbye to his best friend, it was the hardest decision of his life. He warmed to the fact Niko had relented and forgiven him for his deceit, it was after all in the best interests of everyone. She finally realised Mike only agreed to do it because he loved their special friendship and didn't want Sol to suffer.

Standing near the edge of the village, out of sight of the others, the leaving party gathered, Mike hugged Niko tight then kissed her warmly.

"Dad!" said Nicolas, shocked at his mum and Uncle Mike.

"It's alright son, calm down" said Sol. He understood their closeness; besides, he guessed it was a human thing.

"I'm going to miss you Mike, you've been such a good friend to me" said Niko and kissed him back.

"Ditto" he said, "but you won't miss me, you will all be back in no time at all, a matter of minutes so don't even bother sending a postcard. Just be safe."

Niko smiled, "Of course, I could be back before I actually leave, now that would a bizarre, right."

"Right, take care of my adopted nephew, that's all." Mike hung onto Niko, afraid to let her go, but he could see Sol getting impatient.

"I have one question to ask Mike."

"Yes?"

"What does the B stand for?" Niko had known him for more years then she cared to remember, she even asked once or twice, yet he never revealed his middle name. it was missing from his medical files, something she couldn't understand at the time. It didn't seem to matter as the years went on.

"Michael Benjamin Dyland at your service" he replied in a jokey way and they both laughed, even though they had tears of sadness in their eyes. He kissed her again. They parted company and Niko went to stand with her husband. Mike waved, he was choked, speechless.

Always late arriving anywhere came Xander and JT with Po as usual following behind, all three of them with bags over their shoulder loaded with food for the journey. They came fully prepared for the long haul.

"Xander?" Tom said at the top of his voice. "What the hell do you think you're doing?"

The party was set to go, and Sol and Calum were anxious to begin the procedure to activate the artefact and open the portal.

"I told you Just Tom, where you go, I go. JT won't stay without me and Po wants to come along for the ride." Xander said in his best voice, adamant he was going. "And besides, I have my wife's permission."

"This is not a bloody picnic –" Tom was frustrated with the little guy; he wouldn't be told. Xander hovered in front of Tom, his arms folded in an act of defiance, and that one good eye telling Tom *'don't even go there.'*

Tom was speechless.

"I guess that makes ten of us then" said Sol, knowing full well that Tom would not win that argument.

Thet gathered together real close, nobody was getting left behind.

"Ready?" said Calum, standing with Sol to make sure every symbol was correctly done. They turned to see their loved ones standing back, all in tears and heartbroken it had come to this. They had no choice, Tom wished there was another way, but there wasn't, they had a job to do. Sol activated the artefact with a single surge of mental energy pulsating through his veins. He had mastered the artefact so well. He felt he had a hand on his shoulder encouraging his every move, a renewed confidence overwhelmed him.

Some yards away a void opened up, a black hole of nothing, no bushes, no trees, no sky or even the ground, just a huge empty space awaiting them. All they had to do was step through. Nely suddenly had one of his queasy stomachs, something he'd not felt in years. He questioned how he allowed himself to be coerced into volunteering for a mission again. He was sure he had *'sucker'* stamped across his forehead. If he backed out now, he was going to get the shit kicked out of him for sure. That steely look in Darryl's eyes said as much. An arm from Alec round his shoulders told him he wasn't alone.

"Come on buddy, you can do this. It's you and me to save the universe again" said Alec.

"Yeh, right." Nely as usual was not sure, but at least his childhood friend was never too far away.

CHAPTER SEVENTEEN

Aboard their alien ship the Clariziane pilots found themselves in a bit of a sticky situation. They had to deal with just about everything thrown at them in this unforgiving universe. How anyone could survive in this chaotic place was beyond them. This universe was strange, unnatural, hazardous, and very bad for their well-being. The sooner they were out of there the better, at least their own universe was uncomplicated – or it was until the Clariziane hierarchy messed things up. There was even the possibility it wasn't there anymore, and they had no intention of going back to find out.

The pilots were at a loss as to what to do next, they were stumped. No one could agree on anything, except for the fact it was going to get a whole lot worse. The ship remained stationary in space, having been exposed by a sudden spatial distortion seconds earlier, one of many they had encountered in the last few weeks. They began to wonder if it was normal occurrences for this universe, danger lurked everywhere. It was hard to tell what was safe and what was not.

The uninhabited planet the ship was hiding behind was gone, it had been displaced from its normal orbit and sent across space with a new trajectory, one that sent it on a collision course with one of the other planets. A major catastrophe was imminent, the pilots hadn't a clue how to stop it. They only wanted to reach the third planet to speak with the inhabitants, now even that was looking unlikely.

Uncanny forces prevented their every move, whatever was going on outside the ship, this universe was out of control and in danger of destroying itself. All the pilots wanted was to find Sol and get the hell out of there, except they couldn't; they couldn't go home, couldn't find Sol and they didn't have their own spaceship, had to steal one. It was fast becoming apparent their lives were a mess.

Looking at the alignment of stars from the portholes it was clear they were all wrong, that too changed in an instant, no way of navigating the ship out of the system, not without knowing which direction to take. The star charts in the ships data bank didn't match up with this universe. It posed a question about the origin of the ship in their possession.

Whose universe did it belong too?

The occurring events were way beyond the Clarizianes intelligence, they couldn't fathom how they got into the middle of this chaos, it wasn't what they signed up for. *How could they expect to deal with a universe that didn't behave rationally?* The laws of science and reality appeared to have gone out the window.

The only piece of reality the pilots could understand was the warship staring at them that mysteriously appeared on the bow when the planet shifted off course. It too made no attempt to move, probably as bewildered as they were, Don thought, '*what were they waiting for?*' Don already hated this universe, it wasn't normal, didn't behave normal, he wondered what Sol would have made of it.

Could he really have survived this lunacy?

Even more bizarre, still in its normal orbit the unknown third planet was the only constant in the chaos, at least it maintained some normality for now. If it moved the whole sector was in danger of imploding in on itself.

Don began to feel pretty much useless; he tried so hard to be a good leader, the other pilots relied on him to make the right decisions. It just wasn't enough. He was grateful Stella was there, for a teenager she was one hell of a woman. Her presence meant a great deal to the morale of the crew, even if she was a distraction for Rol. That man was heading for trouble, he could never hope to handle the likes of Sol's cousin. She was too feisty even for a teenager. Still, they wouldn't have got this far if it wasn't for her and Ariel, but now it looked like they were at a dead end. They couldn't go on, they couldn't go back, he could see no way out for the pilots, it seemed months of travelling across space in uncharted territory, searching for their friend had come down to getting lost in a universe that wasn't theirs, and one that didn't want to behave itself, and now facing a space battle they wanted no part of. This universe was playing mind games on them for sure, to top it all they were no nearer to finding out what happened to Sol.

A big debate was taking place with some of the pilots as to whether they should rescue the two alien prisoners on the third planet, but if they did the question remained, *what were they supposed to do with them?* Don didn't like the situation they put themselves in, there seemed little chance of getting out of this alive.

What would be the point rescuing prisoners, it was they who needed rescuing.

Don felt his heart sink to a new level, he walked away from the others, they could carry on the debate without him, he wanted time alone and found himself near the stern of the ship and sat down. He couldn't control the goings on in this universe, no mortal could. Space was in the hands of a higher entity, his own mortality was simply shredded, he felt so vulnerable.

The mysterious unnatural forces hampered every part of their journey, so how could they ever hope to succeed when the cards were stacked against them.

Don wasn't even sure that it was only months ago they lost Sol on a routine patrol, maybe that had also changed. He should have realised it would end in disaster after Stella made the guards disappear at spaceport then blew up the place. He couldn't ask her how she did it, he didn't want to know. He never got his head round the fact Sol's little cousin was capable of such a deed.

'What had Sol been teaching her?'.

Strange timeline fluctuations occurred so often it was hard to keep up with the changes, Don had no idea what the date was any more, they were trapped in space in the wrong time, never mind the wrong universe, and probably they would die here in space. It was no way to end their lives. Who would mourn them, not their own kind for sure. The Clariziane authorities wanted them dead in the first place, more than likely they were all dead anyway.

'*What an epitaph*' Don thought, no one to grieve them.

Sitting alone for a while at the stern of the ship gave Don time to reflect on his life, he tried so hard to be upbeat about the predicament he and the other pilots found themselves in. he failed miserably, nothing could make him feel better. He heard voices coming from the control section, everyone talking about what was going on outside their ship. The debate concerning the alien prisoners ended with no solution. They would have to stay put for now, they were the least of their worries.

While talking amongst themselves the pilots watched out the portholes waiting for movement, waiting to see what the warship would do, if anything. Don guessed it might be the case of who blinked first, whoever they were out there probably thought the same about them. He had so many thoughts, unanswered questions pounding his brain his head hurt. This was a futile mission from the start, *why didn't alarm bells go off in his head?* Right from the beginning he should have realised there was no real chance of finding his friend alive. It was suicidal to even leave their own galaxy, finding another universe was more than they could handle.

Who was he kidding to think Sol would hear his pleas and come to his rescue. Resting his head in his hands Don sank deeper into despair, *how could he tell the others they were all going to die in an alien tin can, in an alien universe where not even the universe cared about them.*

"I care," came a voice out of nowhere, "well, are you pleased to see me, or not?"A familiar voice Don thought he would never hear again. *'But what was it doing inside his head? Could it get any worse than this?'* he thought.

"Well say something my friend" came the voice again, it definitely wasn't in his head, it was real. Don lifted his head and opened his eyes, a figure stood in front of him. For a moment he couldn't be sure, he blinked several times not understanding what he was looking at, then the penny dropped.

"Sol!?" He was so startled he slipped off his seat, ending up on the floor, his bottom lip hit basement level. This stranger standing over him looked like Sol, even sounded like him, but he had aged so much, and he was wearing weird clothes.

Was that plant fibre he could see?

What was that black void behind him?

And where the hell was the stern of the ship?

Don was speechless, staying on the floor seemed a good option. Then an outstretched arm gestured to Don to help him up.

"Hello Don. It's so good to see you after all this time. I understand you've been trying to call me, a few times in fact" said Sol smiling at his long-time friend. Don got to his feet, then hugged Sol, just to make sure he was for real.

"Is it really you?"

"Yes my friend, it's really me."

"You mean you really heard me call to you?" Don blurted out.

It was Sol but he was different, Don didn't want to believe what his eyes were seeing. Then things got even more bizarre, appearing from behind Sol, Niko and Nicolas passed through the portal and came into view. Don thought he was hallucinating, or had he fallen asleep and it was just a bad dream.

It wasn't real, it couldn't be. How could these strangers walk out of nowhere onto the ship?

"Sol, what is going on? Who are these people? What's with the weird clothes, where is your uniform?" Don pumped out every question he could think of his mind was racing. The woman sort of looked like a Clariziane female, yet quite clearly she wasn't. The boy he had doubts about his origin. He didn't know either of them. *How did they get here?* That void behind was still there, Don wanted answers, he wasn't sure of getting them, especially from strangers.

"Don, calm down my friend. I want you to meet my beautiful wife Niko, and my son Nicolas" said Sol proudly.

"No, no, no, that's not possible." Don shook his head in complete disbelief, confused now, Sol had only been missing a few months. This was not real; it was not a dream; it was a bloody nightmare. He shook his head again, his expression said it all, he couldn't take it in.

"I can see you are sceptical, I would be too Don, but it's true. I have come here from the future to help. I need to put a few things right in the universe, it's out of control."

"Future?" Don questioned, his face screwed up, perplexed to the extreme. Yes, the universe was at odds with itself but how the hell did Sol think he could fix it.

"I bought some friends to help, they will be here any second." Sol hoped Don would understand, he was obviously struggling. He didn't really have the time to explain everything, he had to trust him.

"Hello Don" said Niko holding her hand out to greet him. "Sol has told me so much about you over the years, I feel I already know you." She smiled at him waiting for a response. Don could only stare back at her odd coloured eyes, they were scary, that couldn't be right. His mind couldn't take it all in, it was too much, he felt sick. Sol had to be wrong; time travel was a non-starter back on Clarizia. His people tried and failed; they probably caused all the problems in the universe in the first place. Nothing was going to put that right. No mortal anyway.

No, his friend was mistaken, he couldn't be from the future. Could he?

"Please Sol, tell me this is real, help me understand. The last few months have been hell for the pilots. You have no idea what we've been through."

"Oh I think I do know Don" he said with a certain smile and a soft giggle Don remembered so well.

It was him!

"But – but where have you been?" asked Don, "and please tell me what you are doing in those stupid clothes, they really don't suit you man."

Sol didn't get the chance to answer. Fisah arrived at the stern after hearing voices, he had assumed Don was alone, then he spotted Sol standing there.

"What the –" he was stunned into silence but elated at the same time. It hadn't occurred to Fisah where Sol sprung from, it was surreal. Perhaps he was an illusion, perhaps madness had finally set in with the pilots. Some of them were certain of seeing and hearing things. Don was heard on several occasions talking to himself, trying to contact Sol. Using the radio might have been a better option. Then Fisah suddenly spotted Nicolas standing close to Sol, and there was a strange looking woman also. He looked straight at Nicolas.

"Wow! A half-breed, where did you come from?" he announced shockingly.Without any warning he saw a fist coming at him right between the eyes, a common weak point for Clarizianes. Fisah fell to the ground howling in agony, blood gushing from his nose. He kept screaming with pain. "You broke my nose, you broke my nose" he yelled out, spurting out blood profusely.

Standing over him Niko yelled back at him furiously, "You call my son a half-breed again and I'll break more than your bloody nose." She was fuming as she stared down at the little jerk squirming about, still with a clenched fist ready to hit him again. All Fisah could do was look up to see that menacing blue eye piercing his brain.

"Mum!" Nicolas was shocked at his mum's action, but he was also perturbed having never heard anyone call him that before. He knew he was different from the other kids, all the same they were all part of the Utopian family. This behaviour he wasn't used to. Sol looked at his wife open-mouthed.

"Remind me not to make you angry my darling" he said meekly. Niko had tried to curb her volatile temper over the years, without much success it had to be said. It take didn't much to upset her, nobody messed with her family and got away with it. That was a big no-no.

Don helped Fisah get to his feet, his nose a complete mess, misshapen and still pumping blood all over his uniform, he looked a sorry state. Sol stepped in. "Here, let me help you Fisah, I am a doctor" he said, that was something he hadn't needed to say in a long time. It felt good.

Don thought *'What? No you're not, you're a space pilot.'*

He wondered if Sol had lost the plot, but with a very dangerous fist flying around he decided to keep quiet for now.

"You okay mum?" asked Nicolas, putting his arm across her shoulders in a protective way.

"I'm fine Nicolas" she replied, calming down now. "I'm sorry about your friend Don but he needs to watch his mouth."

Don didn't disagree with that, Fisah always had a knack of opening his mouth before engaging his brain. He turned to watch Sol who seemed to know what he was doing.

"Hold still Fisah, trust me and stop yelling while I put your nose back in place, unless you want to look stupid for the rest of your life." Sol did try and sound sympathetic, truth was he asked for it. Still looking on Don was feeling Fisah's pain, it was a hell of a fist. She was some woman.

"You're not really a doctor Sol, are you? So what gives?" he asked.

"He is a doctor and a very good one" said Niko proudly, and she didn't regret for one second what she did.

While attempting to stem the blood flow, Sol was almost there, getting Fisah's nose straight as he could, there was obviously too much damage, he was never going to win a beauty contest now. Suddenly they heard a high-pitched voice ring out.

"Sol!" squealed a delirious Stella rushing in with arms swinging around his neck and planting kisses all over his face. "Sol, I'm so pleased to see you." Stella couldn't contain her enthusiasm, to actually hold her beloved cousin again was wonderful.

Trying to maintain a hold on Fisah, it was Sol's turn to be shocked. "Stella, what are you doing aboard this ship?" he hadn't calculated for a reunion like this. She shouldn't be there, what had she got mixed up in; he had to let Fisah's nose go to hug Stella. Lifting her off the ground in his arms. In his heart he was happy she was alive.

"It's so good to see you sweetheart, I thought this day would never happen. But I have to ask again, what are you doing here?"

'Sweetheart?' Niko was going to need holding back if Sol didn't put her down.

"Well, someone had to break these guys out of prison" she replied.

"Prison? What are you talking about?" Sol was worried now, she knew nothing about that sort of thing, she was just a kid, innocent at that.

"Yes Sol, then we sort of stole a spaceship from spaceport and came looking for you."

Sol looked over to Don bemused. *'Prison breakout, stolen spaceship.'* Don nodded.

"Does somebody want to explain?" he asked, something told him he wouldn't like the answer. Stella was far too young to get involved with this bunch. *'What had they roped her into?'*

"It's true Sol, she saved us," said Don, "we couldn't have done it without her help. She's a credit to you."

Sol still didn't want to believe it. *How could she organise a prison break?* He suddenly remembered how heavily guarded spaceport was, something he never understood, there was nothing to protect.

Hearing Fisah squealing like a baby, more of the pilots came to the rear to see what was going on, which sounded more than what the warship was doing right then. It was getting boring just standing there watching the portholes.

The universe had gone quiet for now, how long for they didn't know.

Seeing Fisah in a bloody mess Cora sat down with him. "You look a sorry sight, what door did you walk into?" she said jokingly to lighten the mood, it was clear he was in a lot of pain. Fisah had a dreadful habit of getting hit, good job his split lip had healed that Kat gave him a week earlier for speaking out of turn to the women.

Rol and Hanzon were right behind, followed by Mos and Ariel. The stern was filling up suddenly. The pilots were immediately confronted by strangers, aghast at their presence. *Had they somehow breached the airlock without setting off the alarm?* How did they get onboard was the question they all wanted answered. They were angry now, taking their eye off the ball and allowing it to happen. Rol feared it was a ploy from the alien ship out there. They must have tricked their way onto the ship.

No one had a chance to ask a single question because through the portal that remained open, came the delayed arrival of Tom, Calum, Nely and Alec. As soon as they were clear of the void, the portal closed. The pilots saw it, didn't believe it, simply stared open-mouthed, speechless, words could not describe what they were thinking, none of it repeatable in front of the young ears.

"Sorry we're late" said Tom.

"Yeh, I think we took the scenic route" said Nely.

"What the hell is going on? How many more aliens are going to invade our ship?" yelled Don rather loudly, as if that would make a difference.

"Hi, Rol, Hanzon" said Sol, who still had Stella hanging round his neck. He hadn't quite finished straightening Fisah's nose before Stella launched herself at him. It needed more work; Sol didn't have time.

"Next time Fisah, mind what you say where my family are concerned" he said, having sympathy for him, but nobody spoke like that when his wife was about.

"Family? Sol, what are you talking about?" asked Rol, with a confused look on his face, then so did Stella, she thought she was his only family, they only had each other as long as she could remember. Mos and Ariel simply looked at each other thinking, *'this could be interesting, can't wait for the explanation.'*

"Perhaps you care to introduce us to your friends Sol" said Niko, slightly angry her husband might have an admirer she knew nothing about, and she was just a kid.

"Then may I remind you we have urgent business to attend to, time is precious" said Tom with an air of authority in his voice. They had a mission to complete, one that was time critical. His six-foot six-inch frame towered over everyone, the Clarizianes felt intimidated by his size. It was the one time Tom used his height as a way to get the attention of his audience.

"Let me go Stella, please" said Sol, he was having trouble breathing with her hanging on. Stella still wanted to hug him, happy he was alive, even if he looked strange. Turning to Niko and Nicolas, then his Utopian friends Sol announced, "This is Stella Nussar everyone, my cousin."

"Your cousin?" Niko said, "You never once mentioned you had a cousin Sol." She was however pleased to hear it; it did explain the clinginess. Now she felt a bit silly that jealously had reared its ugly head for a moment.

Nicolas finally spoke. "Hi Stella, I'm Nicolas Nussar, I guess that makes us family" he was happy even if no one else was.

"Pleased to meet you too" said Stella. She had been eyeing him up and couldn't help noticing he was a little different to other Clariziane boys. It didn't matter, she liked the feeling of a family and went over to hug him. Niko embraced the pair of them also. She was happy in the knowledge Sol had family, she supposed he never mentioned it because he thought there was no realistic chance of him ever going home.

Strange they had to travel back in time just to see family and friends. Niko understood why Tom wouldn't allow the artefact to be used without good cause. Earth in the past was not a place anyone wanted to visit. It would have been nice though to see her parents one more time so she could tell them how happy she was, and for Nicolas to meet his grandparents. It was just a pipe dream with no chance of realisation. She shook her head to return to the real world, the stern section of an alien ship.

Sol stepped forward; introductions were needed before they got down to business. He could see Tom was itching to go.

"Don, Rol and the rest of you, these people here are my friends, and we have come from the future to help."

"How?" asked Rol, sceptical this bunch of aliens were any use to them at all, they didn't look ready for anything, not in that get-up anyway, dressed in what looked very much like plant life at one stage. And they had no weapons to hand.

What use would they be?

They were just a bunch of misfits. He didn't dare say as much, he spotted Fisah's bloodied face and guessed one of the aliens did that to him.

"My friend Tom will do his best to explain, we really do have urgent business to deal with, so for now introductions are over, we need to get started." Sol urged his fellow pilots to gather their senses; he would need them to assist, the artefact was clear on that. They weren't too sure how much time they had, best to get started.

The universe was already in a volatile state, total collapse was imminent, this was going to be the biggest repair job in history. Tom had no idea where to start or what tools to use. He was worried about his little buddy, had the Avaans made it through the portal in time. Xander had a habit of not revealing himself, he hoped this was one of those times. He really needed Xander's expertise, he needed his friend by his side.

Fisah hadn't moved from his seat, he didn't want to drip blood all over the place and he thought it safer to stay put. He was still being comforted by Cora holding his hand. He felt sorry for himself, the pain was unbearable, he regretted now opening his big mouth, *why couldn't he ever learn?* His nose was swollen and throbbing. It would never be fixed now, Sol only done half a job.

Before leaving the rear section Hanzon decided to get up close to Sol, he felt he needed to check him out, dressed identical to the aliens, it looked like he had gone rogue. He didn't fit in with his own kind anymore, not looking like that.

"You've got old looking mate" he said bluntly.

"Good to see you haven't lost your charm Hanzon, and for the record, you've put a little too much weight on. Your uniform is ready to burst." Sol was equally blunt, he said what no one else wanted to. Hanzon knew he was right, he was ashamed, but it was only since leaving Clarizia. His metabolism was out of sync, it was never going to correct itself unless his mind realigned with his body.

"Now please, can we get on with our mission?" pleaded Tom, "we have urgent matters to deal with." He had so much pressure on him to get it done; he hoped Sol and Calum got the exact time in history, or they were all screwed. Tom put his faith in them and the artefact, it had to be precise, no margin for error.

The universe could not take much more, it was ripping itself apart, and they, as mere mortals were expected to put it right.

The universe silently urged them on.

Tom and his friends desperately needed to get the job done and go home to their families, beyond that nothing else mattered. But if they couldn't correct the actions that started the collapse of the universe, the integrity of existence would be destroyed, and they would have no home to go back to; that's of course if they survived themselves. Tom knew the consequences, much of it he kept to himself, not wanting to burden the others.

"Who is the best one to explain how you all arrived here and what's happening right now?" asked Tom, "I need as much information as possible."

"Come to the control section and I'll fill you in" replied Don, "Rol, Hanzon, we'll need you also" he added.

Turning his attention back to Tom he said, “Then perhaps you can explain how you actually got aboard our ship, because that black void, I’m not believing.”With that Don walked off to the control section, he needed to check on the alien warship on their bow, no one was keeping watch it seemed, and it was just too damn quiet out there. He wasn’t entirely sure these strangers could solve their dilemma, they didn’t arrive dressed for the occasion, that much was certain, no weapons, nothing, and his ageing friend supposedly married to one of them. She looked mysteriously like a Clariziane woman and hit like one. She clearly wasn’t; maybe Fisah had a point about the half-breed boy, but it couldn’t be possible. Clarizia never ventured outside their own galaxy and had no interaction with other beings. He would have to watch that strange woman, watch all of them until he knew more about them. Sol may trust them, he had his doubts, at the moment he had no choice but to go along with it.

Tom obliged by going after Don although he had the distinct impression Don just ticked him off for telling lies in school. *What was his problem?* He passed Fisah on the way out still being nursemaided by Cora, his uniform a right bloody mess and he was still bleeding

“What happened to you my friend?” asked Tom in all innocence, wondering if this ship might be a dangerous place to be.

“She broke my nose” was all Fisah would say. He was embarrassed he got floored by a woman, and an alien woman at that. Right then he wasn’t sure what felt worse, his nose throbbing like hell, or that fact that he was hit by a woman.

How was he going to live that down?

At least Cora had some sympathy for him along with a few soothing words. She decided to stay and care for him, and make sure he didn’t get into any more trouble.

Tom stood there for a second and thought, *‘She? Who did he mean?’*Nicolas was right behind Tom and simply said, “Mum.”

"That explains it" said Tom, shaking his head and hoped Niko didn't upset the Clarizianes too much, he needed their help. Space was a lifeline to all living beings, they were all involved, whether they liked it or not.

"Stay here for now Nicolas, Calum you come with me to the controls" said Tom. Best he caught up with Don, he thought, time to start the mission, if only he knew where to begin.

Nely and Alec stayed back for now, they weren't needed just yet. They were actually more interested in comparing notes with the Clarizianes about their space travels and the route they took to arrive in that sector. They didn't get a positive answer, simply because the pilots had little knowledge of this universe and with so much disruption going on they weren't sure of anything. It was however good to talk to different beings after so long being isolated from the universe in their paradise world. Nely likened it to a day out and was glad he came now. Alec was also enjoying the attention of Sal and Ariel who both obviously took a fancy to his good looks and rather deep masculine voice. He in turn enjoyed the female company, he wasn't going to say no. The alien women weren't that bad looking, and Niko looked very similar now. It was nice to feel wanted, he never got the chance before; he spent his whole life keeping Nely out of trouble. Now Nely had Carol, he was left alone. Utopia wasn't bad, but it would be nice to share it with someone.

Niko smiled at Alec getting all the attention, she then thought she better check on Fisah, she did give him one hell of a thump. She didn't want to hold a grudge with Sol's friends, it wasn't exactly a good start to the introductions. Fisah wasn't so happy with her getting up close.

"Don't touch my nose" he yelled, scared she might deck him again.

"Oh stop whinging you baby and let me see. I am a doctor as well."

Fisah was in too much pain to argue. Cora held his hand tight while Niko examined him, before finishing what Sol started. At least then the nose would have a chance to heal in the right position. Fisah was screaming with pain, then it subsided. She must have got lucky.

"Are you all doctors?" Cora asked, she spoke softly, having a quiet tone to her voice, although she wasn't sure about Niko yet but for some reason liked her manner, despite hitting Fisah.

"No, we're not, just Sol and me" replied Niko.

"Forgive me but what species are you?" Cora decided to ask, someone had to.

"I'm human, but I do have Clariziane DNA now, that's why I look the way I am" said Niko then turned back to Fisah.

"You're going to be fine, Fisah isn't it? Just watch your mouth in future, okay?"Fisah nodded, he wasn't saying another word for a while. It was safer that way.

Stella and Nicolas sat together, eager to know everything about each other, to suddenly have a new family meant so much to both of them. Ariel watched and listened, she particularly wanted to hear how Sol managed to have a family in the first place. One or two curious pilots were of the same mind, some not able to get their head round the fact. Niko also sat down to talk, everyone had questions. It was time for explanations and the reason for their abrupt arrival.

Nely left Alec with the women, not sure he'd be safe, but he gave them space. Getting comfortable for a while seemed the best option, leaving the important stuff to Tom, Sol and Calum, confident they would work something out with Don. It appeared both parties were happy to have company, even alien company was better than nothing; but no one let their guard down just in case. The strangers appearance was to say the least a little bizarre, but they seemed to know what they were doing.

Tom explained to Don if they could restore the universe to its original state there was a chance of going home, except neither the Clarizianes nor the Utopians had a home in this universe to go back to. Now the Clarizianes had found Sol they had to decide where to go, what direction to take. It was a major problem.

*

'Don't lose faith now mortals'

The universe was close to cracking under the pressure. It didn't know yet whether to forgive the Clarizianes for violating the natural law of the cosmos, they broke the rules and should have stayed put in their universe. Now it depended on their ability to succeed with the Utopians, work together and complete the mission.

They better be quick.

Time was running out.

*

In the control section Tom and Sol were getting a crash course of the ships workings. At the same time Don briefed them on what was happening in the galaxy. There was tremendous upheaval, space and time out of sync with each other. Tom expected as much having experienced it all before. The problem hadn't gone away. Don admitted he didn't understand what the universe was doing to itself. Tom had to agree. He was already feeling edgy being there, knowing this system was once home. He felt anger rise up inside, this was not a good place to be. For now he thought it best to keep their identity under wraps, he didn't want to alert Earth authorities to their whereabouts. It was hard to suppress his emotions, suddenly the face of his one-time friend flashed across his mind, he hadn't thought of Cal in a very long time. Earth had a lot to answer for, this wasn't the time to lose control.

Checking the data the pilots had collected Tom became aware the spatial disturbances had altered the configuration of stars, the whole galaxy was out of sync with space and time, now one of the outer planets was off course and careering who knows where. He was seriously worried they were too late to prevent a major catastrophe. Secretly he wasn't bothered about Earth, there was no love lost there but still he felt an obligation to try and save the people there; save the galaxy from destroying itself. The universe was not helping itself, it couldn't. its very existence was in the hands of mere mortals. The chosen ones had to fulfil their destiny. Tom realised these were desperate times, it didn't make his job any easier.

The pressure was on.

Looking out the porthole Tom recognised the warship sitting on the bow staring back at them, a presence he found very unwelcome. Now his job was made a whole lot worse. Don interrupted his trail of thought as he watched out the porthole.

"We can't understand why they haven't fired on us yet, the ship looks pretty aggressive, don't you think, and there are more of them in this sector" said Don. Tom thought it strange too, the Cynturians were not known to be patient. They were ruthless murdering barbarians. To Don's sheer astonishment Tom declared he knew who they were, and they were trouble.

"Cynturian warships Don, and if, like you say there are more, we have a big problem." Tom shook his head, puzzled by their presence in this system, wondering *if they were not the target, then who was?* Sol sensed Tom's anguish, it was another hurdle they had to deal with, he was just as concerned.

Without warning Xander appeared in the control section floating mid-air, along with JT and Po, having heard the dreaded Cynturians were back. Xander was furious he had to face them again. *Did they not learn their lesson before?* But it seemed the Avaans sudden appearance made Rol fall out of his control seat, Hanzon back-pedalled towards the exit. Sol sniggered as Don next to him nearly staggered into him. He panicked, *who else was going to turn up?* It was now standing room only. These little creatures were definitely not on the guest list. Tiny aliens floating in the air was disturbing enough, coming out of nowhere was terrifying. Rol climbed back into his seat with a worried look, *did these aliens pose more of a threat than the aliens outside?* Now they were inside the ship and too close for comfort.

"What the hell is going on? Someone get this thing out of my face" yelled Rol.

Xander wasn't happy with his remark and glared at him menacingly. Rol sank back in his seat, that weird looking eye out on a stalk was penetrating his brain. *Why was the other one looking down at the floor?* He froze for a moment. Sol reassured his friends, "It's okay guys, these are our friends too, they are here to help" he said.

Hanzon edged forward, not sure what to make of them. Tom smiled, relieved they exited the portal safely. He was pleased and should have known Xander would pull a stunt like that, he couldn't help himself. Xander turned to Tom, the alien could wait until later.

"Just Tom, what do we do now? You know Cynturians will never give up."

There was genuine concern in his voice, he was fearful what they were up to. He floated close to Tom and settled on the control panel right next to the red button. Rol was panicking even more, watching those tiny feet edging closer and closer. One more step and he would have to swat him away.

"We have to weigh up our options first Xander, there are other matters to deal with" said Tom, "The Cynturians can wait, if they were going to fire, they would surely have done so by now." That was one fact Tom was certain of, even if he didn't understand why. Bumping into the Cynturians was a complication they didn't need.

Rol, still squirming in his seat spoke up, there was something he had to mention.

"Sorry, did you just call this little guy, whatever he – it is, did you call him Xander?"

"Yes, why?" asked Tom.

"Yes, I'd like to hear this also" said Xander, still giving Rol the evil eye, he didn't like his manner.

"Shut up Xander. Go ahead, what do you know?" Tom asked, his curiosity racing at that point.

Rol proceeded to explain while watching where Xander was putting his feet, that red button was making him sweat.

"Well, we picked up several conversations from that alien ship. They seemed to know your friend here. Don't ask me how, but apparently they have been searching for someone called Xander who has eyes out on stalks, he fits the description."

Xander was perplexed. "Why would they be looking for me Just Tom?"

"I'm guessing revenge Xander, you did after all kill their emperor" said Tom, they obviously had long memories.

"Him?" questioned Rol. "No way!"

"There is a hefty price on his head" added Don, "I'm afraid we're all in danger if they find out he's aboard."

Don was concerned for the safety of his crew, now he didn't know which intruders to be more wary of. This was getting tricky.

"Don't worry my friend, we will be fine, trust me, and Xander is more capable of looking after himself" said Sol, putting a hand on Don's shoulder to reassure him.

"He has more brains in his little finger than you got in your whole body Don, we need him" said Tom.Xander wasn't so sure, "Just Tom, my brains are not in my little finger."

Tom smirked, "He also can't count, but he is our friend, don't ever try and lay a hand on him. You will have to go through me first."

Tom saw the way Rol looked at him, a mixture of terror and contempt, a dangerous combination Tom thought. Xander was puffed up, he had friends, he had a bodyguard, and apparently brains. He looked at his little fingers wondering about them, before floating up and hovering over the red button. Rol sat upright; he had to distract him.

"So, how did you get the wonky eye? Or shouldn't I ask?" Rol failed to see anyone that size could be a threat. Xander was suddenly in his face, angry he had asked.

"If you think my wonky eye is bad, you should have seen the other guy" he sniggered devilishly in Rol's face then stuck his tongue out.

"Please tell me he's joking, right?" Rol cowered back, quaking in his boots, he was a little squirt, yet he made Rol feel petrified to move.

"Xander, back off, stop winding him up" said Tom and reached out to grab him by his dungaree straps, he was a right mischief maker.

"Sorry guys, he really is harmless, you'll get used to him" said Sol.

"Yes, I'm a class act" said Xander proudly, he had to live up to his reputation. He joined JT and Po on Tom's shoulders pushing JT over, still giving Rol that evil look, just to wind him up a bit more. Rol didn't know what to make of him, this was one alien he was not going to get used to in a hurry. At least he was away from the red button for now. He felt relief if nothing else.

*

The universe was still watching, silently urging them on, hoping Tom would make the right call. More trouble was on the way, events it had no control over, events that would escalate the problems it faced. Tom had the biggest decision of his life to make, he would have to make it against his better judgement. The universe was getting sick of aliens from the parallel universe invading its space, causing so much disruption.

It had to stop.

CHAPTER EIGHTEEN

Being in the galaxy of his home planet made Tom very uncomfortable, as they had travelled back in time there was a good chance the federation were still looking for them. Niko said she was also having feelings for Earth, but they were not good ones. It was best they didn't outstay their welcome. Nely and Alec more or less blocked out all memories of home a long time ago. Earth meant nothing to them now. Tom understood what his friends were saying, it didn't stop him having jitters just thinking about it. He was starting to miss his family; in reality he had only left Utopia less than an hour ago. It felt like a lifetime. He was however keen to get a move on, complete the mission successfully and go home.

The universe deemed it was his destiny to fulfil his duty to save all life in the cosmos. At that point he had no idea of the significance, yet for the last fifteen years he had the belief this was why he was saved from the crash.

Now Tom had to stand tall and show strong leadership, he needed a clear head to instruct the others on exactly what they had to do – once he found out what it was they had to do. The artefact remained silent, giving out no clues to Tom or Sol, even Calum made several unsuccessful attempts to activate it in the hopes the answers would come. Nely made the stupid comment it might be broken. Alec soon gave him a dig in the ribs. He wasn't helping the situation, or the morale. Xander was on hand to give his advice but as usual he wasn't much help, even his sixth sense was letting him down.

There was an even bigger problem to deal with, timeline fluctuations that occurred earlier made it virtually impossible to know precisely how much time they had, even a calculated guess at this stage could prove fatal. Tom felt they had failed before they started. With both crews gathered together, everyone was anxious to hear what Tom had to say. Don allowed him to be elected leader for this mystery mission, the aliens appeared to know more about what was happening in the universe, but Tom still hadn't explained the black void they came through to board the ship. He was sceptical and remained wary, giving strangers control over their ship and the crew hadn't been part of the plan. The weird object Sol was holding was worrying him, *how did he let all this happen, it was a living nightmare, and they were stuck in it.*

Tom pointed out to the Clarizianes he was once a science officer and knew about the crumbling universe, more than the Clarizianes could ever know, but he insisted both parties had to work together when the time came. The burden on Tom to carry them through this crisis was tremendous, if his worried thoughts weren't enough he had the added distraction of Xander sitting cross-legged on his shoulder, tugging at his ear, JT and Po messing about on his other shoulder, *how could he concentrate on the matter in hand?* Whenever Xander sat cross-legged, he liked to look important, intelligent even. He was neither, in the same boat as Tom.

As yet Tom had not formulated a plan, he still wasn't certain why the artefact instructed them to the Clariziane ship. Yes, they had to rescue Sol's friends, but Tom felt there was more to it than that. *Why couldn't the artefact speak to him? Were the Clarizianes part of the plan all along?* He was a bit hazy in his head. He had no clue what to do with the Clarizianes, and there was quite a few of them. They couldn't stay in this universe, that much was certain.

Hanging around, kicking his heals playing for time, time they really didn't have to spare; Tom hoped beyond hope a sign would emerge from the artefact, anything, even one of those strange messages that frequently ran across his brain, something to tell him he was on the right track. Sol and Calum were still having no luck with the artefact.

They were missing a vital detail.

Maybe the Clarizianes were holding the clue, something they failed to mention, something they didn't realise was important.

"Okay everyone, time is running out, it may already be too late. I need answers" declared Tom abruptly. He stood among the Clarizianes looking round at them, one by one.

"I know we have to do something before any more disturbances in the universe. We are missing a piece of information that could solve our problems."

There were nods of agreement, but no answers. Rol at that point was more concerned with that damn alien warship on their bow, it was giving him a bad feeling about the whole set up.

*Why don't they do something? Or maybe it simply belonged to Sol's friends, a*nd that thought scared him even more. He put his concerns to Tom to see what his reaction would be, he hoped at least he would take action to allay their fears. Sol's friends, in his opinion were weird, strange creatures. If the warship wasn't theirs, *how did they know about its identity?*

Were they the ones holding something back?

"Look Rol, I know you are afraid of us, but please trust us. If the Cynturians were going to fire they would have done so by now. We'll deal with them later" said Tom.

"Or I will Just Tom, say the word and I'll fix them up good and proper this time" said Xander swinging his good eye in Tom's face.

"Later Xander, okay."

"Okay" replied Xander disappointed, but he was already hatching a plan. They would not bother anyone else when he finished with them.

Rol and some of his fellow pilots started having doubts about Xander's ability, probably his size didn't give them much confidence. The aliens put a lot of faith in him, Rol thought that rather dangerous. Xander caught a strange look in Rol's eyes, he was sceptical. All the Clarizianes had piercing black eyes, but Xander could tell the difference, his sixth sense was tingling, trouble was brewing. Just Tom had to find a solution quickly before he lost control of the situation. The immense brain power he inherited from his mentor Kanon Garg would not help against a rebellion. Just Tom needed help, more than he realised. JT and Po were playing the fool and teasing the Clarizianes much to Tom's annoyance. After all these years it was too late to say anything. They wouldn't change.

The Clarizianes would need a lot more convincing to put their trust in a bunch of tiny misfits, strange weird aliens even more strange than Sol's friends. Don tried to assist, he continued to explain further, how they arrived in this galaxy, about hiding behind one of the outer planets to give them time to assess their options, except time ran out, and that was when Tom and his friends abruptly appeared out of nowhere, and he was still trying to fathom that bit out. He continued, saying the planet got caught in a spatial distortion and careered off course, heading for another planet in the system he surmised. They witnessed the misalignment of several distant star systems. Everything in this universe was wrong, distorted beyond recognition and it wasn't getting any better. There was no way of navigating their way out, the Clarizianes were stranded there, unable to understand what was happening around them. However Tom did know, he had experienced the same a very long time ago. The past trauma was something he would never fully forget. Returning to the universe in the past brought it flooding back, all the painful memories, the lost lives. He couldn't shut those thoughts out completely. Utopia was a good healer, coming back opened old wounds.

Hearing what Don had to say, Tom knew which planet had been displaced. It wasn't good news whichever way he looked at it. He asked if one of the pilots could compute its new trajectory, he wanted to see what they were up against. The news got worse. Rol was quick to the control seat; he had more experience with the controls having spent much of his time there. Secretly he wanted to keep his eye on the little squirt sitting on Tom's shoulder. He obliged Tom by showing the new flight path. Uranus was now being pulled towards Saturn which had also shifted orbit. Two giant planets colliding would cause a massive impact and a major catastrophe for this system. If space debris made its way to Earth's gravitational pull, it would be raining meteors for months, if not years. Earth would not be able to sustain a prolonged bombardment without consequences. Tom feared they were already too late for whatever the end mission was to be. The artefact directed them to this particular place and time in history, it had to be right. They made no mistake with their calculations. It seemed likely now this galaxy could be wiped out, including Earth, all because of outsiders from the parallel universe, and not just the Clarizianes. Tom was stunned. *Could it actually get any worse?* He hated Earth authorities, but he didn't want this to happen. He had no power to stop it. Xander felt his pain, his heart was breaking also for his friend.

*

The universe was also feeling the pressure.

'Stay with it Tom, don't give up. The answers will come.

*

Checking on the rest of the data Rol pointed out to Tom another smaller planet which so far appeared to maintain its original orbit, the only constant in this disrupted system, and the only inhabited planet. He zoomed in so Tom got a closer look.

"Thank you Rol, I do know the planet, it's called Earth. I was born there." Tom was choked up for a second, he had terrible misgivings about going there, it certainly wasn't on his bucket list of places to visit. Earth was a dangerous place. He wondered if they had any idea what was heading their way. Then again probably not, he guessed, not unless they took their heads out of the sand and realised they were not the most intelligent beings in the universe, not anymore. They lost the top spot when they ordered the destruction of Retriever-2 and its entire crew. Earth authorities lost all credibility after that.

"Better tell Tom about the two alien prisoners being held there" said Don, he wasn't sure it was relevant, he only just remembered.

"Prisoners?" uttered Tom, could things get any more complicated. *What the hell were aliens doing on Earth?*

"Yeh well, apparently two unknown aliens are due to stand trial for multiple crimes, no details yet. But I managed to pick up several other communications, there's complete anarchy on the planet, no ruling government to speak of, nothing to suggest any kind of law and order. To top it all they are only interested in prosecuting these two aliens for just about every crime in the book."

"What the hell –" Tom was shocked. Earth had already gone to pieces, but why? It didn't make sense. Then the sign he'd been waiting for flashed across his brain.

"Rol –" suddenly he was interrupted.

"Tom, the artefact –" called out Sol rushing to his side.

"The artefact, it came to life, I know what we have to do."

"So do I, so do I" replied Tom, dreading the prospect, and the fact Earth was involved.

"Something is going to happen dad, yes?" said Calum, arriving seconds after Sol.

"Yes son, this is it, time for action."

The final destination was indeed Earth, Tom didn't want it to be, but whoever those aliens were, he was certain they shouldn't be there. Maybe they were contributing to the imbalance in the universe all along. He had no choice but to go there. His next task he didn't want to do either, deliver more bad news to the Clarizianes, they had been through enough. Deciding to come straight out with it was the only way.

"I'm sorry Don, Rol, to be the bearer of bad news, but you and the rest of your crew are in the wrong universe –"

"Tell us something we don't know" interrupted Rol rather defensively, of course they were in the wrong universe, but it wasn't their fault entirely. Tom ignored Rol's manner; he did however understand it.

"Your presence here and that of those two alien prisoners on Earth are creating the imbalance that is tearing the universe apart. You have to leave."

"What?" Don was staggered, he froze on the spot, open-mouthed wondering if he heard right, or was Tom jerking his leg? *Did he really think they wanted to stay here?*

"Where do you expect us to go?" asked Rol, "we have no home now."

"Anywhere is better than this universe the way its behaving" Hanzon put in his point of view.

Sol remained quiet, he felt for his friends, this was hard on them.

"I'm sorry guys, but if we are to put things right, stop the spatial distortions, the timeline inaccuracies and finally find a way to seal the rifts permanently, perhaps the universe will recover, well this universe anyway. You all have to return to the parallel universe. Seek out a new life." Tom was sincere, but his words were brutal to hear.

"And what about you? What about Sol?" asked Don, finally able to speak.

Tom spoke, "Sol, that's for you to answer my friend."

Sol turned to his friends, he was glad to see them again, but it had to be a short-lived reunion. "I have a life elsewhere, a family, I can't stay with you. Besides we belong in the future, we have to go back."

"Well, thanks a bunch pal, at least we know what side you're on." Don didn't disguise the fact he was angry with his friend. None of it was their fault, someone somewhere was screwing them over.

Tom was adamant they had to go; it was the only solution he could think of.Remembering the huge crack in the sky over Utopia, he had no choice but to send the Clarizianes back. If the problem wasn't sorted he would have no home to go back to either. He left friends, family, all were relying on him and Sol to mend their world. Seeing Simone in tears when he left broke his heart, that image would live with him always. It was the hardest the decision of his life.

"Okay one-time mister science officer, tell us what we're supposed to do to get out of this mess" said Rol, "we only came in search of our friend, now we find he's been living in the future with another life we know nothing about. Tell us, how is that fair?" Rol wanted to be angry, right then he was upset with Sol, the pilots risked their lives in search of him. None of it was fair, maybe he should get angry and swat that little squirt off Tom's shoulder. It wouldn't solve the problem, but it would make him feel better. Then he worried where the other two were, for all he knew they could be hiding in plain sight, invisible right in front of him. That was a scary thought.

Don was worried about the whole situation, Sol didn't answer him, he was obviously annoyed at the way he spoke to him. The ultimatum was hard to swallow, he couldn't see how they would survive something they didn't understand, and why was it alright for Sol to stay in this universe, and not them? There was more to the aliens than they were letting on. He was suspicious of them, he had no real evidence, just a gut feeling. It wasn't enough to accuse them of anything. He so wanted to be wrong for his friends sake, if he didn't push the doubts out of his head he was sure of a meltdown.

"I can see you're all angry, I would be too in your shoes, we have to deal with the facts as we see them." Tom wasn't convincing them, he could see that. Xander fidgeting about on his shoulder was unusually quiet, the little guy had no answers either.

"So, changing the subject, do we go to this third planet you call Earth, or not?" asked Rol, all the while scanning the control section for any movement, visible or otherwise, he was dying to know where those two missing little squirts were. If they got near that red button he was going to flatten them whatever the cost.

Hanzon, still holding back, not really wanting to get involved, was distressed by what he was hearing. Being told to leave this universe wasn't sitting well with him either. Nobody liked being ordered about, not on their own ship anyway – a purloined ship but that was a minor detail, it was still theirs.

Tom looked at Sol and Calum, he knew the answer to Rol's question, it was hard to believe it had come down to this. Sol nodded; it was time.

"Well, that planet is my home, but we aren't exactly welcome there anymore" said Tom with sadness in his eyes.

"What did you do that was so bad?" asked Rol, "or shouldn't I ask that?"

"You don't want to know my friend" replied Tom. It was too complicated to explain, and even more difficult thinking about it. Sometimes it was good to bury the past, digging it up was more painful than the Clarizianes could ever imagine. Tom turned to Sol again, it was time for action.

"Sol, can you and Don select some of your friends who would be willing to go to Earth, we are going to rescue those prisoners."

"Yes!" exclaimed Rol, punching the air. "That's one thing we can agree on" he said.

"Don, do you have any weapons on your ship?" asked Tom.

He hoped not to use violence, whatever the situation they might need protection. He had half a plan, the rest he would make up as and when. Right now he needed to get Don onside, he wasn't buying any of it, even Xander thought the same and whispered in his ear to say as much. Nobody said the mission was going to be easy, but he didn't expect this much resentment.

The Utopians were there to help. Perhaps Sol would be better to talk him round.

*

After a short heated discussion involving both the Clarizianes and Utopians, it was soon clear the next course of action, the final part of the mission. It meant working together, not that the Clarizianes understood the details entirely. Don was still reluctant but after a heart-to-heart with Sol, he went along with the plan, and he did apologise for his outburst. He trusted Sol implicitly, he always did. If he was honest with himself, Sol's friends weren't really hostile, strange alien creatures, but not hostile. Maybe he allowed his doubts and fears to run riot in his head.

The prolonged journey across two universes had taken its toll, he was tired, mentally and physically. He had no time to dwell on his thoughts and inner feelings, not after Rol announced more trouble.

"We got company guys" he called out loudly, still at his post maintaining a vigil at the controls while the others got on with their discussions. The control section was his baby, having mastered the mechanics of alien technology better than anyone else. Don rushed to the front immediately with Hanzon, the others soon followed behind. Tom was equally swift, making sure Sol and Calum were with him. Xander whizzed past all of them, his sixth sense was tingling, warning him danger was imminent.

Everyone feared another Cynturian warship, it wasn't. It was worse.

"Not them again!" said Hanzon, "please let me use the red button" he pleaded loudly. His voice carried down the corridors, bringing everyone to the front as soon as they heard the words '*red button.*'

"Easy Hanzon, don't be hasty, we all agreed" said Rol. He made sure that button was safe from itchy fingers, and especially when Xander landed on the control panel, he needed an extra pair of eyes. That little squirt was dangerous to have around.

"Who are they Don? I take it you've had dealings with them before?" enquired Tom, it wasn't a spaceship he recognised, no markings on the hull either.

"Yes, we bumped into them a while back. It appears we stole their ship, and they want it back. They call themselves Kangans, I believe" replied Don, his stress levels hit the roof now they had two alien ships alongside, both wanting to annihilate them. He sank into a vacant seat, suddenly he lost all confidence in his own ability to deal with the fallout – *'could it get any worse?'* he asked himself. Sol put a hand on his shoulder, "Stay with it my friend, we can deal with it."

"Kangans?" questioned Tom, that was a name he hadn't heard in a very long time, they were far away from home. *What could they possibly want now?* He assumed they had violated the universal law and forced their way through the space time continuum into this universe, intent on causing more trouble no doubt. Blowing up their planet obviously didn't stop them. They had to be part of the reason of the spatial upheaval.

"Do you know them Tom?" asked Rol.

"Yes, well Kangis-3 actually, an artificial planet we destroyed, or rather Xander did. I guess they have be connected."

"Him again!" muttered Rol, everything seemed to revolve round that little squirt. Tom gave him a look that said, *'watch your mouth.'*

"Sorry" he averted his eyes back to the monitor, promising himself to stay out of trouble.

The Kangan ship was a complication Tom didn't anticipate. They were going to add to the problem.

"Tell me Don, what is the red button?" asked Tom, it seemed significant to them.Rol pointed to it on the panel as Don explained. "We threatened to use it on the Kangans if they didn't back off. I guess they're back to try again."

"We think it's a deadly weapon of some kind, so we're reluctant to try it out" Rol added.

"I'm not" said Hanzon, "I wanted to use it all along."

"Hanzon, go and chat to my friend Nely, I have a feeling you two will get along rather well" said Tom. He sounded so much like Nely they were bound to hit it off.

"I'm not sure I want to be ordered about by an alien, thank you very much" said Hanzon rather indignantly.

"Hanzon, go!" snapped Don, he was no use at the moment. Hanzon left in a huff, nobody ever listened to him, he felt put out and went to seek solace in the food supplies.

"Sorry Don, I didn't mean to interfere with your crew, it's not my place" said Tom, very apologetic.

"Don't worry about Hanzon, he'll get over it."

"He hasn't changed then" said Sol with a smile. Hanzon was always the sensitive one. Then Sol realised it wasn't fifteen years since they were all together, going back in time really screws up one's memories.

Xander was getting curious, he moved closer to the red button, wanting to study it. His sixth sense was saying there was more to it than the Clarizianes would ever realise.

"You get any closer pal, and I'll knock you for six" said Rol raising his voice, he didn't like the way Xander roamed so freely about the ship, and he still hadn't seen the other two yet. Probably up to no good he guessed. He was agitated the little squirt was getting away doing what he liked, then suddenly he realised he should have kept his mouth shut.

"You will never lay a hand on him, understood PAL!" Tom was angered and equally loud, but to ease the tension he picked Xander up, "Stay with me Xander, okay."

"Okay Just Tom" said Xander, swinging his eye menacingly at Rol. He was definitely getting the evil stare.

"Alright, alright, I'm sorry, really, but he makes me nervous."

"Cool it Rol" said Sol, "let's get down to the matter in hand."

"Dad, the artefact is going crazy, I think it's telling us to begin the sequence" said Calum, holding it up so everyone could see the glowing flashing lights. Sol had to hand the artefact to Calum earlier so he could concentrate on his friends, tempers were a little frayed to say the least. The artefact had obviously connected with Calum and activated itself.

"Okay son, start your calculations but don't finalise it just yet" said Tom, he needed more details before they advanced to Earth, their final destination.

"Now perhaps would be a good time to tell me how you knew where to find us, then how you actually got onboard our ship, then what's that strange gadget the boy is playing with?" Don was desperate for answers because it was bugging him why the ships early warning siren didn't go off.

"Don my friend, I'll leave that to Sol, but later" said Tom, besides they would find out soon enough.

Returning to the monitor again, they all wondered which of the two alien ships would be the first to make a move, it was suspiciously quiet out there. Rol continued to check incoming data, when another disturbance was detected.

"Spatial distortion just occurred, and the timeline just jumped three weeks into the past, before shooting forward two months. Don, I – I'm not sure how much of this I can handle, it's way above my pay grade. I don't understand it. We have no idea of the exact date now." Rol was getting out of his depth, confused with the events unfolding. He was nervous on several levels. Monitoring was one thing, watching his life go backwards and then forward was just shredding his brains. He was sure he could handle the alien ship, that was a piece of cake. It was outside in space that was the problem. Travelling for so long, painstakingly negotiating the pitfalls of a fractured universe was enough to send him crazy.

Don could see Rol was struggling with the stress, he himself felt the pressure too, *why else would he start to doubt Sol's friends when they only came to help*. It was just their manner of entrance that freaked him out. Tom put a hand on Rol's shoulder, he couldn't hold a grudge, he needed him in the plan.

"Stay with it Rol, you're doing a brilliant job. Now, tell me where this spatial disturbance occurred, don't worry about the timeline."

"That's easy for you to say" answered Rol nervously, not because of what Tom said, but that little squirt just vanished into thin air and Tom never even flinched. Now there were three of them on the loose, they could be anywhere.

"Okay, I'll zoom in to show you, it's close to the planet you called home. a ring of atomic particles orbiting the outer magnetic field just lost cohesion and are now plummeting towards the planet.

"Oh, shit!" Tom realised they had even less time than he would have liked. This was wrong, *why was the universe punishing them so harshly?*

"Is it bad news?" asked Don.

"Eh, yeh" he muttered, that was the Van Allen belts slipping out of orbit. Eventually Earth's gravitational pull would suck the particles in. The whole solar system was in danger of collapse.

"We have no time left guys –" announced Tom, "It's now or never, we have to act before it's too late, it might already be."

He then realised Xander was gone. "Xander where are you?" he called out.

"Right here Just Tom" replied Xander appearing on the control panel in front of Rol where he'd been all the time, listening, and so he could study the red button in detail.

Rol fell out of his seat again, no way was he ever going to get used the squirt, it was too creepy. Xander on the other hand had the chance to listen to many conversations. The Clarizianes were an interesting bunch of misfits, he could have so much fun with them.

Rol got back in his seat, even Don was having a laugh at his expense, Xander was sniggering, that will teach him not to make threats towards him. Even Tom had to smile, he knew what he was like.

"Xander, when you're finished playing the fool, can you check out the inner workings of that red button everyone is afraid of. See if we can use it to our advantage" said Tom.

"NO!" screamed Rol, "He can't touch it."

Sol looked up from the artefact. "Rol, back off, Tom and Xander will find the solutions."

"This sequence next I believe Sol" said Calum.

"Yes continue" said Sol, they were nearly there.

"Just like old times Just Tom, I believe I know what to do. I will check it out immediately." In a flash he was gone, vanished inside the control panel, hoping there was enough space for him to move about freely. If there was a suitable solution he would find it.

"Bloody cables!" came a tiny voice from inside the panelling right at Rol's feet.

"Right, you are letting that one-eyed little squirt loose inside our controls where the red button is, the exact button we've been avoiding for months." Rol was not comfortable hearing Xander shuffling around there, stumbling over by the sound of it and muttering something inaudible. Tom leaned over the controls to get right up in Rol's face.

"Just one more thing my friend, mind what you call my buddy, you know what happened to your friend Fisah." Clenching a fist, Tom made it absolutely clear his intentions. Rol had stepped out of line once too often, he'd had enough.

"Sorry, but it's creeping me out, he shouldn't be in there. He doesn't know what he is doing."

"Rol, easy, you have to trust us" Sol said, stepping in again. Don might have to drag him away if he carried on like that.

"Xander does know what he is doing, he has more brains than the rest you of put together, have faith" said Sol.

Tom nodded in agreement and unclenched his fist, he wouldn't have hit him, he wasn't that kind of man but as long as Rol thought otherwise, it was enough. He turned to Don.

"Okay Don, I'm pretty certain our first objective is to rescue those two prisoners, and before Earth gets bombarded by millions of electron and proton particles. It's going to get a bit hairy; we have to be quick about it."

"Agreed" said Don, his crew had a similar idea but didn't know how to go about it. He had a sudden aversion about going to that planet now, it was dangerous. If Tom and his friends were exiled from their home planet, the people there weren't very friendly he guessed.

"Don't know how you plan to do this Tom, I can't wait to find out" said Don.

"I'm not sure we want to know" interrupted Rol, he really wanted out of this nightmare, it wasn't going to end well.

"Be quiet and do your job Rol" said Don, he was definitely going to be a handful.Tom looked straight at Sol and Calum. "Time to use the artefact guys."

"Nearly there dad, all we need is a point of entry, or at least the building they are being kept. I need a point of reference to finalise the sequence."

Calum worked the artefact well, Sol watched his every move, the kid was good.

"Well Rol can you?"

"I can certainly try Don" said Rol, doing his upmost to keep his mind on the job.

"Good, get on with it" said Tom, he had a plan coming together finally. With the Clariziane weapons for protection he was confident of pulling it off even though they were heading into danger like they had never faced. The alternative didn't bear thinking about.

Rol was busy scanning the planet, having one eye on that red button, he was having a hard time concentrating with Xander making so much noise under his feet.

"He isn't going to blow us up, is he?" he asked, worried what was happening in there. "And where are the other two?" Rol didn't like the idea of tiny invisible floating creatures, there was no telling what they were up to.

“Ignore Xander, he has a job to do, you need to hurry up and get that information to us. As for JT and Po, they probably found their way to your food supplies.”It was a sure bet Tom thought, all their own supplies gone already.

“Oh nice, as long as they get their priorities right” mumbled Rol. Tom shook his head, letting it go. He was never going to convince Rol.

The long range scanners zoomed in on Earth, Rol was met with a lot of interference with the instruments, the readouts fluctuated. He guessed the particles heading in the planets direction were blocking the signals. This was harder than he anticipated, he made several adjustments to filter through the interference. Looking at the monitor, all Rol could see was a huge meteor storm on steroids, it was brutal; once it hit the atmosphere there was no telling how much damage it would cause. He did his best, Sol was relying on him for the data; he finally managed to cut through most of the interference, then began to triangulate the prisoners exact position.

“Whoops, wrong one again” came worrying words from Xander. Rol was sweating so much he had to keep wiping his palms on his uniform. It wasn’t the best idea of Tom’s to let Xander loose inside the ships mechanisms. *What was he thinking of?*

Rol couldn’t believe he allowed it to happen.

*

Don followed Sol closely, desperately wanting answers from his friend, this so called rescue mission, the reason for their abrupt arrival. Don wasn’t entirely sure his calls were the sole purpose for the strange visit. It was clear Sol was not the same man anymore. *Just what had the universe and these aliens done to him?* He had so many questions to ask, his head was spinning.

Sol and the boy were deep in concentration with a piece of old wood with lights, it seemed like a game. *How was that going to get them out of this mess they were in?*

"What the hell is that Sol?" he had to ask.

"This is an ancient artefact that came into our possession, it's how we travelled here Don, it's how we will travel to Earth."Immediately Sol went back to the artefact with Calum and continued to work on the sequence until the alignments were all correctly in place. Don stood there stunned into silence.

Did he understand any of that?

Like hell he did.

A few months ago they were simple space pilots, now he wasn't sure of his own name even.

"Sol, I need to –"

"Sorry Don, I have important work to do with Calum. You could check on the crew, make sure they are ready to go."

Then Sol walked away with Calum, eyes glued to the artefact. Don was left behind, gobsmacked, *did he just get snubbed in favour of a kid?*

He wanted answers. He wanted his friend back.

Vital minutes ticked by.

Nely linked up with Hanzon near the dwindling food supplies, surprisingly they really did get along, to the extent of comparing notes of their fellow beings. It pleased Nely to know he wasn't the only downtrodden man in the universe. He felt some empathy for Hanzon; telling him to stand up for himself, although Nely wasn't much good at that himself. Growing up with his best friend, it was always Alec fighting his battles. Now he had Carol in his corner. He told Hanzon about his beautiful family and how he could be himself, and that if he got a wife it would change his life.Hanzon thought *'nice idea'*, but it was unlikely ever to happen now, not the way the universe was crumbling around their ears. They had to get out of this crisis first – alive. They laughed together and wandered round the ship, chatting, food in hand.

Alec was still with his female admirers. He never saw himself getting so attached to a woman, now he had two who wouldn't leave him alone. Clariziane women were so overpowering, but he was enjoying the attention. Unfortunately it would have to stop soon. The mission would take priority. Alec was needed, he didn't know it yet, but he was going to Earth.

Nicolas was getting to know his new family member, Stella was full of stories for him, and Nicolas was the first person she told, that Rol was the one for her, she would agree to marry him, once they got off the ship. For her, having a new cousin was a different level of love, much the same as she felt for Sol, Niko watched on, happy for her son, she was happy to be part of two cultures. Now in the company of several Clariziane women, Elia, Mos, Kat and Cora, who finally left Fisah's side, all quizzing Niko about her appearance, and why she had all the characteristics of a Clariziane woman when she clearly wasn't. They were confused. Niko had a hard job explaining her alien DNA courtesy of Sol and his life-saving devotion. They warmed to her immediately, Kat saying she fought like a true Clariziane woman, that right hook on Fisah was a beauty. Niko was embarrassed; still for a brief time it was nice to relax from the reality of their situation. She sensed that fireworks were about to start. Catching a glimpse of Sol along the corridor, she could see his stress lines quite clearly. The ridges on his forehead deepening, he had a lot of pressure on his shoulders.

Attempting to finalise the end sequence of symbols Sol and Calum were almost there, they were now waiting for the last piece of information from Rol, the entry point to Earth and location of the alien prisoners. Rol couldn't give them the data; he was finding it difficult; in the end he had to ask Tom to help. There was so much interference giving false readouts he wasn't making any progress. Another timeline distortion occurred moments earlier, taking them hours into the future. It messed up the previous calculations he had already computed. Precious time was lost. Sol continued to readjust the sequence on the artefact in another attempt to finalise their own calculations; the artefact would only tell them when the alignment was in place and only then would the portal open.

Having to keep resetting the symbols was getting to Calum, the pressure was on his young shoulders too. If this was what it felt like to be a grown up, he wished he was back on Utopia playing with Annie, Josef and Maria. Now he just wanted to be a kid again. He had to accept he was the chosen one to control the artefact, he couldn't break the circle now. He was glad Sol was there; he couldn't do it alone.

The alien ships made no attempt to make contact or even issue demands, the Kangan ship alongside, only two hundred metres away, and the Cynturian warship on the bow remained constant in their positions, even after another spatial distortion close by, causing more displacement. Several of the natural satellites of Jupiter shifted out of orbit, some finishing up outside the galaxy drifting into oblivion.

*

The universe could not prevent the fallout.

Another of the warships that found itself in Earth's upper atmosphere earlier started to feel the effects of the particles from the Van Allen belts hitting their ship with devastating impact. They assumed, wrongly, they were under attack and fired their weapons in all directions, some hitting the particles which backfired on them in spectacular fashion. A huge explosion ripped through the ship, destroying it completely. Chunks of twisted metal and debris crashed through the stratosphere and plummeted to Earth. The other warships watched on from afar, aware of the events, deeming it an act of aggression from the planet below. They would pay dearly for their actions. Unfortunately the few warships left were stuck in stasis, caught in a spatial flux, the ships could not respond to the controls. Aware of two alien ships in the vicinity was infuriating them, the Cynturians wanted to fight, but without helm control they were powerless, their ships too far across the galaxy to be a threat.

*

Being familiar with the Van Allen belts Tom realised the reason for the static interference. He couldn't believe they had got this far only to be thwarted by a few particles misbehaving in space. The time wasted on this one task was making it hard for them to complete the mission with any degree of success. Sol was already frustrated with the delay; he needed the information urgently.

"Would it help if we tried to manoeuvre closer to the planet?" Rol asked Tom, they were after all sitting far out from the inner planets, he thought their proximity could be a factor.

"I don't think so Rol, keep at it anyway. We need that data" said Tom, who then caught sight of Niko and Nely standing close by. They finished talking with the Clarizianes and were keen to know what progress Tom had made, the waiting about was getting to some of them. Tom's face said it all. They were at a point of no return, effectively screwed if the mission didn't begin soon.

"Anything we can do Tom?" asked Niko, putting a hand on his arm to let him know he was not alone in this awful time. Tom shook his head, not sure what any of them could do.

"Sorry Tom, I know its hard for you. I'm sure your friend here is doing his best" said Niko.

"I am, thank you" said Rol, pleased someone had faith in him. Tom had other matters on his mind.

"Do you know if the volunteers are ready?" he asked, at the same time glancing at Nely.

"Why are you suddenly looking at me when you mention volunteers?" Nely was put out, it seemed everytime volunteers were needed he felt pressured, he always got roped in. It wasn't fair.

"Because you are the go to choice Nely. You and Alec go with the Clarizianes, Sol and Calum will need plenty of support, they will be busy concentrating on the artefact, and make sure you both have weapons."

Nely wasn't so sure about handling weapons again; he suddenly had a dreadful flashback to the last time he was shanghaied into a mission. If he got out of this alive, Carol was going to kill him anyway. His stomach started churning over, he really didn't want to do this.

"It's important Nely, I need you on this mission" pleaded Tom.

"Hell man, the whole bloody universe is falling apart."

He couldn't let the team down.

Nely muttered several expletives under his breath and left to find Alec. It looked like he had no choice.

"Poor Nely" said Niko, she had so much sympathy for him, he was a good man.

"He'll get over it" said Tom, he had faith in his friend. He went back to the monitor to help Rol, still trying to adjust the instruments to allow the long range scanner to cut through the static interference.

Don stepped into the control section seconds later, to see what the hold up was. "What's wrong with your friend who just left?" he asked.

"Nothing, he's fine" said Niko, she never heard words like that before, she guessed Nely forgot she would hear every word, but then Don would have heard as well.

"He just gets a little nervous Don" she added.

"Okay, I hope he can hold it together. Rol, how are you doing?"

"Don't ask." Rol was still struggling to pinpoint the prisoners location; at this rate he might have to guess.

Don turned to Tom. "Then what about our unwanted visitors out there Tom? Because I tell you, dealing with them would be my first choice of action." It seemed Tom and his friends didn't share his concerns about their presence. *Could he really be certain they wouldn't open fire?*

Don had serious doubts over their safety.

"All in hand Don, all in hand, no need to panic my friend."

But Don was panicking.

"Second choice would be getting Xander out from under my feet" chirped in Rol, he was increasingly perturbed by the weird noises going on inside the panelling. He dreaded what the little squirt was doing.

Tom ignored his remark, Xander would take as long as he needed.

A very impatient Sol entered the control section in search of good news. Surely Rol had done his job by now. He needed that final piece of information.

"Hi Sol, how are you and Calum doing?" asked Tom, he too was hoping to hear good news. He had an awful feeling time had already run out for them. The universe was in such bad shape he feared they had little chance of saving it. He was certain it would take more than superglue this time. The consequences he didn't want to think about. He kept a mental picture of Simone and his beautiful daughter Annie in his head, the one thing keeping him going.

"Just about there Tom, I've managed to calculate a time differential to go back just before the planet is bombarded by those particles, I'm waiting on Rol now for the location, only then can we complete the sequence, activate the portal and go."

"That's brilliant Sol, well done" said Tom, at least it was some good news.

"Thank your son, he's been the real brains, a great help to the mission. He should accompany us to the surface. I believe he will be needed. The artefact works better with two brains."

It was sucker punch for Tom, he was hoping to keep Calum safe by leaving him aboard the ship. This mission was more dangerous than the first one, he was reluctant to allow it, but in his heart he knew Sol was right. He himself needed to stay on the ship and hold everything together, direct operations, something he felt he was best suited to.

Calum appeared alongside Sol, with the artefact in hand, half the lights lit up, waiting for the final symbol.

"Dad, you know I have to go with Sol. I did the first mission okay, didn't I?"

Tom sighed; he really didn't have a choice if the mission was going to succeed.

"I can do this dad."

Tom nodded reluctantly; unhappy his son was heading into danger. He had to trust Calum, trust Sol to look after him.

Sol turned to Niko. "I can't take you my darling, you must stay with Nicolas. I promise we will be only minutes."

Niko wasn't happy either, she promised herself they would never be parted again. Tears started.

"I'm sorry, after this I will always be by your side." Sol kissed his wife and wiped her cheeks.

"You get back safe, or else" her piercing blue eye glared up at him, it meant only one thing.

"Yes, my dear." The one human phrase he knew and when to use it.

"Tom –" called out Rol, "we have another problem" and it wasn't Xander under his feet.

"What is it?"

"Another spatial displacement just occurred, there was a single satellite orbiting your home planet a second ago – it's gone."

Tom didn't think his heart could sink any lower, it just did. Niko gasped in disbelief.

"Tom, Earth cannot survive without the moon. Is there nothing we can do?" she pleaded. It was the worst possible news at this perilous time.

"Like what Niko, we can't exactly go looking for it, besides, Earth already has other problems being pounded by millions of particles." Tom rubbed his hands over his face, he was tired, hungry and no solution to the ongoing crisis. The whole matter was totally out of control, the universe was breaking up, rifts opening up everywhere, the timeline in complete confusion with itself. He started to doubt himself, questioned whether it would be better just to give up.

Was any of it worth saving?

*

'Don't give up Tom.' The universe put its trust in him as the chosen one, he had to complete the task with Sol and Calum. He would succeed if he just had belief in himself. Life was important, it was the very essence of existence across the cosmos. Without structure there would be no life, no existence, no universe.

'Tom – it is time for redemption – complete the task.'

*

Slapping himself in the face brought Tom back to reality, he thought about a bucket of cold water, only there wasn't one around.

"Rol, any luck yet?" asked Sol impatiently. Earth was being pummelled from the skies, very little would be left in a few hours' time, and the moon off who knows where, the effects were having repercussions across space. Any more delay those prisoners would be the least of they worries.

"Almost there Sol, you be ready when I say." Rol made the decision that a calculated guess was better than no guess at all. Time had run out; they had to move now.

Sol turned to Niko, he was heartbroken he couldn't take her with him, the mission was dangerous enough without worrying about his wife getting hurt. She would be safe on the ship. Luckily she had calmed down slightly, realising it was the right decision.

"You better go then my darling; just remember I will be here waiting for you. I love you." She had tears pricking her the back of her eyes, trying to hold them back until Sol was gone. Sol kissed her again, then turned round and hugged Tom.

"Take care of my family, won't you."

"Sure thing my friend, you take care of my son, and we'll see you in a few minutes from now."

It was hard to let go, this was the biggest most important thing any of them had ever done. They hoped the universe would soon be back to normal, and that it was grateful for what they were about to do.

*

'I AM.'

*

"Okay Sol, I've done the best I can, here are the co-ordinates you require." Rol interrupted the goodbyes, he sensed the genuine warmth between Sol and his wife, and his alien friend. It was tough on them.

"Okay my friend, go" said Tom, "go before I start with the waterworks. I instructed Nely and Alec to go as well. You will have all the support you need."

Nicolas and Calum were also saying their goodbyes, they grew up together, almost as brothers. The goodbyes felt almost permanent; they were praying silently they would see each other very soon. Yet there was that horrible doubt hanging over them – going into the unknown and never coming back.

"Time to go" said Calum, "see you on the other side."

"Likewise buddy" said Nicolas. He so wanted to go on the mission with his dad, prove he was a man, but he knew his mum would need his support. Besides he thought, he better stay and make sure she didn't break any more noses. He had no idea she had such a powerful punch.

Nely went off to grab Alec from his admirers, his friend was having too much fun at a critical time in their lives.

"Come on, I need you" said Nely grabbing an arm, hoping the Clariziane women didn't whack him one.

"We're going, it's time."

"What –" Alec for once was the reluctant one, he had no idea he'd volunteered for the mission.

"You said we would save the universe together right? Now move."

Alec had no choice; his childhood friend would always come first. He had definitely grown up now.

"Sorry girls, I'll see you later, unless either of you wish to come as well."Nely dragged him along the corridor to join the others.

"What are you like?" Nely muttered.

"First time in years a woman has paid me any attention and she has to be an alien, what can I say?" Poor Alec was hooked. So much for the single life.

"You are full of shit mate" said Nely.

They joined the leaving party near the stern, the point they first materialised from. Sol and Calum prepared to activate the final sequence to open the portal. If Rol got it right, the pathway to Earth was seconds away. The Clariziane women, Kat, Mos, Stella and Elia arrived, weaponed up, pumped up and raring to go.

They were pilots no more.

"Where's our weapons" asked Alec, he wasn't planning on unarmed combat in any situation.

"There you go guys" said Stella, handling them both a quantum energy blaster.Nely took his and thought *'Shit! Which end is the dangerous end?'*

Alec turned it around for him. "Idiot" he said.

Sol turned to his mission crew. "Stay close everyone, I am about to open the portal; be prepared when we enter the other side."

Calum stood by his side, full of confidence, perhaps a bit much, a bit cocky even. He knew what to expect having done it before. Of course now he thought he was an expert. Sol told him otherwise; each mission was different. The lad might have saved his life before he was actually born; this was unlike any rescue he could imagine. It wasn't just the alien prisoners they had to break out, but ultimately it was the universe and everything in it that needed rescuing.

Both Sol and Calum memorised every symbol on the artefact, what it represented and in which order to use it. The artefact reacted to Sol instantly by glowing stronger than ever before; the centre piece rotated several times, aligning up each symbol until the sequence was complete. They all prepared to enter into the darkness of the void. Nely, once the reluctant volunteer, stood boldly with his friend, his wife and children in his heart. He told himself over and over they will succeed; he will see his family again, even if that included his bullying brother-in-law. Maybe after this he would see Nely in a more favourable light – but he doubted it any time soon.

"Ready?"

"Ready!" came several voices.

The portal opened. A huge void appeared in front of them. The Clariziane women hadn't exactly prepared themselves for the rear of the ship vanishing like that. It was a bit daunting, for a split second they were speechless. But in true Clariziane style they didn't back down, they were fearless.

"Weapons up girls" said Kat, her finger firmly on the trigger. They were ready for action. Nely and Alec pretended to be. One by one they walked into the void, disappearing into oblivion.

The portal closed.

CHAPTER NINETEEN

A slight miscalculation from Rol, which was inevitable; he was under so much pressure to deliver the co-ordinates to Sol, it meant the rescue team emerged from the portal in the wrong place. They were only a few feet away from the correct entry point but on the outside of the building, out in the open and exposed to danger if spotted. Standing in a narrow access road facing a huge windowless building, it was soon clear they needed to be inside that structure, but no doors, no windows, no visible means of entry meant extra problems.

Mos and Kat immediately stood back to back facing both ends of the road, their blasters ready to shoot anything that moved. They were so pumped up for action they probably would have shot anything that didn't move. Elia and Stella guarded Sol and Calum, then instructed Nely and Alec to back them up. They had to protect the artefact at all costs – their only means of returning to the ship.

All eyes scoured the vicinity for unwanted visitors when voices, or rather screams were heard in the distance, and getting alarmingly closer by the second. Suddenly people were rushing frantically past both ends of the access road, running from something, or someone. Sheer panic in their voices. Strangely they were oblivious to a group of aliens standing halfway along the access road close to the building, completely out of place; the Clarizianes in their white uniform jumpsuits and the Utopians in their woven plant attire, odd they thought why no one came along and questioned them. But they were taking no chances; blasters were primed, ready to go.

The incoherent screams and yelling, said something was going on, but the crew had a job to do. Sol pondered their next move, how they would get inside, when out of nowhere JT appeared, shielding himself behind the women. The safest place he thought.

"JT, what are you doing here?" whispered Sol, the little guy was not part of the plan. He had enough responsibility taking care of the others. The last thing he wanted was JT floating about in the air causing unnecessary attention.

"My dad said I had to come, you need me" replied JT, doing his best to stay hidden in the middle of the group. He didn't want to get shot or end up like his dad with a wonky eye.

"Now what?" asked Nely, "where the hell do we go from here?" he was more concerned whether the Earth people would spot them, it would mean he would have to learn to fire the alien blaster – he hadn't got a clue.

Luckily JT had the answer. "The prisoners you want are on the other side of this wall, sitting in a cell. There's another prisoner in the next cell, we don't want him" he said, he knew exactly where they were, having teleported straight from the portal into the building to search for them. Sol had no idea how close they were to the correct entry point.

"Okay, well done JT" said Sol. Before he had a chance to say more, it began raining particles from the skies, a full blown meteor shower with devastating effects had begun. No wonder the Earth people were running for their lives. Sol guessed, another miscalculation, but from him this time. The Van Allen belts had already reached the Earth's atmosphere. Sol was sure he had more time.

"We have to go now" he said, "no time left, JT, now you're here, go inside and move the prisoners to a safe corner, Mos, Kat, keep us safe from overhead. Blast everything."

"On it" said Kat.

"Now you're talking" added Mos, they were dying for action.

"Stella, Elia, make a new entrance, and Alec and Nely, be ready to rush in and grab the prisoners. Got that?"

Everyone nodded. Sol instinctively knew what had to be done, it was as if the artefact was guiding him, sending messages to his brain. It felt strange to be issuing orders to his crew after all these years. He kind of liked it.

"What if they don't want to come with us?" asked Nely, a valid question he thought. The prisoners wouldn't have a clue who they were.

"Persuade them Nely" said Sol sharply. "There is no time for messing."

Everyone moved to one side as Stella and Elia prepared to blow a hole in the side of the building. Calum watched the lunatic humans running about aimlessly, trying to escape the heavy bombardment of meteors. It was pointless, huge chunks of rock fell on them relentlessly. Buildings were hit, some collapsing almost immediately. He looked up to an invisible safe zone being created by Mos and Kat. The girls were good.

"What shall I do Sol?" he asked.

"Just stay close to me Calum. I might need you."

Stella and Elia were a split second from firing at the building when JT poked his head through the wall.

"Okay Sol, ready when you are."

His freaky appearance alarmed Stella and Elia.

"Sol, tell your little friend never do that again, I nearly vapourised his arse" said Stella.

"I wish he wouldn't keep doing that, it scares the shit out of me" said Nely in a panic. Sol signalled to shoot, ignoring JT. He could take care of himself.

Supporting masonry came crashing down in a cloud of dust, the blasters doing the job in seconds. A huge hole in the wall soon appeared as the dust settled. The aliens were cowering in the far corner, shaking with fear; JT wasn't helping the situation hovering over them and scaring them as much as that wall disintegrating in front of them. They assumed their time had come, perhaps their captors were dispensing with the trial and going straight for the death sentence. They didn't want to die, but they were helpless.

"Go and grab them guys" said Sol, "quickly."

Nely and Alec climbed over the rubble and went in. Sol scanned the area around them. It didn't look good. Buildings were crumbling, some burning, there was mayhem; the humans weren't interested in entering the access road, they were frantically running in all directions, trying to stay one step ahead of disaster. A huge tsunami of coastal water was heading their way, the tidal rush reaching several miles inland. Sol realised they had seconds left to make their escape.

In the cell Alec and Nely had a problem.

"We don't want to go with you" squealed the dwarfed alien, hanging onto his friend for safety, shaking uncontrollably. With the blasters pointed in their faces, they guessed this was it; they were being taken out and shot.

"Look, if you want to live, move it" urged Alec. Sol was calling for them to hurry.

"Get outside now!" ordered Nely, grabbing one of them by the arm, but still they wouldn't budge. "We don't have time to mess about with stupid aliens, out now!" Nely and Alec were getting nowhere. With the blasters still in their faces, they thought *'why don't they just shoot and get it over with?'*

Suddenly there were voices approaching the cell from inside the building. The noise from the blasters and falling masonry alerted the guards that something was happening. Several guards closing in on the cell, none of them actually wanted to be there, the need to escape the horrors outside would be a better preference, except a huge fat bonus was promised if they maintained the tight security on the only two occupied cells.

Sol looked in the cell, they should have been out by now. "Calum, take the artefact. Begin the sequence to open the portal, we will need to go in a hurry." Sol stormed into the cell stumbling over the rubble in his haste. He spotted the aliens.

'What a pathetic pair' he thought, and they were risking their lives for them.

“They refuse to budge Sol” said Alec.

Sol was having none of it, and leaned in. “If you two don’t move your useless, ugly little butts right now, I will have to shoot you my bloody self. Now move your arses!” he was furious, staring at them with his piercing black eyes. He never had to use such an evil stare in his life before.

This was a good time to start.

“Oh, very forceful, very humanlike Sol” muttered Nely, even he was quaking in his boots.

Gingerly the aliens shifted from the corner and got to their feet, more terrified by an even stranger looking alien looming over them without a weapon, he looked more dangerous than the ones with the weapons, his eyes said it all. Maybe it was better to go.

“Now get outside before I kick your butts, and no funny business” said Sol.

Alec pushed them along and poked the tall one in the back with his blaster, just to let them know who was in control. He was relieved not to use his weapon; he wasn’t sure he wanted to. The prisoners were unarmed, it wouldn’t have been a fair fight. His conscience was clean, and it was staying that way.

“You sound so human my friend” Nely said to Sol, patting him on the back on the way out. Sol didn’t know whether it was a compliment or not, he would ask Niko later.

Outside Calum was concentrating on the new calculations, he was almost there, just a few more symbols to align. The prisoners emerged into the open. More aliens, more weapons, they were terrified to even speak, they were a crazy looking bunch, but at least they hadn’t shot them yet.

“We don’t know who you are, or what you’ve done but you’re coming with us whether you like it or not” said Alec, “now stand there, don’t move until I tell you, got that?”

They nodded. No one could understand why these pathetic, wretched harmless pair were locked up in the first place. *What could they have done that was so bad?*

Sol was last out, thinking to himself, *'the humans were odd people to lock aliens in that manner?'* He wasn't sure now if he wanted to be likened to a human. Maybe he'd lived with them so long it had to happen.

Calum finished the final sequence of symbols, having just escaped certain death when a large section of the building fell away. Mos was quick to redirect her blaster skyward and vapourised every last particle. Calum never felt so relieved and grateful for an alien saving his life.

"Thank you" he said.Mos gave him a sneaky smile; she thought he was rather cute and decided to investigate that thought later.

The tsunami was almost upon them, they all stood tightly together as Mos and Kat, and now Stella and Elia kept them safe from above. Calum hoped he got his calculations right this time, he didn't want to screw up on the return journey.

The portal opened, they swiftly entered, dragging the prisoners with them. They were reluctant to walk into a black hole in the middle of the road. They panicked, *could it get any worse for them?*

Stella and Elia were last going in, still firing at the relentless meteor shower, then they heard the cell door being unlocked, a split second before the entire side of the building collapsed. The portal closed as the tsunami swept along the access road, a wall of sea water fifty feet high, bringing with it tons of debris.

*

High above the stratosphere the outer layer of Earth's atmosphere was destabilising, spatial distortions across the galaxy now taking its toll. Earths only natural satellite, the moon, was now on an intercept course with Mars.

No one on Earth saw the devastation coming, no authority left to monitor the skies, no one in control to deal with a major crisis. They were stupid enough to believe Earth would always be safe, the citizens hadn't realised until it was too late they were not impervious to outside forces causing chaos in the galaxy. Now it was too late, the universe was crumbling. Yet the leaders of Earth deemed it more important to investigate how two notorious prisoners escaped their clutches and somehow vanished into thin air. They wanted them back to stand trial for their crimes, someone had to pay for the destruction of the galaxy. The prisoners would have a whole new list of charges against them.

Just as soon as the tsunami died down?

CHAPTER TWENTY

Patience was a virtue Tom thought he had in abundance, having adapted to living a quiet relaxed existence on Utopia, and a happy one at that. But right now his patience was very much lacking. He was getting concerned the mission had failed; his only thoughts were for his son, *how could he ever hope to live with that loss*. His family was the most precious thing in his life. Then again, if none of the rescue team came back he and the others had no way of getting home, back to the future, back to their peaceful lives.

Tom's thoughts were tormenting him to the extreme, he could be stuck aboard an alien ship in the past and forced to live the last fifteen years all over again in a completely different environment, and in a universe on the brink of collapse. If they survived this it would be a miracle.

Outside the ship was utter chaos, the galaxy was breaking up before their eyes, planets colliding with each other. Uranus and Saturn already gone, shattered with devastating effect. Nothing was going to repair that damage. Tom wasn't sure what to feel, at times he just felt numb to the core, if he dragged his emotions to the surface he was certain he would lose control of his faculties altogether.

The monitors showing the events unfolding were sickening to watch. Earth was in serious trouble; the moon got caught in the crossfire earlier, and still on a collision course with Mars, Mercury was heading for the Sun. Tom could only hazard a guess how that was going to play out. The Van Allen belts continued to pummel the Earth with destructive consequences. The timeline fluctuations occurring at random were not helping Tom's nerves, which were already shot to pieces. He hoped and prayed the rescue team left planet Earth in time.

If they had – *where the hell were they?*

They had been gone an hour, it could have been more, it could have been seconds ago. There was no way of telling.

The waiting was killing them all.

The only one aboard the ship appearing to be busy was Xander. He said he had totally reconfigured the red button but wouldn't elaborate further for now. Tom was desperate to know if it was going to help their circumstances or not. Xander remained tight-lipped. He also teleported to the other Kangan ship and did a little rewiring there, as he put it. They were in for a big shock. Xander had reprogrammed their computer mainframe to instruct the ship to make a course correction that would eventually take the Kangans back to the parallel universe. They would be unable to prevent it as Xander had effectively locked them out of their own system. The journey would not be stopped or corrected.

Another minor adjustment was going to fry their brains good and proper, Xander had a wicked glint in his eye when he told Tom he had programmed the computer to emit a signal to confuse the thought process to the Kangans positronic brains. He remembered all his scientific knowledge that Kanon Garg instilled in him. The Kangans own computers revealed their one weakness, being half organic, half machine beings, he decided to mess them up once and for all, they were becoming an annoyance to him. They hadn't a clue what was heading their way. Xander gave out one of his devilish sniggers.

As for the Cynturians, what was left of the fleet after their defeats, Xander plotted their demise with great delight. He hated them with a vengeance. Remembering what he learnt on their last encounter many years earlier from Ti Glish, when Xander was the novice, he thought it a good idea to have some fun at their expense. He would taunt the Cynturians by revealing himself and declaring his name, just to provoke them even more. If indeed there was a price on his head he wanted to make sure they got value for money.

Xander never had so much fun, and no one to tell him off. Swiftly, after the deed was done, he teleported out of each ship before it exploded. One by one the Cynturian empire was destroyed, they would trouble the universe no more.Xander's work was done.

Finally coming to rest on Tom's shoulder, with Po not far behind, Xander could now relax, he was pleased but exhausted. All that teleporting across the galaxy from ship to ship drained his energy, a feat he had never attempted before, and one he had no wish to repeat. It was a one-time offer. Now the Kangans and the Cynturians would not get the better of him and his friends ever again. Xander made it his life's obligation to protect the people who saved his species from extinction, and most of all Just Tom, his friend for life.

Xander would never desert him.

No sooner had Po come to rest on Toms shoulder, he was asleep, exhausted following Xander in his quest to nobble the enemy. Xander had to take him to keep him out of trouble, but really he was no help, pretty much useless on the job, he didn't have his father's intellect.

"Don't be sad Just Tom" said Xander, wrapping his tiny fingers round his ears as always.

"I feel your pain, but they will succeed – have faith. My son is with them too, he will be a great help."

It wasn't until that moment Tom realised JT was missing, now he was extremely worried. JT could be wild, reckless at times, just as Xander was in the beginning. He tried to smile, Xander meant well. His little friend was a big comfort to him over the years, but he was also a big pain in the backside at times; especially when Simone had banned him from the marital bed on several occasions and he took no notice. He rolled his one good eye at Just Tom that melted his heart, he always got forgiveness.

He was sneaky like that.

*

It was all kicking off outside the ship with massive explosions shaking the universe to its core. The Cynturian warship that was stationary for so long on the bow, abruptly veered off and burst into flames before disintegrating into small fragments floating away aimlessly in space. Tom could not save this galaxy or his home planet, it was doomed. He never wanted this to happen, surely the universe could have found a better solution to chaos, he thought. It could have shown leniency. *Did it have to destroy everything?*

If Sol and Calum and the others didn't return soon they would all end up as space debris. For now it appeared Xander had saved their lives yet again, for how much longer was down to the universe not throwing another hissy fit.

Tom wondered about his friend, for one so small he was a giant in Tom's eyes, with intellect to put them all to shame. But this mission troubled Tom, he feared it was a step too far for the little guy. The Avaans had evolved so much over the many centuries to become who they are now – Tom loved to hear the stories of old, although he was sure Xander embellished some of them. He didn't care. Now he despaired they had bitten off more they could chew. The mission was a failure, Tom was sure of it. Xander's irrepressible enthusiasm refused to be defeated. He was having none of it, and he told Tom as much.

Niko sat close to her son, they were feeling pretty much the same as Tom – wretched. They were stuck in a metal box in a galaxy that was slowing tearing itself apart, they felt helpless.

The universe could not or would not intervene.

Niko felt so remorseful it had come to this, she really wanted to take Nicolas to Earth to show him where she was born. She had no idea if her parents were still alive, it would have been nice to tell Nicolas he had grandparents. Now all that was gone, her dreams crushed, no chance of ever returning home. That was the hardest part in all of this.

Tom still hadn't come up with a solution for the Clarizianes, they didn't deserve to die either; they were trying to help put the universe back on track, but the longer they stayed in this universe, the worse the situation was becoming. Their only crime was their devotion to finding their friend. *Why should they be punished for loyalty?* Other star systems could well be experiencing similar upheaval. *How was he supposed to solve the mess they were in?*

The universe failed them.

It seemed like the artefact had failed them.

Now Tom felt as if he had failed his friends. He felt duty-bound to act, but he was a mere mortal, *what was he supposed to do?*

Now something deep down in his soul was urging him on, pushing him to seek the answer. It was somewhere in his mind, in his heart, yet he could not concentrate until his son was back safe. Xanders fingers playing with his ear really didn't help him to think. Po in his other ear snoring wasn't helping either. *How could he say anything to his little friend?* Without them Tom was nothing.

Xander was best man at his wedding ceremony, they were best friends from the day they met. Xander even named his first born after Tom. JT had a lot to live up to. *Was it all for nothing?*

Dragging his thoughts away from the crisis, back to when they first met warmed Tom's heart. Xander had an infectious smile, a positive outlook on life, he was full of confidence to the point of recklessness, and those eyes swinging in all directions made everyone fall in love with him, his small stature, like his fellow beings, in no way held him back. His wonky eye always a reminder he nearly didn't make it. That was when Tom thought he was a jammy little bugger, then wondered how many more lives he had left – because right now he was going to need every single one.

"How are you holding up Tom?" asked Niko, sliding along the seat to be closer. She thought he looked sad, desperate; he was struggling inside. She could tell. They were all suffering, but Tom was taking the burden of responsibility on himself.

Tom didn't answer Niko; he had nothing to say. He couldn't put into words how he felt, he wanted to give up, still that nagging deep down feeling inside was telling him not to.

Something wouldn't let him go.

Niko sat with Tom taking his hand to give him reassurance.

*

The Clarizianes were mostly at the stern of the ship as if waiting for their fate. They needed the portal to open and see everyone come through the void safely. None of them in a position to be any help, this strange phenomenon the Earth people brought aboard was out of their league, they couldn't understand it's meaning, or why Sol was in charge of it. Pacing the floor, leaning against the bulkhead, sitting down, getting up, pacing the floor again was the only way to relieve the frustration of doing nothing, feeling helpless. They were all boxed in together and the walls were closing in

Don returned to the central section of the ship where Tom, Niko and Nicolas were sat. He thought they might want company, they'd been very quiet. Rol was left alone at the controls, refusing to leave his post. He couldn't do anything either, except monitor space, watching the destruction as it unfolded out there. Their ship was the only object in this galaxy staying constant. Rol didn't know why, or if it was a good thing or not. He wondered if any of it was real. *Was there an unseen force at work out there? Was it protecting them or wanting to destroy them?* Rol wished he could understand even a small part of the madness. The truth was, he hated this universe, it made no sense to tear itself apart, he so wanted to go home. the Clarizianes own universe was never like this. This was one crazy existence, who would choose to live in a volatile environment that was on the verge of destabilising at its core?

Now more trouble was occurring, Rol just witnessed a far off star system disappear from the long range monitor, leaving a huge black hole sucking in everything in close proximity.

'*Like that was going to help*' Rol thought.

The universe was definitely intent on destroying itself, unable to contain the rifts turning into cracks with disastrous results.

*

The crack over Utopia was getting bigger, even though it wasn't in the universe. It was supposed to be a safe haven outside reality. The effects were far-reaching beyond the parameters of normal existence. It was as if the universe had exceeded its limitations.

It was not helping itself!

*

Rol sat in the control seat watching his life ebb away, he questioned why he tormented himself by keeping a vigil, constantly looking at the monitors, as another crack opened up in a nearby constellation. More of the universe was about to disappear, and that one was too close for comfort. Rol was feeling the heat, he couldn't take much more of the stress, he'd kicked the rest of the crew out earlier, saying he would manage it alone quite well, or so he thought. Now he had no one to share his fears.

Could their ship be next?

Rol didn't mind admitting he was scared. Fate was dealing them a shit hand and the cards were well and truly stacked against them.

*

"Shouldn't they be back by now Tom?" asked Don, his crew were going stir crazy waiting for Sol and his rescue party to return. They wanted answers, not more misery dumped on them.

Tom shook his head. *'How the hell did he know anything?'*

He was more worried they weren't coming back at all. His faith in the mission, in the artefact was waning fast, his depression was in danger of rearing its ugly head again, he didn't want to deal with it. This was a mission too far, they had no choice but to get involved, but it was too big a task to handle.

"My dad will succeed, I know he will" announced Nicolas, listening in; Niko put her arm round her son, she admired his faith in his father, but even she was already grieving his loss.

"Nicolas is right Just Tom; Sol will succeed and so will Calum. My tingling sixth sense tells me so. They are coming back, give them time" said Xander, leaning forward into Tom's face. He was certain everyone would return safely.

Strained expressions were followed by more silence, none knew what to say for the best. Tom's worry was the simple fact they were stranded in the past and not knowing if they could survive here; the universe was on the verge of collapse, survival was doubtful after that. The very existence of life would be snuffed out in an instant – all because of a stupid mistake, an error by reckless irresponsible aliens who thought life would be better in the past and by doing that destroyed their own future as well as life everywhere in the universe.

Don wanted to help these friends of Sol's, he couldn't, he still wasn't entirely sure about them, it was their manner of arrival that perturbed him.

Could they really help?

They came with a plan, that wasn't going too well. Then again he could offer no solution to the situation either. He was struggling to work out how they managed to get drawn into this insane mess, he and his crew were innocent pilots who got stitched up by the authorities, then managed to escape their clutches to end up as outlaws of their own kind. Now Clarizia was no more, he was at least certain of that, destroyed by their own stupidity. It was a lot for Don to take in.

'And what did Tom mean, they had to leave the universe and live elsewhere?'

Where else was there?

How many universes were there?

Knowing what was happening outside the ship, there was very little chance of this universe surviving its own devastation.

Where were Tom and his friends going to live?

All had their own thoughts at that moment as they sat together in silence – yet each one of them felt alone.

*

Without warning, loud voices and jubilant cheers shattered the silence running throughout the ship, it was coming from the stern. Niko, Nicolas and Don heard it immediately, so did Rol from the control section. Don looked up realising Niko had acute hearing also, her eyes saying, *'Is that them?'*

Rol had already launched himself out of his seat in a flash and heading along the corridors. The one person he wanted to see back safe was Stella. She never left his thoughts for a moment, perhaps now she would agree to marry him. He had no idea that she had told Nicolas she would. He rushed past the others like a tornado, calling out as he passed, "I think they're back."

Don followed in hot pursuit.

"Let's go Tom" said Niko, grabbing Nicolas by the arm as they hurried along, Don and Rol already disappearing into the next section. Tom got to his feet sharply, he'd forgotten Po was still asleep on his shoulder. Startled by the rude awakening, Po nearly landed headfirst on the floor. Tom suddenly had a dreadful flashback when Xander went flying from his shoulder escaping from Kangis-3.

He froze.

If he caused another accident to one of the Avaans he would never forgive himself. His confidence, his mood was already rock bottom. One more failure in his life would send him over the edge for sure.

Po was fine, his levitation skills stopped him short one inch from the floor, then he was upright again. A close examination of the metal panelling covering the floor of the ship was not high on his list of things to see. He hoped not to do that again.

Tom breathed a sigh of relief.

"I'm ok Just Tom" he said, it did give him a bit of a fright though, he didn't want to wonky eye as well. Rubbing his sleepy eyes in a weird way, he was gone. The near miss meant no big deal to him.

Xander was already gone, teleported at speed, desperate to see his son.They were back!

The first thing Sol did was seek out his wife and son, hugging them both. It was such a relief to be back.

"This is the last time you ever leave me behind" Niko whispered in his ear sternly. "I'm never letting you out of my sight again" she added, but in a way that Sol knew he was grounded for the rest of his life. All the anxiety and worries melted away as they hugged and kissed; being grounded was not so bad Sol thought.

Tom threw his arms round Calum, so relieved to have him back. He quickly forgot how depressed he'd been worrying about the boy.

"We did it dad, we did it" said Calum excited to see his dad, not so much the hugs though. He looked across at Nicolas and they winked at each other.

'Parents, huh?!' But they were happy.

Mos, Kat, Elia and Stella were greeted warmly, heroes in everyone's eyes. Sol told the crew how they defended the rescue party with real courage. They were fearless, the success of the mission was largely down to the women.

Stella could see Rol in the background waiting for her, no one prouder than he. She decided not to hold back any longer, it wasn't fair on him; he'd been so patient. She pushed through the crowded stern section to get to him.

"Hi" he said, for once he couldn't think of anything else to say.

"Hi yourself" she smiled, "Well, do I get a kiss or not?"

Rol was only waiting for a green light, and that was it.

Nely and Alec came through the portal dragging two very reluctant aliens.

"This is what we risked our lives for Tom" said Alec, "This little one is Qrotei, and the other is Oston, a right bloody pair of idiots."

Alec and Nely finally released their grip on the aliens, they weren't going anywhere now. Neither of them seem grateful for their rescue, being dragged through a black void on a journey to nowhere. They crouched together on the floor, frightened to speak.

"Well done everyone" said Tom, no one was more pleased and relieved than him. This was a good day. Don nodded, his crew did well, he though still had concerns.

"Well Tom, what next?"

Tom looked for Xander, it was up to him now to reveal his great plan, he assured Tom he had one. But Xander wasn't concentrating on the conversation, or the excited congratulations, he had something else on his mind. He stared at the portal as it was about to close, it was disappearing before his eyes. JT hadn't returned. He was always late; this was a step too far.

At the very last second, as the centre of the portal vanished JT came flying through.

"Phew! That was close" he said, not sure how he managed to lag so far behind the others. It might have had something to do with stopping to admire the colourful nebulae through the wormhole, like a corridor between space and time – but he decided not to let on about that bit, it could have been very embarrassing. Xander was delighted to see his first born, but livid at his slow departure from the portal.

"Don't you ever do that to me again JT" Xander snapped, then relented. "But well done my son, you did well."

JT was puffed up his dad was pleased with him, his very first mission, and exciting, even if he did get distracted.

"Okay, okay, listen up everyone –" said Tom clapping his hands to get everyone's attention, the celebrations were rather loud in a confined space. It was only to be expected, Tom didn't want to dampen their enthusiasm, they did a good job, now there were other priorities. It was time for Xander to deliver.

"Xander, now will you tell us your plans. Can we actually fix the universe?"

It was a tall order Tom was asking, it certainly got everyone's attention, one or two Clarizianes thinking it a damn fool question in the first place, but what did they know.

"Sure, no problem" said Xander rather nonchalantly, he had it all worked out.

"Well?" came several voices from all directions, eyes zooming in on the little guy, back with his son sat in his favourite place, cross-legged, always appearing to look important.

"First, my sixth sense is warning of imminent danger, we must exit this system immediately before it implodes on us completely. It's too late to save this galaxy, it's gone."

Xander delivered a harsh statement for the humans. It wasn't what they wanted to hear, even though they could see with their own eyes space had finally rebelled against the natural order of existence to destroy all life. If they didn't get out of there soon, they were next.

"Sorry Just Tom" he was genuinely sad that his friends home planet could not survive such a violent upheaval. The devastation would be total.

"But the rest of the universe we can fix" announced Xander, he was certain of his facts. He was very meticulous in his calculations.

"More sticking plaster I suppose?" said Nely in a rather flippant way, and not expecting a sensible answer.

"Precisely!" replied Xander, or words to that affect he thought. Then Kanon Garg flashed across his memory, he would be so proud of his pupil.

"I'm not hearing a valid solution Xander, we need something concrete to work on" said Tom with some urgency. Time was critical.

Don stepped in. "Rol, Hanzon, get to the controls and get us out of here fast." He had to trust the aliens sometime; this was a good time to start. Besides he was hearing explosions happening too close to their ship, moving away seemed a sensible idea.

"Thank you Don" said Tom, at least he was working with him now.

"Right, once we're away, Don and I will discuss strategy with Xander" he said waving his arms, gesturing everyone to move, they all had a part to play. Departure from this place was paramount.

*

Niko took it upon herself to tend to the newcomers, they looked frightened and in a pitiful state, tired, hungry and showed clear signs of several vicious beatings during their incarceration. *What did the Earth people think they were doing to these poor souls,* she wondered. Surely that was against the intergalactic treaty, the very same treaty Earth had established two hundred years ago. *How could they violate their own treaty?* Niko wondered what had happened to the Earth people, maybe they deserved everything that was coming to them.

Whatever the crime, these poor souls didn't deserve such appalling treatment. The little malformed alien appeared to be in a lot of pain, he had taken the worst of the beatings. The sight made Niko's blood boil to think this could happen on Earth.

"Come with me you two, I'll get your wounds dressed, then we'll find you some food. How's that sound?" she said quietly.

Qrotei looked at her. "Thank you." It was the first bit of compassion shown to him in a long time. Whoever she was she had a nice soft voice – he did worry about those evil looking odd coloured eyes, but she seemed genuine enough. Then he winced in pain. Niko called out.

"Stella, can you help? Where can I take these men to tend to their wounds? I take it you have at least some basic medical supplies? And have you food and drink to spare?"

Stella called her friend Ariel; they were more than willing to help. Stella had family ties now, of course she would help. Rol would be family too, she was buoyant, hoping it would last long enough to survive this dreadful crisis they found themselves in.

Stella and Ariel assisted getting the aliens to their feet. "Don't be afraid, we only want to help" Stella tried to reassure them they were safe now.

"Thank you Stella" said Niko as she glanced away for a second to see Sol and Nicolas in conversation, catching up with events she guessed. She was happy to see them together again. The thought of losing Sol inside the portal sent shivers down her spine.

Qrotei and Oston stayed close together as they always did, then taken deeper into the ship, every step was painful for Qrotei, Oston urged him on. They were unsure of their new surroundings, they had no idea who the aliens were, a strange mixed bunch of beings Oston thought, obviously from different worlds. He didn't know what to make of them, they seemed friendly, but could they be hostile? Maybe the women, with those powerful weapons that disintegrated their prison cell – they looked the most terrifying of all.

Niko kept reassuring them they were safe now, no more beatings ever. "You're in safe hands here."

She spoke in her softest doctors voice as she tended their wounds, medical supplies were sparse. She did what she could. Stella and Ariel brought food and water. It wasn't much but they were grateful – but could they really let their guard down? Everyone was being far too nice to them.

It was strange.

CHAPTER TWENTY-ONE

The alien ship sped away from the galaxy, leaving it to destroy itself. Planet Earth was close to annihilation, total destruction was imminent. The humans tried not to think about it, there was nothing to be done to save their once home. In the end it wasn't worth saving. The people were despicable and brought it on themselves. Now thoughts turned to Utopia and whether they could get back there to save it.

Tom and Don sat down with Xander, it was time for action, time for Xander to reveal his plans.

"I'm sorry about your home planet Tom, I guess we're in the same boat now" said Don, it only just hit him, the pilots were actually homeless. They found Sol, but they hadn't a clue what they were going to do afterwards. At the time, no one wanted to think about the future. They were fixated on finding their friend, he then would solve all their problems.

That was the plan.

How wrong they were.

Tom thanked Don for his kind words, it meant a lot to him.

"My people were homeless once Don" said Xander, he felt their pain, it was a sad thought to think they were all homeless at one stage in their lives.

"My friend Just Tom found us a new home" said Xander sounding more upbeat.Don nodded, smiled, suddenly he could see the friendship between this giant of a man and the little guy, not many people had that affinity with someone. He was beginning to understand the aliens – a little.

"Business Xander" said Tom firmly, "we need to know the next stage, and by the way, how far must we travel to escape the effects of this galaxy?"

Tom was afraid if there wasn't enough distance between them and the entire galaxy implodes, they might get sucked back in.

"Good question Just Tom –" Xander was unusually hesitant. It wasn't like him.

"You don't bloody well know, do you?" Tom was frustrated, Xander wasn't helping his blood pressure. Definitive answers were needed, not uncertainty. This wasn't a good feeling for Tom.

"Are you telling me he hasn't got the answer Tom, after all that messing about inside our controls?" asked Don equally frustrated, annoyed now he put so much faith in these people to solve their dilemma.

Xander resented Don's remark. It wasn't his fault; he was doing his best. "The universe wants us to fix it, so why is it thwarting our every move Just Tom?" he asked.

"Good question Xander" said Tom who had no answer of his own. Xander had made a very good point.

"I rest my case" Xander said smugly. He did have the answers, he just needed to get them in the right order in his headfirst, he was playing for time – not just playing this time.

*

Sol and Calum found a quiet spot on the ship to work on the artefact, if a quiet spot was at all possible with the non-stop chattering going on. It was more disturbing for Sol to concentrate fully. He had to rely on Calum a great deal. They had to recalculate a different re-entry point back to Utopia, this time it wasn't going to be so easy, and then they still wouldn't have the final sequence until the ship reached its destination point. That couldn't happen until Xander had completed his repairs to the universe itself. An added problem they had not anticipated was the calculation of returning to the future at the precise time they left. The artefact would not allow going deeper into the future, but neither did they want to return to a time before they actually left, that would have serious consequences.

Without warning the artefact shut down, the sequence was wrong, the symbols couldn't align themselves, more data was required. But while the ship was travelling at great velocity, there was little chance of accurate calculations. The artefact knew it, so it closed down.

*

Don listened to Xander with his so called scientific explanation, the dreaded red button had a new function it seemed. Don was getting more and more confused, the science didn't make sense, the red button was a weapon of immense power, *how could this tiny alien turn it into something else?* None of it made a lot of sense to him, his face said it all. He wasn't a scientist, but Tom was, and he appeared to understand every single word Xander said. It was then Don realised Tom and his friends had done this once before when aboard their own ship years ago, or at least it was Xander who had a major part in that. *Wonder what happened to their ship?* Don thought.

One thing that really puzzled Don, he had to ask. "What is superglue?" it was bugging him not being able to understand the logic of Xander.

Tom did his best to explain in simpler terms to Don, except this time it was on a much larger scale, and no guarantee of success. As for the superglue, he told Don it was a metaphor and not to worry about the details.But Don did worry.

The alien ship in the Clariziane possession all these weeks also had to leave the universe; it didn't belong. At that point Don had to question where Tom and his friends came from – what part of the universe did they belong to. Tom said he wouldn't believe him if he told him and thought it best to leave Utopia out of it for now. Don would definitely not understand that bit.

*

The other Kangan ship had already left the system, taken off heading for a rift that would lead it to the parallel universe – courtesy of Xander. He had confused its occupants somewhat, having no idea they had an intruder meddling in their mainframe. Now they had difficulty thinking independently, something was blocking the thought process from the computer; messages were garbled, even reading backwards. They couldn't function when their computer brains were being fried trying to decipher the rubbish being fed to them. The three Kangans were totally muddled, and it was only going to get worse for them.

*

Now it was down to the final part of the mission, the real business of saving what was left of the universe. Xander made it absolutely clear what both crews had to do, everyone had a part in their own survival.

Nely was almost right with the sticking plaster, the idea worked before, this time Xander upgraded it slightly.

Now every alien back in their own universe – the Cynturians were finally defeated at last. Whoever was left on their miserable home planet would be too afraid to try again. They had failed in their quest for supremacy. They would never murder again, or trespass into this universe. It was time to seal the rifts, close the cracks so no one could enter uninvited ever again.

The red button was now altered to intricately emit a high frequency sonic impulse beam as the ship travelled space, hopefully fusing the rifts together, filling in the cracks so they could never open again. It was then hoped the crack over Utopia would also heal itself. It was a huge risk to take, but one Xander knew he had to take. He had confidence in his own ability. Kanon Garg would be proud of him; he had finally grown up. He now prayed the universe would play by the rules, once the task was completed, the universe would return the favour.

*

Sol and Calum asked Tom to assist for a short time, with the artefact closed down, it needed all three minds to re-establish the link. They had to activate it again before calculations could resume. Sol did point out to Tom the complication with the alien ship they were occupying.

How were they supposed to dispose of it?

At present that looked impossible. Then, with the ongoing problem of not being able to locate the exact entry point to Utopia because of the shifting position in space – which continued to alter at will – was going to prove even more difficult to solve, Sol could see no way of correctly calculating the right time period, effectively, with all that going against them, they were screwed, this time really screwed. Tom could see his point, it was a valid one, but he just said Sol was sounding more humanlike in his words every day, there was hope for him yet.

Secretly Tom had concerns, he had no real answers to offer, yet the problem was never going away. Like Xander, he was banking on the universe to help them out, give Tom a sign to complete the task, tell them how they could dispose of the alien ship.

Why couldn't the universe send him a message? Give him the vital information to read in his mind's eye.

*

The universe had mysteriously gone quiet.

*

Finally the ship drew close to the edge of the universe and came to a halt, they could go no further. The rifts were newly sealed up to Xander's satisfaction, no one was going to rip the sticking plaster off this time. He was happy and sniggered loudly.

He job was done – too well done.

Xander had unwittingly sealed the alien ship with them aboard in this universe, with no means of escape. The ship couldn't stay, that fact had been established, neither could it go through the portal, it was deemed too great a risk. Tom unusually didn't seem too concerned about the problem; he was sure there was a plan – he just had to think of it first.

Rol was joined at the controls by Tom, he thought he could help with the monitoring. Rol couldn't understand what they were waiting for, but he was glad of the company, he decided the aliens weren't all bad. They did after all rescue two defenceless beings. Now though it was they who needed rescuing. He did ask Tom what the plan was, but Tom didn't reply. He just sat down to watch the monitors, watching and waiting, his eyes rarely left the screen. All that was needed was a significant sign, something to let them know they were even in the right sector.

Tom wanted that black void to reappear like it did before. It would certainly be big enough to take the ship through, he wasn't sure what to do with it after that. Yet still they couldn't go anywhere without the final sequence.

The artefact refused to play ball.

*

Sol and Calum were left to work alone as Tom had nothing to offer. They strived tirelessly for hours to find a way to activate the artefact. A light flickered occasionally, a faint glow emanating from the centre suggested there was still life in the artefact – but nothing more, not yet anyway.

*

Waiting and watching space hour after hour, day after day, Tom and his friends had time to discuss the prospect of taking the Clarizianes with them to Utopia, if of course they made it themselves. Utopia would take a lot of explaining to the pilots. Tom could only hope they were ready for it, that they would understand they had to leave the universe altogether – permanently. It made sense to the humans; a new life would await them. The Clarizianes deserved to live, they proved themselves worthy of life.

Tom wasn't so sure about the rescued prisoners, not after he discovered who they were and the dreadful deeds their people had committed. He was however persuaded to show leniency. They had taken a brutal beating on Earth; it wasn't their fault they got dragged across the universe to boot.

Life in the parallel universe could have suffered the same fate as this one and was possibly non-existent now, they couldn't afford to throw away a single life, not even the Naasooks.

*

The universe had to fulfil its commitments, to sustain and nurture all life – or what was the point of its own existence?

*

Paradise – Utopia awaited any and all believers. As Xander always said.

"We will succeed, have faith."

www.ingramcontent.com/pod-product-compliance
Lightning Source LLC
Chambersburg PA
CBHW030518310726
48979CB00010B/1719/J
* 9 7 8 1 8 3 6 1 5 3 5 2 8 *